WHERE THE DESERT MEETS THE SEA

WHERE THE DESERT MEETS THE SEA

WERNER SONNE

Translated by Steve Anderson

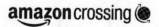

Text copyright © 2008 by Werner Sonne
English translation copyright © 2019 by Steve Anderson
All rights reserved.

Previously published as *Wenn ich dich vergesse, Jerusalem* by Berlin Verlag, Berlin, Germany, in 2008. Translated from German by Steve Anderson. First published in English by AmazonCrossing in 2019.

Published by AmazonCrossing, Seattle

www.apub.com

Amazon, the Amazon logo, and AmazonCrossing are trademarks of Amazon.com, Inc., or its affiliates.

ISBN-13: 9781542043908 (hardcover)
ISBN-10: 1542043905 (hardcover)
ISBN-13: 9781542043915 (paperback)
ISBN-10: 1542043913 (paperback)

Cover design by Faceout Studio, Jeff Miller

Printed in the United States of America

First edition

WHERE
THE
DESERT
MEETS
THE SEA

February 15–16, 1947

They have to be out there somewhere, she thought. *If they spot us, it's over.*

The wind surged and the rain whipped at her face, running down her legs, combining with the seawater grabbing at her feet through the railing. It was a moonless February night. The storm had swept in from the northwest and sent temperatures plunging.

Judith Wertheimer watched the captain as he scanned the horizon with his massive binoculars, again and again, his greasy dark-blue cap pushed far back on his head. The Cypriot's sharp features, framed by a stubbly gray beard, didn't betray any concern. But she could make out a subtle clenching in his jaw.

She, too, stared into the darkness, toward the west, beyond the waves' white crests and into that dark-gray mountain of clouds that seemed to merge with the churning Mediterranean Sea. Again the thought raced through her head. *If they catch us, it's over. What then? More barbed wire, more barracks, more camps?* She couldn't bear it, not again.

Judith pulled her old gray wool overcoat tighter around herself. It had once kept a German Wehrmacht soldier warm. Altered by a German housewife, it had changed owners numerous times before a Red Cross nurse pulled it from a pile of worn-out clothes and thrust it into Judith's hands right before she left. Judith anxiously felt around in the pocket for the postcard, then calmed down once she felt it between her fingers, still safe and dry.

"You need to live. Come here," he'd scrawled in old German script. "Come to my home, in Jerusalem. Your Uncle Albert." In the upper left corner, squeezed in really small, was the address. "Albert Wertheimer, Ben Yehuda Street 112, Jerusalem, Palestine."

How old would he be now—sixty-four? No, sixty-five. Her father's brother, Albert Wertheimer, PhD, had been a lawyer and notary—back then.

Lost in thoughts of her uncle, Judith didn't see the huge wave until it slammed against the bow. The ship lurched, then reared up, rising high, and smacked back down, a loud creak coursing through its old hull. The impact ripped the front lifeboat from its mount, and it tipped over the ship's left side, dangling there a few seconds and banging against the hull until the last chain gave way and the boat was swallowed up by the dark water.

From below deck came the combined screams of many, then the piercing cries of a child, then nothing. Silence. It took Judith a moment to grasp what had happened. The engine laboring to propel the heaving ship had cut out, for the second time since departing Cyprus. The first time, they'd lost three precious hours firing it up again.

She knew time was running out. They had to arrive before dawn; otherwise, they'd be caught along the shore. She looked to the captain. He put down his binoculars, pushed his cap forward, and hurried down the short ladder from the bridge, disappearing below deck with a young crewman.

The *Morning Cloud* started to lurch out of control, a toy on the waves. An old woman appeared from the hatch; she staggered the few steps across the deck, clamped on to the railing, and threw up. Judith rushed over to hold her up. It was Esther, the little Polish lady who'd lived next to her in the barracks of the British internment camp on Cyprus. She was only fifty-seven but looked much older, emaciated and broken from forced labor in Hitler's Germany, her narrow back hunched. She stared at Judith with her eyes wide, flashing with fear. She threw up again.

A dull rumble rose from inside the ship, first stuttering, then growing steadier as the engine returned to full speed. The captain climbed back onto the bridge and resumed scanning the horizon. The *Morning Cloud* gradually turned its bow back toward the east.

Judith had Esther by the arm and was holding her tight.

"Easy, easy! Just a few more hours and we've made it," Judith heard herself shout into the wind.

Esther squeezed her eyes shut and nodded. Judith led her out of the rain that seemed even heavier now, back to the hatch, back to the nearly 250 exhausted people packed together below deck. The hold stank of fear and vomit, but the passengers seemed to feel that anything was better than exposing themselves to the storm's fury.

Judith helped Esther down, then pulled herself back up along the thick, frayed rope railing. She glanced around the deck. Then she saw him, at the rear of the ship. A man in a black leather jacket, dark pants, boots.

She strained to make out more details. A red glow flickered, apparently a cigarette. His legs had a slight spring to them, balancing on the rolling waves. A realization hit Judith: she had seen him briefly when they'd come on board, together with Ari, the man from the Haganah. She remembered his jet-black hair, his equally dark mustache. About thirty-five, slim, fair. Under different circumstances, his figure might have been called athletic. Even more striking than his hair were his eyes—blue, very blue. Something about those eyes had disturbed her deeply.

She kept her own eyes fixed on that figure defying the rain and smoking in the darkness just ten yards away. She took a deep breath and concentrated. She was more and more certain that she had seen those eyes before, long before coming on board.

She turned back toward the bow. The wind still whipped at the waves, but the wall of rain had let up for the moment. She believed, or rather guessed, hoped, that she could detect some bright dots far ahead. *Lights,* she thought, and not on the water—lights on the shore, the lights of Tel Aviv.

"The ship's coming." Uri Rabinovich pressed the binoculars tighter to his eyes. "They're coming," he repeated, more urgent now. He waited a moment, wanting to be certain. "It's them. Give the signal!"

Daniel Wyzanski sprang up and directed the spotlight at the sea. Three long flashes, two short, three long. Uri held his breath a second. What if he'd gotten it wrong? What if the *Morning Cloud* had already been intercepted, like so many ships before her? Seconds passed, feeling like minutes. He glanced at his watch. Half past five—they were late, far too late. Soon it would be light.

"Again," Uri shouted to Daniel. He squinted through his binoculars. Still nothing. "Goddamn it," he muttered. But then, there it was: flashing on the other end, three long, two short, three long. He lowered his binoculars.

"Quick! Prepare the boats."

Five young Haganah men sprang up from behind a dune and ran down to the beach where their gray inflatable boats lay. Only two of the five had a motor. The others had to be rowed, roughly three hundred yards out over the roaring surf.

The *Morning Cloud* was now clearly in view. Uri reached the beach close behind the others, short of breath after his sprint. Just as he went to jump into an inflatable boat, a glistening light shot up high over the *Morning Cloud,* illuminating the old ship. Light from a flare. Uri raised the binoculars to his eyes, searching for the source. Then he saw it, far beyond the refugee ship, cloaked by the rain.

The British were here, and they were closing in fast.

Judith shielded her eyes, blinded by the light. For a moment, the spectacle fascinated her—the waves rolling, their ship bobbing, the rain now reflecting the white flare, the tattered clouds racing across the sky. Then shock set in. She now could see, barely, its outline against the dark-gray horizon of rain and sea and clouds: a British destroyer.

She instinctively turned her back, as if she could deter fate by not looking. She clapped her hands to her face, taking deep breaths. The events of the previous forty-eight hours replayed in her mind—their escape from the camp, the Haganah trucks rushing them to the ship, the British in pursuit, the throng of people scurrying up the narrow gangplank, the cramped and overloaded ship.

Judith knew what would happen if the British caught them. Esther had gone through it already. They'd be returned to the camp on Cyprus where the British had crammed in thirty thousand Jews, all survivors of the Holocaust and all with only one goal: to reach Palestine.

Suddenly, there was frantic commotion all around her. Three Haganah men were bringing up their human cargo from the belly of the ship. Frightened figures, unsteady on their feet, the crying children holding tight to the adults' legs.

"Throw out the ladder!" Ari shouted.

As the rope ladder splashed into the water, another harsh jolt passed through the ship. The *Morning Cloud* had hit a sandbank. All eyes turned to the captain, who was trying to reverse course. To no avail— the *Morning Cloud* was stuck. The crew frantically grappled with the remaining lifeboat and lowered it down over the restless waves. Then they began handing out life vests, but there were only fifty for two hundred fifty passengers.

"Give them to the children, hurry!" Ari screamed.

Judith saw Esther put her life vest on a little girl.

She heard Ari shouting: "Hurry, faster!"

Judith grabbed the girl and pulled her close to the rope ladder. The girl hesitated.

"Where's your mother?"

The girl gaped at her.

"Get going already! Go!" Ari yelled.

"You go with her," Judith told Esther. "I'll be right behind you."

The Polish woman reached for the girl's hand, helped her climb over the railing, then reluctantly climbed over herself.

"I—I can't swim," she whispered.

"Don't worry, you can do it," Judith reassured her.

Judith watched Esther struggle down the ladder, then followed, fighting the waves. Below, she could now make out a gray inflatable boat, where two Haganah men were reaching for the people abandoning ship. About five were already on board. One of them grabbed the girl, now howling in despair, and swiftly pulled her over and handed her to one of the women.

Next was Esther. She clung to the rope ladder, unable to move, frozen with fear. A hand reached out for her, but the *Morning Cloud* rocked wildly back and forth atop the sandbank. Esther hung with both hands clamped to the ropes, her face to the hull. A man finally grabbed her by the right leg, but she panicked, flailing. Then suddenly, unable to fight him anymore, she let go. Her leg slipped from his hands. She tumbled down headfirst.

Seeing Esther disappear into the waves, Judith didn't shout, didn't even think. She pushed off from the rope and dropped feetfirst into the depths. The shock of the cold water only hit her when she came back up spluttering, kicking to stay afloat. She frantically peered back and forth, searching for Esther. For a moment she thought she saw the woman's head in the crest of a wave. She immediately began paddling in that direction, but her progress was painfully slow, damned from the start by her heavy coat and the ice-cold water.

"Esther," she screamed. "Esther!"

Judith's arms kept thrashing, yet she couldn't gain even a yard. Her movements slowed. When the next wave crashed over her head, she swallowed a huge mouthful of water, then coughed it back up, retching.

"Esther," she gasped.

Suddenly, she felt someone roughly grab the back of her neck, an arm wrapping around her torso. She flailed and fought, trying to free herself.

"Stop it," said a male voice. "Stop, there's nothing you can do for her."

Yet she kept fighting, more violently now. The man tightened his grip.

"Hang on, the boat's coming!" he shouted.

"Esther," she muttered. Then she was right up against the gray rubber of the boat. Hands reached out to her, a face hovering, framed by jet-black hair. Blue, very blue eyes. More hands seized her overcoat. The man in the water released his grip and pushed her forward. Gradually, as if in slow motion, they pulled Judith on board.

Esther, she kept thinking. The woman had survived the German labor camps, the death marches, those uncertain days after the war, the British camp on Cyprus, and now she was dead. Drowned, only a few hundred yards from the shore of Tel Aviv. Judith's eyes slid closed, and she passed out.

When she came to, she was lying between wool blankets, among sand dunes. The black of night had given way to the gray of daybreak. The rain had stopped. Several trucks waited on the sand with motors running. People were crammed on the cargo beds, their faces weary and drained. Mothers held their children tight.

A face leaned over her. She perceived what resembled a smile. It belonged to a man in his midtwenties. Short, dark-brown hair, dark and determined eyes, and a gentle mouth that didn't seem to fit him.

"How are you doing?" he asked.

She sat up. It was a simple question to which she had no answer. Reflexively, she replied, "Um, fine, thanks."

The man kept smiling. He held out his hand. "We already met in the water. Uri. Uri Rabinovich."

She accepted his hand, shaking it gently.

"Judith Wertheimer." Only now did she notice that she was wearing nothing but panties under the wool blanket. Her wet clothes lay next to her. She realized how silly their formal introduction was under the circumstances, and turned red. Yet Uri had already turned his eyes away and was waving over a young woman.

"This is Yael," he said. "She'll look after you."

Yael smiled broadly at her. She was Judith's age, with dark-blond hair, khaki shorts, and a dark wool sweater. She looked athletic, nearly tomboyish. She pulled some clothes from a paper bag: khaki pants, khaki shirt, and a sweater like hers.

"Put these on; it's the kibbutz uniform."

She gathered up Judith's wet clothes and was about to stuff them in the bag when Judith stopped her. She reached for her overcoat and searched its right pocket. The postcard was more like a wet cloth now, the ink running. But the picture on the front was still discernible. A photo of the Wailing Wall, the Dome of the Rock above it.

Uri had been watching her. Now, he lit a cigarette, then offered the pack to Judith and Yael. Yael took one out, letting Uri light it. Judith just shook her head. From a distance came the sudden howl of sirens. Uri's face hardened.

"Shit, the Brits. The destroyer must have radioed them."

He tossed his cigarette in the sand and waved at the trucks.

"Go, go!"

Yael pulled Judith to the rearmost truck. She was barely on the truck bed before the driver hit the gas pedal. Judith watched Uri run over to a dark car. She could make out the contours of a figure in the back seat. It was the man with the jet-black hair and mustache. Uri slammed the door, and the car sped off.

February 17, 1947

A banging on the door jolted Uri from his sleep. He heard a woman softly call his name.

"Uri, Uri, open up."

He threw off the bedsheet, which left Yael lying naked and exposed. She muttered in her sleep. He tossed a blanket over her, then wrapped the sheet around his hips, pulled out his revolver from under the pillow, and rushed over to the door. Few people knew his address in Tel Aviv. He turned the key with his left hand and opened the door a crack.

Before him stood a full-figured woman in her late twenties, with bleached blond hair. Her shapely lips were painted red, and her blouse was open one button too many. Uri lowered the revolver and opened the door a little wider. She brought her face close to his.

"The Brits," Hilda whispered. "They're heading to the laundry today." Her gaze wandered over his shoulder. "Sorry, I see you have a visitor."

Uri looked and saw that Yael had woken up. He turned back to Hilda in the doorway. "Thanks, Hilda. You've been a big help, as always."

He pushed the door shut and hurriedly threw on a pair of pants and a shirt. Then he put on his hat, a type of flat cap. Yael watched in silence. She'd arrived last night from Yardenim on a truck full of vegetables headed to market. Now she sat on the bed, her knees pulled up and her arms crossed around them, staring at him. Uri threw a glance toward the door.

"Hilda works for us."

But Yael kept staring at him in pointed silence. Uri retrieved her clothes from a chair and tossed them to her.

"Here, get dressed. I need to warn the others."

Yael put on her clothes without speaking.

"Let's go," she said finally.

They climbed into the old Ford together. Uri drove north. Yael looked out the window, slightly turned away from him.

"How's that young woman, the one we pulled out of the water?" he asked, hoping to distract her. "What's her name again?"

Silence for a moment. "Judith. Judith Wertheimer."

"So? Is she settling in?"

"Not really. She's been through quite a lot. First a concentration camp, then the camp on Cyprus, and now that cold bath on arrival," Yael said. "That'll take it out of you."

Uri turned off the road. "Nearly there."

On the edge of Tel Aviv, on the Ma'agan Michael kibbutz, stood the low laundry building. A truck was dropping off uniforms and shirts.

"British uniforms." Uri grinned. "Good business."

He stood outside for a few moments and watched. Nothing looked conspicuous. He signaled for Yael to follow him in.

Inside the laundry, a few young girls were ironing uniforms. Uri passed them by and continued through the large building. In a back room, he stopped at a trapdoor built into the floor. He knocked three times with his foot, then waited a moment and knocked again. Someone pushed open the hinged door from below. Uri and Yael descended the stairs into a cellar. Bare light bulbs illuminated a workshop where about a dozen men and women sat at unfinished wood tables crammed with gray cardboard boxes. In a corner was a lathe as well as a milling machine and other equipment.

"Take a look." Uri pulled a handful of metal capsules from a box and held them up to Yael. "Meant for lipstick, imported directly from Great Britain, original packaging." He reached into another box. "And out of those, we make these." The lipstick capsules had been turned into large-caliber gun cartridges. "We also make hand grenades, small mines, explosives, whatever's needed. I'm hoping to arrange a shipment to Yardenim soon."

There was a sudden commotion near the stairs. A young woman who'd been ironing ran down, looking flustered, and whispered something to Uri.

"Everyone out of here!" he shouted. "Now!"

They all rushed up the stairs, and the men pushed a heavy cabinet over the trapdoor.

"Everyone go for a walk," Uri said, "until they're gone." Then, turning to the girls at the ironing boards: "The British are coming. Just do your work; don't act nervous."

He escorted Yael back to his Ford.

"I'm sure they just want to pick up their laundry, but it's better that they don't see us here." He lit a cigarette. "By the way, about Hilda. Most of her, uh, customers are British. She's one of our most successful agents."

He leaned over to Yael and kissed her. She returned his kiss and wrapped her arms around his neck.

"Let's go back to your place," she said. "I still have another hour before the truck heads back to the kibbutz . . ."

She placed a hand on his knee, sliding it upward.

He grabbed the steering wheel with both hands and stepped on the gas.

February 19, 1947

The bus jerked to a stop before the mukhtar's home, an imposing building in the center of Deir Yassin. Hana Khalidy stepped on board. A full half hour more, and then she would see him. She couldn't wait.

She wondered if he'd find an opportunity to talk with her this morning beyond the course of their official duties. The notion made her stomach tingle. *Butterflies,* Nurse Sarah had once called the feeling, and Hana looked up the English idiom in the dictionary: "a fluttering sensation," it said.

Deir Yassin, a village of modest prosperity, lay just a few miles west of Jerusalem. Many inhabitants of this Arab community of seven hundred souls worked in the city, and relations with the Jews were friendly.

The bus cleared the village after a few hundred yards and soon reached the road connecting Jerusalem with the coast. *Twenty-five minutes,* she thought. *Still so long.* Should she greet him first? For months, they'd been trading smiles and shy looks, but she didn't want to be too forward. He was her boss, after all.

Hana clutched her purse tight and drank in the view of Jerusalem while the village disappeared behind her. She didn't look back. Although she didn't want to admit it, it became clearer every morning where her future lay: before her, in that big city, not in the village, not in Deir Yassin.

She could still hear her mother's words in her ears. *Hana, it is time.* In the last few weeks, she'd been hearing it more often, more urgently. At twenty-three, she was practically too old now for a traditional life. Her younger sisters had long ago been married off to young men in the community and already had children. Both her brothers were married as well. And she herself had been promised to a neighbor's son, Youssef Hamoud, who was to inherit a large bakery from his father. Youssef was twenty-five, and others in the village teased him for still being a bachelor. She had put him off again and again, but she knew that things couldn't continue like this much longer.

What Hana wanted more than anything was to complete her training as a nurse. Then they could see about marriage. But, as she well knew, this only fueled his resentment. Youssef couldn't bear for her to be trained in a profession where she had contact with other men every day, especially ones who weren't Arabs but came from cities like Vilnius, Kraków, Berlin, London, and even New York—Jews from across Europe and America.

From America, she thought, *from New York.* What did the women in New York look like, the ones that *he* knew? Had there been many? She glanced down at herself. She surely couldn't compete with those women. She, an Arab, a nurse trainee. What could he ever see in her—in her of all people?

It is time, Hana, she heard her mother saying again, *time for your marriage to Youssef.* Only her father had stood by her side. He was a respected man in Deir Yassin, prosperous. He owned a few apartments in Jerusalem, some of which he rented to Jews. Hana was his favorite daughter. He couldn't say no to her. He was secretly proud of her work, she knew it, of her getting to meet people from all over the world.

The trip didn't take long. At the bus station in West Jerusalem, on the road to Tel Aviv, Hana transferred from the National Bus Company to the Hamekasher line that would bring her to Mount Scopus. An Arab news vendor was announcing the day's headlines at the top of his lungs. Hana bought a copy of the *Palestine Post*, the English-language paper in the British Mandate region.

Asher Leibowitz was the kind of young man who'd rather be riding a horse on the kibbutz than driving an old bus, but this was his job for now. As long as he could spend weekends training with his comrades in the Palmach, best of all with hand grenades, it was okay with him.

He grinned at Hana and glanced at her paper. *"Boker tov*, Hana. Good morning. Those people in London are starting to get serious now. About time too."

Hana cautiously glanced around: the usual Arab passengers' faces looked indifferent. So she quietly replied in Hebrew: *"Boker tov."*

Hana lowered the newspaper. In the British House of Commons, Foreign Secretary Bevin had announced that His Majesty's Government intended to shift all responsibility for resolution of the Palestinian issue over to the United Nations. What would be the consequences of that? Her gaze turned out the window. She studied the passing ads for businesses bearing Arabic, Hebrew, and English lettering, depending on the neighborhood. She noted with satisfaction that she could understand them all. She'd worked hard to master Hebrew as well as English, along with her mother tongue, and in the hospital had even learned some basic Yiddish.

The British, Youssef, her mother, her career—they all spun around in her head. And yet again, she had that one thought she didn't want to have but couldn't stop: *David. David Cohen.*

Hot blood rushed to her face, and she tried to bury herself in the *Palestine Post*, in the article about Bevin's speech from London. But the lines seemed to blur before her eyes. Only a few more minutes. Then she would see him.

The bus came to a stop before the massive Hadassah Hospital building, the most modern medical facility in Palestine. It sat high atop Mount Scopus, in East Jerusalem, in the middle of the Arab part of the city.

Hana climbed out and spent a couple minutes enjoying the view. At her feet lay Jerusalem. Rising from the Old City walls crowned with battlements is the Temple Mount, which Arabs call Haram esh-Sharif and Jews call Har Habayit. The mosque's golden dome shone in the morning sun, above the rock upon which Abraham had nearly sacrificed his son. From here, tradition had it, the prophet Mohammed had ascended to heaven on his horse, accompanied by the Archangel Gabriel. After Mecca and Medina, it was the most important site of Islam, built by the Muslims right where the Temple of the Jews had once stood. When Roman legionnaires destroyed the Temple two thousand years before, they'd left the part of the foundation now known as the Wailing Wall. On the hills beyond lay the newer parts of this city that three religions claimed as their own. Hana spotted the King David Hotel, the British headquarters whose south wing the Irgun had blown up in July of last year. Right behind it, she could make out the prominent tower of the YMCA building. She clutched the cold metal railing in front of her. The British no longer wanted responsibility for this city. They were fed up with the constant attacks, the violence from both sides, the impossibility of reaching a political solution that would satisfy everyone, and only wanted to bring their boys home. Hana knew what everyone in Palestine knew. If the British left, it could only mean more violence.

Another full bus stopped behind Hana. Nurses, doctors, patients, and hospital visitors stepped out. A man carrying his white doctor's coat on one arm, late twenties, slim, and dark-haired, passed by Hana and then stopped a moment once he noticed her.

"Good morning, Hana. How are you?"

She spun around with a jerk.

"Me? Oh, uh—thanks." Then she recovered: "I'm fine, thank you, Dr. Cohen."

He gave her a warm smile and looked like he wanted to say more, then blushed. He turned and disappeared through the hospital entrance. She picked up her purse and followed. It took her some effort not to run.

February 20–21, 1947

The night was moonless and cold. In February, day and night temperatures fluctuate heavily in Galilee. Judith tossed and turned, half-asleep. Her cough had worsened.

Woken by her roommate's restless slumber, Yael got up and lit a candle. She felt Judith's pulse.

"Are you sure you should be going anywhere? I think you still have a fever."

Judith coughed again, from deep in her chest, wheezing. But she nodded. Yael held her hand.

"Listen to me. You should stay here until you're fully back on your feet. Be sensible."

But Judith needed to see him. It was the first time since being sent to Dachau that she would see a member of her family. Her father had clung to life for forty-eight hours after SA thugs beat him up on Kristallnacht, before succumbing to complications of a basal skull fracture. Her two brothers, Josef and Hermann, had been sent to England as children, on the last transport the Nazis had allowed. There was no way to track them down. She'd remained in Berlin with her mother until they were torn apart and sent to different concentration camps in 1944.

Judith was desperate to see her last remaining relative, even though she barely remembered him. In 1935, already over fifty, Uncle Albert had emigrated to Palestine after being barred from practicing as a lawyer in Berlin. At first, the Wertheimer family had thought him a naive idealist, an incorrigible Zionist who'd rushed to abandon his country, because the Nazis would soon vanish from the political stage—or so the family believed—along with so many others. If nothing else, they'd surely become more moderate once the Olympic Games proved successful. Yet now he was the only one left—a remnant of her identity, of her family, of herself.

Judith pushed off her blanket. She slowly sat up.

"I'll be fine. We survived worse in Dachau," she said, partly to herself.

Yael shook her head.

"You don't need to play the hero here. Give yourself some more rest. What do a few days matter?"

She gently tried guiding Judith back onto the pillow of her narrow bed. Just then, the window shattered with a bang. A bullet struck the wall across the room and lodged in the wood. Yael reflexively dropped to the floor. She pulled Judith off the bed, dragging her under the table.

"Stay down," she whispered, and rose again only long enough to blow out the candle.

They waited a few endless minutes in case the shooter outside targeted their window again. Judith fought to suppress a coughing fit, her upper body aching from the strain. Suddenly, Yael sprung up, rushed over to her bed, and folded back the mattress to reveal an old rifle. She chambered a round with expert skill, then used the barrel to bust out the jagged remains of the shattered window and crouched below the windowsill, her rifle at the ready.

Outside, they could hear rushing footsteps, a male voice shouting in Hebrew: "Spread out, go, go!"

Shots rang out, at first single ones from rifles, then the clatter of a machine gun. Judith stayed under the table. She watched Yael stare into the darkness down the barrel of her gun. She slowly bent her finger around the trigger, then pulled. A scream pierced the night, faded to a whimper, then finally fell silent.

"I think I got him," Yael reported soberly as she chambered another round.

Judith had pressed her hands to her ears with her elbows bent inward. She was shaking uncontrollably. Cold sweat formed on her forehead. Outside, all was calm again now, apart from the sounds of the Palmach men using oil lamps to search the fields for any remaining attackers. But gunshots echoed inside her head. Endless machine-gun fire at the edge of the camp, where the SS was slaughtering the Russian prisoners of war. A deep rattle rose up in her chest, erupting as a violent, convulsing cough.

Only now did Judith notice that Yael had placed a hand on her head, stroking her hair to calm her.

"Come on," she said gently. "I'll help you lie back down. It's all over."

Judith woke to Yael standing before her, holding a tray with a cup of tea and a plate of scrambled eggs and bread garnished with cucumber slices.

"Breakfast," she said.

Judith bolted upright. "What time is it?"

Yael glanced at the old clock on the nightstand.

"Just after eight," she said. "You're not still going, are you? Not after last night?"

Judith nodded fervently.

"Here, take it, eat something. The bus doesn't come till nine." She set the tray firmly on Judith's lap. "Please."

Judith began eating, mechanically.

"They found him. It was Mohammed," Yael said. "A boy from the neighboring village. I used to play with him sometimes when we were kids. He was already a hothead back then. Now the mufti's men are inciting them all, going through the villages, turning them against us. That was the third attack on our kibbutz this month."

Judith looked up. "How is he?"

Yael gave her an irritated look. "How is he? He's dead. I shot him."

Judith dropped her plate back on the tray.

Yael eyed her with impatience. "Just eat it. Come on."

Judith shook her head. "I can't."

She jumped up and pulled on the dress she'd worn on the ship. She squeezed into the old leather shoes she'd brought from Germany and grabbed her gray overcoat. She quickly ran a comb through her long black hair. Then she picked up the crumpled postcard with the picture of the Temple Mount from the nightstand and slid it carefully into her pocket.

"All right, fine. I'll take you to the bus," Yael said with a sigh.

"How's Uri?" Judith asked.

"I haven't heard from him for days," Yael replied quietly, as if afraid of being overheard. "He's almost always on the move now."

Boarding the bus behind Judith was a young man in his early twenties, slender, his hair shaved so short she could see the skin on the back of his head. In the five days she'd spent in Yardenim, she'd only seen him once, briefly, in the kibbutz mess tent. She sat in the rear row, tucked into the corner, and rested her head against the window. From the corner of her eye, she saw the kibbutznik take a seat at the other end of her row.

The bus picked up speed. Judith watched the kibbutz fields rush by. This morning the young settlers were excavating a long sewage ditch with shovels. At the edge stood two men with Sten machine guns primed, their eyes on the Arab village just a half mile away.

Judith had fallen asleep. The diesel engine's annoying growl woke her as the driver shifted gears to cope with the incline. The hills rose steeply to the left and right of the narrow road.

"Bab el-Wad," explained the young kibbutznik, who'd moved over to sit next to her. "The Arabs call this stretch Bab el-Wad. The canyon's especially narrow here. Occasionally, they sit up top there and fire down onto the road. I'd do the same in their shoes. There's really nowhere for a person to escape here."

He pulled up his shirt and showed her the pistol stuffed into his waistband.

"Don't worry, we can defend ourselves."

The bus crawled up the rise so slowly that Judith could've walked faster. She broke out in a sweat.

The young man spoke again. "We'll show the Arabs. The only language they understand is violence."

She noticed his lively dark eyes darting back and forth, almost frantically.

"Abraham Horowitz," he said, and put out his hand. Judith shook it with hesitation. He held on firmly for a moment.

"You're burning up. Fever?"

Judith pulled her hand back. "It's not so bad," she said, but Horowitz didn't look convinced.

An armored scout car was coming their way. Waving at the tip of its bobbing radio antenna was the British flag. The soldiers casually waved to them, holding their red berets.

"Goddamn Brits," Horowitz muttered, forming a fist. "Twice a day they send their scout cars down this road, from Jerusalem to Tel Aviv. That's about the extent of it for them—then they can officially claim the road is clear. Don't want to know any more about it. And the Arabs pull back, of course, whenever the Brits come."

The bus struggled to pass a donkey cart laden with sacks.

"Just look at them," Horowitz said with a sneer. "A primitive people, donkey drivers and fellahs. They've been squatting on our land for centuries. Our land. It belongs to us, always has."

Judith shrank deeper into her corner, overcome by the shivers that had reappeared over and over in the past few days, the result of her leap into the freezing Mediterranean.

"We all saw last night how much bolder they're getting. But you can be sure of one thing: we'll show them."

The higher the bus climbed the hills of Judaea, the colder it grew. Judith huddled in her coat.

"These people don't understand peaceful coexistence," Horowitz started in again. "It's either them or us."

On the distant crest of the mountain, high above the road, they could see the jagged peaks of buildings in the now-blue sky.

"There!" Horowitz waved excitedly toward the east. "There, you see? That's it. That's Jerusalem."

Judith rang the bell again. Then a third time. She pulled out the old postcard and again checked the building number. Ben Yehuda Street 112. His name was even listed by the door: "Albert Wertheimer, PhD, Attorney." It had to be right. A woman came up to her, holding the hands of two small children, a shopping basket over one arm.

"Can I help you, dear?"

"I'm looking for Mr. Wertheimer," Judith said. "He doesn't seem to be home."

The woman winced. "You know him well?" she asked cautiously and dug around in her basket for a key.

"I'm Judith Wertheimer. Albert is my uncle."

The woman inserted the key in the lock.

"Please . . ." She opened the front door. "Come inside my place a moment. I was his neighbor."

It took Judith a second to respond. *"Was?"* she asked. "Did he move away?"

The woman pushed the door open wide, let the children through, and waved Judith inside. "Uh, no. Just, please, let's go up first."

They took the stairs to the third floor. On the way, Judith had to stop twice for coughing fits.

The woman eyed her with concern. "Are you unwell?"

Judith shook her head. "I'm fine, fine. I'll be all right."

The woman's apartment was untidy, like that of any family with small children. Judith noticed a lot of books and newspapers lying among a few toys.

"Excuse the mess," the woman said. She gestured to the sofa. "Please, have a seat. I'll make us tea real quick if it's all right with you."

She disappeared into the kitchen without waiting for Judith to answer. The two children moved closer to Judith, shy but curious.

Judith turned to the girl, who must've been about six years old. "What's your name?"

"Ayelith." She beamed and handed Judith a ragged old doll. Judith stroked the doll's shaggy hair, which clearly delighted Ayelith. She chuckled.

"And this is Shimon." She pointed at her brother, who was a little bigger.

The mother came back holding a pot of tea and two cups.

"I see you've already gotten to know one another," she said. "I'm Tamar Schiff. My husband, Yossi, is at work." She placed the teapot on the little table and started pouring. "Children," she said in a firm tone, "please go into the other room."

The two kids exchanged a look, but obediently disappeared. Tamar gently pushed the door shut behind them. "Sugar?"

She waited until Judith had stirred her tea and taken a sip. Then she sat up straight and cleared her throat. "So, about your uncle—" She raised her cup to her mouth, set it back down. "It's like this. He'd already been ill for a while, pretty weak, I'd say. No surprise after those two heart attacks." She paused again. "And then this young British officer came along. That was about two weeks ago. He appeared at his door, exactly like you today, and I was just leaving, about to pick up the kids, so I happened to notice him from the stairwell. Your uncle looked stunned. I don't know what it was about, but he seemed really, really surprised. Then they went into his apartment."

She took a sip of tea.

"Later, when I got home, I went to check on him. You see, we'd always looked after the elderly gentleman. He had no one else. He was practically part of the family. He'd often help the kids with their schoolwork. In any case, I went to see him. When he didn't answer my knock, I went inside."

She looked past Judith at a spot on the wall.

"He was sitting there in his armchair. He was dead."

Judith's teacup clattered against the table. "Dead?"

Tamar gave a helpless nod. "Yes, it was his heart, the doctor said. His third heart attack. Didn't survive it this time. It was possible he'd gotten too excited."

Judith couldn't breathe. "And the Englishman?"

"He was gone." Tamar placed a hand on Judith's arm. "I'm sorry. Really sorry."

It was silent for a while in the room. Eventually, Judith asked, her voice shaking, "The Englishman: What was he doing here?"

"I don't know, I'm sorry. The only odd thing was that they both were speaking German. As far as I could tell, the Englishman spoke it quite fluently."

Judith reached for her tea and took a sip. "Did you hear his name?"

Tamar thought about it. "Yes! I think he introduced himself as Goldsmith, Lieutenant Josef Goldsmith. Jewish name, sounds like."

Judith tried recalling that name, rolled it around in her mind, looking for some kind of meaning, but nothing came to her.

She was overcome by coughing again, from deep in her lungs; it shook her whole body. And with her fit came the realization that she was now alone, completely alone—on another continent, in a country called Palestine, where she'd seen little more than violence and death in the few days since her arrival. Different than in Germany, different than in Dachau, but violence and death just the same. She slumped down, the teacup slipping from her hands.

"For God's sake, are you all right?" she heard Tamar say as if from a great distance.

She tried to focus her eyes.

"Is there anyone who can care for you?" Tamar asked.

Judith shook her head.

"Listen, your uncle's rent is paid until the end of the month, still a week off. I have the key to his apartment. You can stay there until you recover, and I'll take care of you. Come on."

She grabbed Judith's hand and gently pulled her up.

In Albert Wertheimer's apartment, Tamar laid Judith down on the broad sofa and covered her with a blanket.

"Get some sleep. I'll check on you later."

Darkness descended over Jerusalem early on February days like this. Tamar pulled the pot of chicken soup off the stove.

"I'll be right back, darlings," she told Shimon and Ayelith, who were playing in a corner of the living room. "I'm just taking our new friend something to eat."

She opened the door to Albert Wertheimer's apartment.

"Hello? It's me, Tamar," she called, switching on the light in the hall, then continuing on to the living room. It was dark.

"Hello?"

She used her free hand to find the light switch on the wall. The dim bulb bathed the room in a soft light.

"Oh my God!"

Tamar hurriedly set down the soup pot on a sideboard and ran over to the sofa. The beige blanket over Judith's body was soaked with blood, her left hand hanging down. On the floor lay a kitchen knife. Blood still pulsed from an artery. For a second, Tamar froze. Then she erupted:

"Help! Somebody, help!" She heard footsteps in the stairway. A moment later, her children stood next to her, looking distraught.

"No, you two, go back, quick, run back to the apartment." Tamar shoved them out the door.

She ran down the stairs, too, into the produce shop on the ground floor.

"Where's your phone?" she panted.

The salesman stared at her blankly.

"I need an ambulance, quick!"

"There, back there in the corner."

David Cohen snapped the lock of his worn-out briefcase shut. He was pulling off his white coat when the telephone rang in the physicians' room.

"It's an emergency," said a voice on the other end of the line. "Urgent."

David rebuttoned his coat. "On my way."

A few minutes later, he pushed open the door to the emergency room. The ambulance medic was standing over the patient. "Heavy blood loss," he said in David's direction. "Still alive but not conscious. Slit her wrists. But she did it wrong—across the wrist instead of the artery."

"Let me have a look." David leaned over the woman.

The ambulance medic had tied off her arm and stopped the bleeding. David felt her pulse and noted her temperature. He pulled out his stethoscope and listened to her chest.

"Hmm. This doesn't sound good at all," he muttered. "Well, Nurse Sarah, let's get to it. She needs a transfusion immediately. But first we need to determine her blood type. Plus an antibiotic for the fever—and x-rays, as fast as possible—I'd say we're looking at severe pneumonia."

The nurse nodded. "We'll get right on it, Doctor. Hana?"

Hana was standing behind her, listening keenly. She pulled a syringe from a drawer.

"Good. You take a blood sample, Hana," Nurse Sarah said kindly.

"Looks like you have a handle on things," said David. "Call me when you have a blood type. I'll be in the doctors' room." He turned to the door. "Looks like overtime again, Hana," he added with a wink.

Blood rushed to Hana's face. "I—I don't mind at all, Dr. Cohen."

The door flew open. Two orderlies wheeled in a man on a stretcher. The sheet over him was drenched with blood.

"Grenade attack," one of the orderlies explained. "At Jaffa Gate, in front of the bus stop. Some guy threw a grenade right into a group of Arabs. Bald, around twenty, took off in a car. The witnesses say he's a new guy, supposedly named Horowitz, probably with the Irgun. Done his share of butchering, apparently. This man here got it bad. Don't think the leg can be saved."

David pulled the sheet away. One leg was shredded, the bones showing. "Are there any other victims?" he asked.

The orderly shrugged. "We took them to the morgue. Mother and a little kid. Nothing we could do."

When Nurse Sarah knocked on the door later, David was washing his hands. His doctor's coat was smeared with blood—the orderly had been right about the young Arab's leg needing to be amputated. At first, David wasn't sure why Nurse Sarah was standing there.

She flipped open a thin folder with the lab results and made a grave face. She first looked to Dr. Cohen, then to Nurse Trainee Hana, who she'd brought along with her.

"AB," she said in a grave voice. "The patient, she's blood type AB."

David nodded. "A rare type, but, all right, give her a transfusion right away."

Nurse Sarah's somber expression didn't change. "The problem is, we don't have any more. Too many injured in the last few months, and the number of donors keeps falling."

David took the folder and stared at the lab results. He knew there was no delaying this. The patient had lost too much blood.

"So, we're supposed to just let her die?" He looked helplessly at the two women.

Nurse Sarah was staring fixedly at the floor.

Then Hana stepped forward and cleared her throat. David gave her a quizzical look.

"I—" she began, "I'm type AB."

"You are?" The surprise in his voice was unmistakable. "You're sure?"

"I'm sure, Dr. Cohen. It's in my file."

"And you'd be prepared—I mean, are you aware that you—?"

Hana nodded. "Of course, yes."

David placed a hand on her shoulder. "Thank you, Hana." Then he added, businesslike: "Let's hurry. We really can't lose any more time."

When Judith woke the next morning, it took her a while to grasp the situation. She was lying in a clean bed in a large, bright room with five other beds. A tube was sticking out of her left arm, leading to a bottle with liquid dripping from it. Her left wrist was bandaged. Her bed stood next to a broad window. Through the glass, she could see a patch of blue sky, below that a bare, light-brown hill with green stretches. In the distance, she thought she could make out tents with a flock of sheep grazing before them.

The door opened, and three people dressed in white, a man and two women, walked directly toward her bed. The man smiled. "You're awake," he said.

Judith tried to smile back.

"I'm Dr. Cohen, and this is Nurse Sarah and Nurse Hana." The doctor pointed to the two women, one in her early thirties, the other about ten years younger.

He reached for Judith's right hand and felt her pulse. "Better already. The fever also seems to have come down somewhat." He took his stethoscope. "May I?" He opened her nightgown and leaned over her. "Well, the lungs don't sound good, but no surprise there." Dr. Cohen straightened up again. "You were lucky," he said matter-of-factly. "Despite everything."

He turned to the younger nurse, who handed him Judith's medical chart.

"You have severe pneumonia, considerable blood loss from that, uh, cut on your arm, and a fever, of course." He handed the records back to the nurse, then waved her forward. "This is Hana Khalidy. Without her, you'd be dead now."

Judith took a closer look at the young woman.

"Hana donated blood for you. Considering your rare blood type, it was the only way."

Judith wasn't certain, but she had the impression that Hana looked Arabic. The doctor seemed to guess what she was thinking.

"Hadassah Hospital is supported mostly by Jews from America, but we're an open institution. We don't discriminate. We welcome patients from many countries, Jews, Arabs, Europeans, Americans. And that applies to staff as well." He gave Judith a brief pat on the hand. "I'm thinking a few days of antibiotics and everything will be much better. Can we call someone? Relatives, friends?"

Judith shook her head. Dr. Cohen looked baffled for a moment.

"Then how about Nurse Hana looks after you for a bit? I mean, since it is her blood flowing in your veins."

Judith smiled weakly.

"Good, then. Get some rest for now. We'll check on you later."

He turned to go, but then pivoted back as if something had occurred to him. He took her hand and held it tight a moment. He made eye contact, then said softly, "And no more foolishness. Promise?"

She lowered her eyes.

"Promise?" he urged.

"Promise," she said.

He let go and strode to the door, followed by both nurses. Judith saw Hana turn back to glance in her direction.

"Now, what about that young Arab they brought in yesterday?" Dr. Cohen was asking as they left.

By the time the bus cleared the hill to the village, nearly everyone had gotten off. Hana had fallen asleep from exhaustion. She only woke up when they came to a stop at the house of the mukhtar of Deir Yassin.

She was shivering. The day had blessed Jerusalem with its first spring temperatures, but the nights were still cold. At the bus stop stood Youssef, his hands buried in his pockets.

"Where have you been?" he demanded.

She stopped before him. "At the hospital," she said defiantly.

"At the hospital, with your doctors?"

"At the hospital, with patients."

"All night?" he railed.

She withstood his glare. "All day, all night, and another whole day, until this evening."

His eyes were cold. "So? What are you doing there the whole day and whole night in that Jew hospital?"

She stood erect, straightening her back. "Surely you remember Ali? Ali Heikal? About your age."

"Ali? What about him?" he asked, annoyed.

"They were operating on him for half the night, and I was helping," she said. "He's lost a leg, but he's alive."

He stood there motionless a moment. Then he looked at her sharply. "Why did he lose a leg?"

She bit her lip. The truth would soon get out anyway. "Grenade attack, at a bus stop."

"Those Jews! Every day there's another attack. And you?" His voice broke. "You're still helping them. This must stop, you hear me? I will not tolerate it anymore! God will punish me if I put up with this any longer."

"We help everyone at the hospital," she replied. "Arabs too. I just told you we were saving Ali. Hadassah is everything this land could be if we could all just let it."

"Didn't you hear me? I will not tolerate this. We're getting married, and my wife will not work in some Jew hospital!" he screamed.

Hana lowered her head for a long moment. Then she raised it and stared defiantly into Youssef's face. Her eyes flashed, but she remained silent. Then she turned, picking up speed as she walked away. A stone flew past her head, only missing her by a couple inches.

February 26, 1947

Uri tossed the cigarette to the ground and tried, like he did so often these days, to get the constant thoughts of Yael out of his head. Should he have asked her to stay in Tel Aviv? There was plenty to be done around here too. Uri knew it was dangerous for her to be on the kibbutz in Yardenim, that the Syrians were attempting to stir up unrest in Upper Galilee, and he couldn't protect her there. But Yael was a sabra, a Jew born in Palestine—she was sure to put up a fight if he tried to coddle her. And the Haganah needed him here, in Tel Aviv. He was one of their commanders.

Right now he had to take care of the German. He climbed the stairs and knocked. When the door creaked open, he found himself looking into a pair of remarkably blue eyes. The man opened the door and let Uri step inside. Uri immediately noticed he had a Luger on the nightstand, within easy reach.

Uri held out his hand. "Let me see that, Adolf," he said in German.

Friedrich Paulsen handed him the pistol. Uri weighed it in his hand. "Not bad. How many Jews you kill with it?"

The question seemed to hang in the air. Paulsen sat on the edge of the bed with his shoulders drawn in and did not move. He stared at his bare feet.

Uri handed back the Luger. The German accepted reluctantly and returned it to the nightstand.

"Okay, Adolf, time to get ready. We still have a lot to do."

"Stop calling me Adolf. My name is Friedrich, which you know, and people call me Fritz." He paused. "At least, when they want to be my friend."

"All right, fine, Fritz." Uri stretched out a hand. "Call me Uri."

Fritz shook it. Then he stood and went over to the little sink.

"Just need to shave real quick," he said, lathering his face.

Uri looked out the window.

"How long do I have to keep up this masquerade with the black beard, the dyed hair?" Fritz asked.

"Just a little while longer," Uri told him. "We can't take any risks."

Fritz placed the razor back by the sink, checked that the Luger's safety was on, and stuffed the gun into his waistband. The two men went down the stairs together.

The streets of Tel Aviv were full of life. Buses puffed black billows from their exhaust pipes, expelling their human cargo, ingesting new loads. Clattering trucks headed for the many construction sites that were changing the face of Tel Aviv day by day.

A city on the rise, far removed from the European image of picturesque, Oriental Palestine. Most of the buildings were whitewashed, the lines of their facades stark and clear, the streets straight and wide.

"Three thousand," Uri declared. "We've put up three thousand buildings—all in the same style. The Bauhaus architects were really able to pursue their vision here after Adolf kicked them out of Dessau."

Small white clouds hung in the west, over the sea. The street cafés were as full as ever on this warm spring afternoon.

"Let's sit," Uri told Fritz.

A waitress came and asked in halting Hebrew what they'd like.

"Coffee, white bread, butter, and a couple fried eggs," Uri ordered in German.

The waitress gave him a grateful smile. "Coming right up, gentlemen," she replied in German.

"You'll meet plenty of your countrymen here. Folks call them *yekkes*," Uri said. "Came in the thirties, most of them. When Hitler started driving them out. First from Germany, then Austria. In the beginning, the Nazis were happy to deport their Jews to Palestine. Eichmann even worked on it with the Zionists. Pretty unbelievable today, but true. He only wanted one thing: to get rid of them as fast as possible. He was proud of every person he was able to dump in Tel Aviv. But in '41, they shut down the borders for good, and then, well! You know, don't ya?"

Uri reported this without any visible emotion as he attacked his fried eggs. Fritz just squinted at his plate grimly. At the next table, two middle-aged women were having a lively chat in Polish.

Uri turned to them, switching to perfect Polish. "Would you pass the salt?"

One of the women handed it to him.

"Dziękuję bardzo," he said in thanks, then met Fritz's quizzical eyes.

"Lemberg," Uri said. "My family comes from Lemberg, or L'viv, take your pick. Poles, Germans, Ukrainians, Jews. We were a multilingual home. I was fourteen when we left, 1936. My parents were Zionists to the core, idealists, you know? To them, Theodor Herzl came second only to God, or maybe even before him. The fact that everyone around us was a brutal anti-Semite naturally encouraged them to see Eretz Israel as paradise. They went to a kibbutz right away, of course, and they're still there, dreaming their socialist dream. Of course, Lemberg is socialist now too—Comrade Stalin saw to that."

He offered Fritz a cigarette and lit himself one.

"If they'd stayed, they probably would've exited out the chimney at Auschwitz. Or Sobibor, Treblinka."

He expelled smoke from his nose.

"And me with them," he added, gazing into the bright-blue sky. He fell silent a moment. "Now we're coming from all over Europe, from Hungary, Romania, France, Holland, and of course from

Germany—though the Brits are making things much more difficult at the moment. As you yourself experienced."

He sucked on his cigarette again.

"But we're going to fight for everyone who wants to come. We'll need every goddamn new arrival here if we want to become our own country. Every one. Otherwise, we won't be able to protect ourselves against the Arabs."

Uri's voice quavered slightly, and Fritz looked up in surprise.

"We need to be fighting on two fronts at once—against the Arabs and against the British. There are one hundred thousand British soldiers stationed here in Palestine alone. And we've got just a few thousand fighters. But we have to prevail. We must drive the British from this land as soon as possible."

Uri set a few bills on the table. They strolled the streets awhile, until they came to Allenby Street. A woman was leaning against the corner of a building, her makeup too garish for a sunny afternoon, balancing on pointy heels. She eyed the two of them expectantly.

"Hello, Hilda," Uri said. And turning to Fritz: "Believe it or not, Hilda's from Lemberg, too, from the same part of town."

He patted her behind.

"Here." He pointed at Fritz. "A new friend, right off the boat. He saved some peoples' lives. Do him a favor, *moja kochana*, my love," he coaxed. "I don't think he's seen anything as fantastic as you for a long time, at least not up close."

Her lips curled into a smile.

He quickly added: "For free, understand?"

She hesitated a moment, then gave in. "You owe me one," she whispered.

"Yeah, that I do," he said, grinning.

He took Fritz's hand and placed it in Hilda's. Surprised, Fritz tried to pull away, but Hilda dragged him to the building she was standing in front of, pushed the door open, and led him up the stairs and into a small apartment on the third floor, its windows covered with black curtains. In the corner stood a wide bed, and above it, a large mirror. She began undressing without further ado. Fritz stood before her, undecided.

"What's the matter?" she asked in Polish.

"I don't understand," he replied in German.

She smiled and switched to German. "That's fine, honey. I'll show you."

She undid his belt, and the Luger fell to the floor with a thump.

"What do we have here?" she said, only slightly startled.

Her practiced hands pulled down his underwear and held his member. She looked surprised, but then smiled.

"Now that's interesting," she said as she led him to the bed. "I haven't seen that in a long time."

"What?" he asked, clearing his throat in embarrassment. "What's so interesting about it?"

Hilda looked him in the eyes.

"You're from Germany, but you're not one of us at all. You're not circumcised."

"I—"

"Not now," she said and pulled him to her. "We can talk after."

March 1, 1947

Judith stared at the ceiling. In the bed next to her, she could hear the Bedouin woman breathing deeply as she slept off her appendectomy. The four other beds facing the window were empty.

Right next to the door was a woman from Dresden—Roswitha Goldfarb, about sixty, emaciated, pale. For years she had hidden in cellars, somehow managing to elude the Gestapo. During the February 13, 1945, air raid, she was in the city center, hiding in a hole built into the far end of a cellar. Everyone sheltering closer to the entrance died, suffocated by fumes from the firestorm. Luckily, she knew of a tunnel that led to the air raid bunker in a neighboring building. In the turmoil after the first night of bombing, as the people of Dresden wandered the streets, no one paid any attention to this Jewish woman, just one of the ten thousand homeless. She persevered until the Russians came. After the surrender, a Jewish officer in the Red Army got her a seat on a train to Berlin. And from there, she'd made it to Palestine. Now she lay in Hadassah Hospital, with incurable stomach cancer.

Judith felt the bandage on her wrist. She had survived. But for what? At Dachau, she and the other prisoners, they had one goal. All they thought about was making it to the next day, and the one after that, and the one after that. They shared a kind of solidarity in their misery. Now, here she was, in a clean bed, but she had no goal. Make it to the next day for what? She was alone, alone in a strange land.

Roswitha was sitting upright in her bed and reading the news-paper, oversize glasses balanced on her nose. The rustle of the pages sounded unusually loud, dampened only by the Bedouin woman groan-ing. Occasionally, Roswitha would glance over at Judith, her eyes sharp and alert in her sunken face, and smile at her. Stacked beside her were magazines and books from the hospital library. Judith got the impres-sion that Roswitha read practically nonstop.

The door swung open. Dr. Cohen strode in, Nurse Sarah and Hana in tow. He planted himself next to Roswitha and took her hand.

"Doing your morning reading already?" he said with a sad smile. "The nurses are here with your injection. I hope it helps you get through the day more easily."

She nodded gratefully. The morphine injections were the only thing that helped ease her pain.

"By the way, I still have a few magazines from New York around here," he said. "Do you know enough English? Would you like to have them?"

Roswitha nodded.

"Good, good. Hana will bring them to you in a bit."

He turned to Judith. "And how are you doing this morning? Better?"

Before she could respond, he checked the chart hanging on the wall behind her bed. The doctor felt her pulse and listened to her lungs. "So, already much, much better. A few more days and we'll be there. Today the bandage is coming off." He nodded to Hana. "You can help with that in a minute."

He'd already moved over to the Bedouin woman. He checked her pulse and took a look at her surgical wound.

"Looks good. She's sure to be waking soon. Then we'll have another look at her."

He gazed around the group and attempted one of those broad all-is-well smiles that doctors do, yet Judith noticed the dark rings under his eyes.

"Well, then, see you tomorrow morning," he said.

He stopped by Roswitha and put a hand on her shoulder. "Hana will be back with the magazines."

Roswitha held his hand tight a moment. "I'm looking forward to it, Doctor."

After a while, Hana returned with two issues of *Life* and placed them on Roswitha's nightstand, then fluffed up the woman's pillows.

"Would you like some tea?"

Roswitha was already buried in *Life*. "Oh, not at the moment, but thank you."

Hana turned to Judith. "May I?"

Judith offered up her wrist, and Hana cut through the plaster holding the bandage in place. Her skilled hands unwrapped the gauze. The wound was healing well. Hana halted a moment, as if weighing whether her next question was appropriate.

"The number tattooed on your arm—what does it mean?"

Judith jerked her arm away and hid it under the covers.

"Excuse me," Hana said, startled. "I didn't want—I mean, I didn't mean to hurt your feelings."

Roswitha set down the magazine and stared through her huge glasses. Hana just stood there helpless, her shoulders drooping.

"Just tell her," Roswitha urged. "There's no shame in it, is there?"

Judith slowly pulled her arm out from under the covers. "It's from the concentration camp. All the prisoners got one."

Hana gasped. "I didn't know." She looked at the ground, her face red.

Judith shifted to one side of the bed. "Please, take a seat. Just for a moment."

Hana found a spot on the edge of the bed, her hands folded in her lap.

"I know that you saved my life," Judith said. "Sorry this is a little late in coming, but—thank you, Hana." She placed her hand on Hana's.

Hana sat completely still a moment. "What was it like there? In the camp, I mean."

Judith's head spun. She felt ashamed and yet relieved when the tears poured out. Her body shook, like an earthquake. She wanted to scream, wanted to scream it all out, all those years of silence, suppressing it, numbing it, but all that emerged from her chest were deep sobs.

Hana didn't know how to react. Then, finally, she leaned down to Judith and took her in her arms, squeezing her gently for a long time while she wept.

"I—I'm sorry," Judith said, falling back on the bed in exhaustion and relief. She tried to wipe away the tears with the back of her hand. "I'm sorry. I—I can't talk about it now. Perhaps later." She attempted a cautious smile.

"That's all right, Miss Wertheimer. I don't want to upset you."

Judith grabbed her hands. "Please, Hana, please call me Judith. And you aren't upsetting me. It's the opposite, just the opposite. I'm grateful you asked. It's just—I don't know. It came as such a surprise."

Someone knocked on the door. Nurse Sarah stuck her head in.

"Hana? Dr. Cohen needs you urgently."

Hana went to stand, but Judith held her hands tight another moment.

"You have no idea how grateful I am to you."

Hana smoothed out her white smock. "I'll see you soon, Miss Wertheimer. Judith."

Judith took a deep breath, feeling liberated. This young woman had triggered something inside her. She wasn't exactly sure what it was, but one thing was certain: Hana was the first person to ask her about her time in the camp since she'd arrived in Palestine.

Uncle Albert was dead, her final link to her old life. But he did have a grave. She would try to find it. She recalled Tamar's words, what she'd told her about his final hours—the British officer whose appearance had upset him so much he'd suffered a fatal heart attack.

Judith turned to Roswitha. "Is there a telephone here?"

"I think there's one in the doctors' room."

Judith pushed back the covers and stood up. She was light-headed and needed to steady herself on the end of the bed for a moment. Then she went out into the hallway and found a nurse.

"Where is the doctors' room?"

The nurse gave her a disapproving look but nodded toward the end of the long hallway. There was a door with a sign bearing Hebrew and English: "Physicians' Room, Entry Prohibited." She knocked and turned the door handle at the same time. Dr. Cohen, bent over a patient file, looked up in surprise.

"Well, who do we have here? Do you need me?"

"No, no," she countered. "I just need to make a phone call. It's urgent."

Cohen pushed the file aside. "To whom, may I ask?"

Judith took a deep breath. "To British headquarters."

Jonathan Higgins flipped through the file, then paused on a page, taking a closer look.

"Bloody bastard," he growled. It was the third such incident this week, and again it pointed to the same suspect. "Horowitz, Abraham," he read in the British police report. "Early twenties, noticeable feature: bald head. Brutal assassin. Previous offence: hand-grenade attack on a British jeep, one deceased, two severely injured. Attributed to the Irgun . . ."

The telephone rang. He set his cigarette in the ashtray.

"Office of General McMillan, Sergeant Higgins speaking," he said.

He heard a female voice speaking English with a strong German accent.

"You wish to speak with whom?" he said. "Lieutenant Goldsmith?" He reached for his cigarette. "Regarding what, if I may ask?"

He listened to the woman with half an ear as she prattled on. Some nonsense about her departed uncle.

"And how does this concern Lieutenant Goldsmith? . . . I see, you aren't quite certain yourself—do I understand correctly?"

Higgins was in a sour mood. Those Jews out there were becoming more and more brazen. And more dangerous. Every report of an attack on British soldiers passed across his desk here in the outer office of the commanding general of British Armed Forces in Palestine. Higgins had been at this for twenty years—India, Yemen, then the invasion of Normandy, finally Germany. He'd been with the troops that liberated Bergen-Belsen concentration camp. In the beginning, he felt compassion for the victims of the Nazis. But then he was transferred to Palestine.

Higgins had been in the King David Hotel in Jerusalem when the Irgun bombed it. He had escaped with an ear injury. Over seventy people had died. Since then, the Jews' attacks on the military had only increased. British headquarters in Jerusalem resembled a fortress now, surrounded by rows of barbed wire. They called it Bevingrad, after Foreign Secretary Bevin. As with most soldiers, Higgins's sympathy for the Jews had vanished completely.

Also like most of the soldiers, Higgins now wanted only one thing: to get home to his family in Lancashire. If the Jews and Arabs were so keen on war, then they could solve the Palestine problem themselves. No one had a solution, neither the men in London nor the British Mandate government. Now the United Nations was supposed to find a way. *Please do,* Higgins thought, *and best of luck.*

"Yes, Lieutenant Goldsmith does work here. But he's not in the office presently."

He pressed out his cigarette in the ashtray.

"When's he returning? . . . See here, miss, it's not at my discretion to reveal official business to strange callers." Adding a sigh, he reached for a pencil. "What did you say your name was?" He scribbled on a piece of paper. *Wertheimer, Judith.* "Very well, I'll pass along the message."

Higgins hung up. Lieutenant Goldsmith was on an official trip to Cairo. He'd only recently arrived, transferred from the British occupation force in Berlin. And wasn't he a Jew as well? At any rate, he was one of the few around General McMillan who wasn't openly anti-Jewish.

March 13–14, 1947

Hana knew what was coming. And she almost felt bad for her father. As much as he wanted to, a leopard can't change its spots. Her father had to make sure that certain conventions were followed.

Mohammed Khalidy stood at the window and looked out, his hands clasped behind his back. Though already past fifty, he still had a thick head of hair, even if steadily graying. As always, he wore a dignified suit and tie in the Western style. His own father had been a doctor and he, too, had studied medicine, in Egypt and London. Along with Arabic, he also spoke Hebrew, English, and French. But then his father had died, and Mohammed never finished medical school. He used the money his parents bequeathed him to build housing in West Jerusalem, apartments mainly rented by newly arrived Jewish immigrants.

Hana followed his gaze. Outside, his driver, Ali, was using a feather duster on the windows of the new Chevrolet.

"I understand you, Hana," he said finally, "but you must understand me as well. Youssef belongs to one of the oldest families in Deir Yassin. His father is your mother's cousin. I cannot simply reject him. You are promised to him, so we must adhere to that. Our family's honor depends on it."

Hana took a deep breath. "You know he doesn't suit us, Father. You know that just as well as I."

Mohammed Khalidy turned and eyed her keenly through his metal-rimmed glasses.

"He's becoming more and more radical," she said. "The mufti has too much influence on him. And on top of that: I don't love him."

Khalidy suddenly looked tired. Youssef was, without a doubt, the black sheep of the family. He'd stopped going to school, his work at the bakery bored him, and he had no professional ambitions—instead he'd attached himself to followers of Hadj Amin al-Husseini. The former mufti of Jerusalem had relocated to Cairo after a time in Berlin cutting deals with the Nazis. The man had devoted his life to fighting the Jews in Palestine, and now he was finding more and more eager followers in his mission to drive the Jews back into the sea.

Khalidy took a step toward his daughter and opened his hands in a gesture of helplessness. "You know how proud I am of you," he said. "I wanted to become a doctor myself once, and now you're the one helping people."

Hana didn't respond. She did recognize the difficult situation her father was in. He had allowed her so much freedom thus far, but how long could he go on postponing the wedding? It had been arranged long ago, when both of them were still young teenagers. But in the years since, Youssef had turned out to be a terrible hothead, and one of just a few men in Deir Yassin who had joined the mufti's crusade.

Khalidy agreed with the mukhtar that it was important to maintain good relations with the Jews in Jerusalem. Everyone benefited from the situation remaining calm. The village leaders had contact with the Haganah as well—they had negotiated a type of standstill agreement, and it had functioned well enough so far.

"I will speak with your mother's cousin," Khalidy said. "He should give Youssef a good talking-to."

Hana kept her head lowered. "I have to go. I have the late shift today."

She would've liked to add: *I don't love Youssef no matter how many thousand times he tries pressuring me. I only love David.*

Hana had bought a bouquet of spring flowers. She carefully arranged them in a vase before bringing them to Judith's bedside.

"For me?"

Hana nodded.

"Oh, Hana, that's so—I really don't know what to say."

Hana timidly picked at the flowers.

"They're to say goodbye," she said.

Judith abruptly sat up in bed and stretched high enough to wrap her arms around Hana's shoulders. She hugged her so hard the young Arab could barely breathe.

Judith was crying. "My God, Hana, I don't know how to thank you. For everything that you've done for me."

Hana had trouble holding back her own tears. "What are you going to do, Judith?"

"I'm going back to the kibbutz. They're willing to take me in there. It's the only place I can go. What about you?"

Hana's face darkened. Her voice sounded defiant. "I will stay here and complete my training as a nurse."

Judith felt weak. She repeatedly had to stop on the stairs to rest. She propped herself against the wall with one hand, holding Hana's bouquet in the other. She heard a noise behind her. Shimon Schiff came running, his face flushed, a soccer ball under one arm. He looked up at Judith in surprise.

"Is your mother here?"

Shimon nodded, ran up the rest of the stairs, and rang the doorbell like mad. Tamar Schiff opened the door.

"That lady is here, you know, Judith, the one with the hurt arm!"

Tamar stepped into the hallway and spotted Judith standing on the stairs. She rushed over and propped her up.

"Come on, I'll help you."

She took Judith's arm. They walked up the final steps together. Inside the apartment, Tamar led Judith to an armchair.

"Sit, sit. I just made some lemonade."

A few moments later, she set a glass before Judith, who took a little drink.

Judith's voice was faint. "I just wanted to say goodbye, and of course to thank you again."

"You're going?" Tamar asked. "You're really going to leave Jerusalem?"

"I am. I have too many bad memories here. Uncle Albert, my—" She searched for the right words. "My reaction to his death, the hospital—"

"Just stay. We'll find something for you. We need young people in Jerusalem," Tamar insisted. "You can live here with us for a while. It's not a problem, it really isn't."

"Thanks, Tamar, thank you so much, but I can't live here. And on the kibbutz, at least I can make myself useful somehow. I simply need a place where I belong."

A piece of her homeland, she wanted to say, but she couldn't bring herself to utter the words. Homeland? What was her homeland? It couldn't be Germany. And here, in Jerusalem, that last link to her family had died. Home was gone forever.

Judith rose. Tamar sprang up to help her, but Judith waved her off.

"I'm fine, thank you," she said. "I have to go. My bus to Yardenim leaves in fifteen minutes."

Tamar ran into the kitchen. After a few moments, she came back with a package.

"Here. Half a cheesecake, for the road. It's all I have in a hurry," she said, placing it in Judith's hands. She kissed Judith on the cheek.

"Shimon," she called out. "Be a good boy and take Judith to the bus. And come right back here after, you hear?"

Shimon came out with his soccer ball still under his arm.

"Can I stay out just half an hour, Ima?" he begged. "Menachem says I'm the best goalkeeper."

Tamar stroked his hair.

"Fine, half an hour."

The bus squealed to a stop by the road to Kibbutz Yardenim. Judith was the only passenger who got out. In her arms, she balanced the cheese-cake from Tamar and the flowers from Hana. Yael was waiting for her.

"You're finally back," she declared in a pleasant tone and gave Judith a quick kiss on the cheek. "Thought maybe you were going to give us another scare."

"Yes, I'm back," was all Judith said.

She looked around. While she'd been gone, the residents of Yardenim had started constructing two wooden buildings to replace some of the tents. The roofs had just been finished. Yael was one of the lucky ones who'd already landed a room, as she informed Judith on the way to a tent.

"I'm sorry, we'll have to put you up here for now. Later, you can share a room with me, if you want. But today—" She gave a bashful smile. "Uri's coming."

A Palmach man rode past them on a brown stallion, submachine gun at the ready.

"It's been calm the past few nights," Yael said. "The Arabs apparently learned their lesson. But that doesn't mean we can give the all clear, I'm afraid. The stronger the Yishuv becomes, the stronger the resistance as well."

Inside the tent, Yael found Judith an unoccupied bed. Judith looked around.

"Is there a vase somewhere?"

Yael smiled. "I'll be right back."

After a few minutes, she returned with an empty jam can filled with water. "This is all we have," she said. "We live modestly, you know."

Judith carefully arranged the flowers and set them next to her bed.

"A goodbye present? From some nice doctor?"

"It is a goodbye present, yes," Judith said. "From Hana. She's an Arab."

The campfire flames blazed high into the sky, the heat radiating all the way over to their table and their bottle of wine.

"From Mount Carmel," Yael said, and handed Judith a glass. *"L'chaim."*

Judith took a hesitant sip. She wasn't used to alcohol. Yael cheerfully emptied her glass. She kept looking at her watch.

"He said he's coming." She giggled. "And he always does." She filled her glass again. "Come on, Judith, don't make me drink alone."

Judith took another drink and coughed. Yael patted her on the back. "Anyone who works hard," she said, "should celebrate just as hard."

They heard engine noise in the distance.

Yael beamed. "That must be him."

An old Ford rolled up a few minutes later. Two men stepped out. Yael jumped up and ran to the larger man, wrapped her arms around him, and kissed him on the mouth. Uri freed himself from her, laughing, and reached into the Ford's back seat. He pulled out a bottle and presented it to her.

"French champagne," he said. "Believe it or not. From Tel Aviv." He didn't mention that a Haganah man had stolen it from a British depot.

Then he reached into the car again and pulled out a red rose. "Happy birthday," he said so loudly that all could hear. He kissed her, grabbed her by the waist, and spun her around three times. Setting her down gently, he gestured to the man who'd come with him.

"This is Fritz. He's a friend."

Ben Zvi, a newly arrived immigrant from Romania, had already pulled out his accordion and was giving the thing all he had. The young kibbutzniks stood and joined hands, with Uri and Yael in the middle. They danced the hora around the fire, slowly at first, then faster and faster, in a circle spinning to the right, each dancer in rhythm, three steps in one direction, then a step back, putting out the left foot first, then the right. The circle turned faster and faster. Yael cheered. When she noticed Judith still sitting at the table, she waved her over.

"Come on, come join us."

Judith stood reluctantly and joined the circle. The wine was hitting her; she had trouble trying to keep in step. The blood was rushing to her head, the flames blurring before her eyes. If the two dancers on either side hadn't been holding on so tight, she probably would've fallen over. She let them carry her along like this, and finally, she became one with the rhythm.

The accordion ceased, everyone out of breath. Judith had a little trouble finding her way back to her seat. The red wine glasses were refilled at once. She looked around for water, glancing around the tables. On the far end, well apart from the others, sat the man Uri had brought along. The flames leaped up when Uri threw on another piece of wood, the fire's glow illuminating the man's face. Their eyes met, and Judith's heart skipped. Now she was sure of it. Those blue eyes—she knew where she'd seen them. Dachau, April 1945.

Judith tossed and turned on her narrow bed. Occasionally, she'd wake up and pull the blanket over her shoulders before falling back into a restless sleep. The nights were still cool in Upper Galilee. In her dreams, the wine, the dancing around the fire, and that unexpected memory all blended into a wild mix of reality and fiction.

She couldn't get his eyes out of her head. They'd stood out to her back then, too, when the vengeance erupted in Dachau. He was standing in the middle of a group of American GIs who'd crowded around to shield him. Several prisoners had planted themselves a few yards away, some carrying weapons they'd taken from the SS guards, the Americans looking the other way. While taking over the camp, the GIs had discovered the train full of hundreds of corpses, skin and bones in striped uniforms, prisoners who'd been starved, died from exhaustion. The SS hadn't been able to dispose of them all, so these mountains of corpses became even more gruesome evidence of the terror they had wreaked in Dachau. The newsreel images soon spread around the world. Only then, during those spring days in Upper Bavaria, did it become clear to many American soldiers what the Nazi regime had stood for and what this war had been about, and they were full of rage and disgust. Some allowed the prisoners to take their revenge. The prisoners killed several dozen SS guards, without any intervention from the US Army.

Judith remembered this one German, in his uniform, with no rank insignia except those SS runes on his collar. And yet the Americans had shielded him from the prisoners, from their thirst for vengeance, from their wild and pent-up rage. They led that one man out of the camp in a jeep, to safety.

Judith pulled her blanket over her head. She tried in vain to drive the image from her head. Only when daybreak was finally filling the tent did she fall back into her restless sleep.

Uri was sitting at the head of the long table, eating with gusto. Yael was leaning close to him and holding her coffee cup. Fritz Paulsen had found a spot at the other end of the table, alone. The kibbutzniks left three places between themselves and the stranger. An intense aroma of orange blossoms wafted into the tent. Yardenim had started growing orange trees, all of them now in full bloom. Judith noticed the gap separating the German and sat down next to him. She reached for the coffeepot and poured.

"Would you like some?" she said.

Fritz nodded.

They sat in silence awhile, next to one another.

"I have to thank you," she said.

Fritz didn't respond.

"You saved my life, on that rubber boat offshore."

He gave her a restrained smile but didn't respond.

Judith held out her hand. "Judith Wertheimer, from Berlin," she said. "Most recently, Dachau."

Fritz reluctantly took her hand, then quickly let go. "Fritz Paulsen," he muttered. "I'm from Berlin too."

Judith sloshed the coffee around in her cup. She steeled herself. "I've seen you before, in Dachau. You were in uniform. An SS uniform."

Fritz abruptly set down his cup. Judith noticed him give Uri a quick, startled glance, but Uri was chatting with friends, his arm still around Yael's waist.

"In Dachau?" he said finally.

"Yes, in Dachau. On April 28, 1945, to be exact," she continued. "Or maybe you'll say I'm mistaken?"

Fritz lowered his head. He eventually shook it. "No, you're not mistaken. I survived the camp, just like you."

Judith sat up straighter. "What's that supposed to mean? Survived? You were on the other side, with the murderers!"

Fritz grabbed her hand. "Not here. We can go outside if you want."

Judith rose warily, then followed him toward the tent's exit.

They walked to the orange grove. Judith breathed in the aroma. The spring sun was already gaining strength. It was a clear morning, the sky a pristine bright blue. Circling over the fields was a falcon. It plunged downward, then quickly rose again, a mouse in its claws. It turned away in the direction of the Arab village, where thin pillars of smoke rose from chimneys. Atop the wooden watchtower at the edge of the kibbutz, a man from the Palmach, his rifle slung on his back, scanned the surroundings with binoculars. Judith felt his presence as a blight on the peaceful scene. For a moment, she had even blocked out the reason for their stroll.

Fritz jolted her from her thoughts. "If the Americans had come a day later, I would be dead."

Judith stopped short. "How do you mean?"

"Dachau was where they sent SS deserters—to execute them," Fritz said.

"Deserters? From the SS?" She stared at him in disbelief.

"Yes. There were some, even in the SS. Men who'd stopped believing the Führer, who didn't want to go along with it anymore."

Judith could see it all again: Fritz Paulsen, surrounded by the Americans, in SS uniform, but no rank insignia.

"I was one of them," he said.

Judith started walking again. Fritz followed her.

"But you were in the SS," she insisted.

"Yes. Completely voluntarily, I'll admit that. As soon as I was old enough, right after the Hitler Youth."

The falcon had returned from its nest and was circling directly above them.

"You said you're from Berlin," Fritz continued. "Can I ask what part of the city you lived in?"

"In Dahlem. How come?"

"You ever been to Wedding?"

Judith shook her head.

"That's where I grew up. Back of the building, sixth floor, toilet in the hallway. Working class. My father returned from the Great War a cripple, his left arm shot off. There were six of us. At first, he still had a job, as a night watchman. Then came the Depression. He had no work for years, like millions of others. I don't know about you, but where I lived, it was chaos in the streets, everyone hungry. It can mess kids up, you know, always being hungry? And then came Hitler. He stopped the chaos, nearly overnight. He had his own methods, sure, but things were looking up. My father joined the Nazi Party—enthusiastically. And soon, so did I."

Judith just stood there, unsure.

"Of course, he also drove out the Jews, first from public life, then from Germany. The Jews were to blame for the Depression, for the country's downfall—that's what they told us in the Hitler Youth. They were bloodsuckers. We were young; we believed it." He gave a bitter laugh. "Then came the war, the big victories, the world belonging to Germany all the way from Norway down to the North African desert. No one could stop us. Hitler in Vienna, in Paris—'Führer, command us, we follow.' The SS had another slogan: 'Our honor is our loyalty.' I was there, yes, sir. I was one of them."

"But you must have seen the murder behind the front lines, the mass shootings, the manhunts."

"I did. Yes, I saw it all. At first, I thought it had to be that way; it was a part of war, eye for an eye, tooth for a tooth. The toll that must be paid to make Germany great again. And then came the doubt. Not just because of Stalingrad. The British air raids were getting more severe every night. My father died in the bombing, my mother six months later, and then of course, the concentration camps. I wasn't there myself, but I knew about it. I can't sugarcoat it—I'd taken part in too many other things. But at some point, I saw that it was wrong. I tried to help where I could. Maybe not decisively enough, maybe not bravely enough, maybe too late. But one day, when I was letting an elderly

Jewish woman escape, they caught me, labeled me a deserter, traitor. And sent me straight to Dachau. I thought, now it's over for me too. And I felt relieved, despite it all."

Judith listened without interrupting, overcome with a mix of fascination and horror. Suddenly the idyllic morning seemed empty to her, inappropriate. She didn't know how she was supposed to process what she was hearing.

Again she recalled that day in Dachau, visualizing the scene where she'd seen this Fritz Paulsen for the first time. Something didn't fit. She could see him before her, his eerily blue eyes, the Americans placing him in the jeep. Then it came to her.

"You were blond then. The proper Aryan, blond and blue-eyed, a storybook Nazi. Why, Herr Paulsen, did you dye your hair black?"

He didn't answer.

"And what are you doing in Palestine?"

Again, nothing. But she didn't let up.

"If you don't tell me—what's preventing me from going to the others and telling them a former SS officer is hiding here, right on a Jewish kibbutz?"

Fritz met her eyes. "Do what you want, but I think that would get you into a load of trouble with Uri."

March 15, 1947

On the other side of the valley, across from Mount Scopus, the lights of Jerusalem twinkled under a starry sky. Calm had returned to the hallways of Hadassah Hospital after a hectic day. Only the shuffling of slippered feet sounded occasionally, patients on their way to the toilet.

David Cohen sat at his desk and rubbed his eyes. He closed the folder documenting a complicated case from Tehran and set his feet on the table. Only now, with the telephone having been silent for an hour, could he feel his exhaustion. He reached for his cup of coffee and discovered it empty. He took a pack of cigarettes from the drawer, pulled one out, and fiddled with the matches. *You shouldn't,* he told himself, *not now and not later.* He smoked too much, a bad habit from his army days. He set the cigarette next to the folder. Then came a soft knock on the door.

"Come in," he said.

Hana's kind face appeared. "I just wanted to see if there was anything else you needed."

David glanced at his watch. Just after midnight.

"No, thank you, Hana."

She started to leave, but he didn't want to see her go.

"Actually, it would be great if you could rustle up one more cup of coffee."

She nodded, her eyes shining, then withdrew silently.

David hauled himself up out of his chair and went over to the window. He usually rejected self-pity, but for this one moment, he savored it. *What the heck are you doing here anyway?*

He'd been asking himself this question repeatedly over the past few weeks. Right now he could be sitting at home, in Brooklyn, waiting to take over his father's well-run Manhattan practice. His father would be grateful, very grateful even. His mother wouldn't need to worry all the time in the face of increasing bad news from Palestine. And he? He'd probably be bored to death. And smoking even more. And waiting for something to happen.

He thought about Lea. She'd always wanted it all and right away. She wanted the apartment on Central Park, two kids, at least two nannies. She wanted the vacation home in Nantucket, the winter trip to Florida, and she wanted him. It had nearly come to that, but only just.

If David was honest with himself, Lea was one of the reasons why he'd applied for the job at Hadassah Hospital. She had opened his eyes to how his life wasn't supposed to go. Lea, deeply hurt, had made a huge scene. Eight weeks later, she was engaged to a banker.

He'd spent the final months of the war as a young army doctor in the Pacific, where they were still fighting for weeks after the last guns in Europe had already fallen silent, and he'd seen what the atomic bomb in Hiroshima had done to the people there. At first, he hadn't seen the newsreel footage from the camps with names he'd never heard before: Auschwitz, Treblinka, Bergen-Belsen, Dachau. Only when he returned to New York was it clear to him what had happened in Europe. He had never been a devout Jew. The only time his family actually ever practiced was on Yom Kippur and a little bit at Hanukkah, to compensate for the Christmas festivities all around them. But after the war, David started becoming interested in his own history, his roots. His grandparents had emigrated from Ukraine at the end of the nineteenth century; he remembered them still speaking Yiddish at home. After the war, the news kept growing that attested to the unimaginable: the Nazis had killed millions of European Jews. Systematically. It had made David feel like a Jew for the first time, a survivor of a race the Nazis had designated for total extermination. So, when he read in the *New York Times* about Hadassah Hospital, he applied on impulse. That was a year ago now, in early 1946.

A knock at the door. Hana came in with a pot.

"Your coffee, Doctor."

He went back to his desk and let her pour him some.

"Won't you join me, Hana? Please," he said and pulled a second cup off his shelf.

She hesitated briefly, but then sat on the front edge of the chair before his desk, her knees pressing together, her posture erect.

"I'm happy to, Doctor."

"Please, don't be so formal," he said. "You and I are closer than that, aren't we? It's David, please."

She turned red. "I'm happy to, David."

He anxiously fiddled with his cigarette. *What was he doing?* It was the middle of the night and here he was sitting with this beautiful woman in the physicians' room. He'd been sure he could keep his crush under control, taking pains to avoid putting himself and especially Hana in any risky situations, and now he'd thoughtlessly initiated one. He snatched up the matches, thinking, *to hell with good intentions.* He exhaled smoke through his nose with relish.

Hana sat on her chair as if nailed there, her hands on her legs. As much as he'd tried not to notice, her face was so thoughtful and so, so pretty. Well proportioned, finely chiseled. And that thick, black, shoulder-length hair she wore pinned up under her white nurse's cap . . .

He took another drag of his cigarette. If this had been New York, he would have known what to do. But here in Jerusalem, the rules were different, and he was still struggling to figure them all out. Hana was Arab, and Muslim, but surely her family was open-minded if they allowed her to work at Hadassah.

He smoked his cigarette down to the filter and kept himself together just enough to light a new one. How incredibly rude, to invite her to coffee and then say nothing. But the only words on his lips were ones he didn't dare to say. If he liked this woman, shouldn't it be okay to tell her? Would she reject him for being Jewish? Would her family?

David let out a sad sigh. "Excuse me, I don't know where my mind is."

Hana smiled politely. Her face revealed nothing.

He stood up, came around the desk, took her hand, and led her to the window. The sliver of a waxing moon floated above the city, reflected in the gold of the Temple Mount.

"Jerusalem," he said. "Everyone here is crazy."

Hana didn't respond, but he felt her lean tentatively against him.

"I guess I'm just as crazy," he continued.

He stepped behind her and undid the clip holding her cap. Her hair fell down. He cautiously caressed it. She pressed her back against him. He hesitated, terrified. Then she abruptly turned, wrapped her arms around his neck, and passionately kissed him on the mouth.

April 3, 1947

Judith held the tattered textbook on her knees. She was perched on a boulder alongside the pasture strewn with stones and wild spring flowers. *"Boker tov,"* she spelled out. Then she practiced it several times out loud.

"Boker tov, good morning." She ran her finger farther down the vocabulary list. *"Laila tov,* good night. *Mazal tov,* all the best."

A sheep nudged her leg with its nose. She looked up and gazed at the herd. The roughly forty sheep were grazing quietly, the lambs seeking milk from their mothers' teats, a scene of nearly biblical tranquility. Judith turned back to her book.

The sheep's bleating was drowned out by kibbutzniks hammering away as they nailed down the roof of a new wooden house over in Yardenim. The village was growing at a rapid pace. Judith had gotten used to keeping an eye on the little herd. At first she'd protested, but soon realized that there was no other way for her to contribute to the kibbutz. She was completely lacking in any knowledge of agriculture and still too weak to do the hard fieldwork that was a part of everyday life here, even for the women. Yael had tried to console her.

"We plan to raise a huge herd, and you can help," she'd argued. "Everyone here has to contribute whatever they can do best."

This morning, Yael had even brought her coffee out in the pasture. She was beaming. Uri had arrived late last night for a brief visit. He'd also brought, hidden under a blanket, three rifles and a crate of ammo along with several homemade grenades.

Judith used her time with the herd to improve her miserable Hebrew. Yardenim was a babel village of languages—Yiddish, Polish, Russian, German. Hebrew was supposed to be the common language, but many of the new arrivals had a tough time getting used to the language of their ancient forefathers.

The hammers fell silent and the workers climbed down to pause for breakfast. Judith saw the falcon circle overhead. Anxious swallows flew back and forth, their nervous chirping blending with the sheep's bleats.

Suddenly, she heard the drone of an engine coming from the road. A dark-gray jeep was approaching the village at high speed, leaving a long trail of dust. Sitting at the wheel was a man in uniform.

From her rock, Judith observed the kibbutzniks jump up and surround the jeep as it came to a stop in the middle of the village. She saw them gesturing and eventually pointing in her direction. The uniformed man made his way over to her. He was wearing sunglasses, the lenses coated with dust. Atop his head was a red beret, with short dark hair under it. His khaki uniform was ironed, his boots clean, his dark mustache precise. *A thoroughly British officer,* Judith thought. The British man stood before her and stared, his eyes concealed by his sunglasses. He slowly removed them, then his beret.

"Judith, is it really you?" he asked in German.

She dropped her book, her eyes widening. She clapped a hand over her mouth. She had opened it to shout but couldn't get any sound out.

For a moment they faced each other, frozen. Judith could feel her eyes welling with tears.

"Oh my God." She flung her arms around the man. "Josef, Josef," she whispered.

He held her tight. Eventually Judith separated herself from him and took a step back, to get a look at him, to make sure this was no mistake. He smiled, that same boyish smile. It was him, no doubt about it, despite the British uniform. Her brother.

Josef took her hand, sat down on the rock, and pulled her next to him. He picked up the book, patted off the dust, and placed it in her lap.

"Mazal tov." He smiled.

"Mazal tov," she replied softly.

"It took a few days for me to find you," he began. "All I had was a piece of paper with your name on it, a message saying you'd called head-quarters. I went by Tamar Schiff's again and learned about Uncle Albert dying right after my visit. Then Tamar told me about you showing up at her place, about your stay at Hadassah Hospital. At Hadassah, they told me that you'd gone to this kibbutz. So, well, here I am."

"But the uniform, and your name—Goldsmith?" she argued. "I never would've guessed."

"When I first got to England, I lived together with other kids, in a type of camp. Then I lived with a farmer and eventually a Jewish family, the Goldsmiths. They adopted me."

He turned his red beret in his hands.

"As soon as I was old enough, I joined the military. To fight the Germans. I served all over, in Normandy, in Bergen-Belsen, in Berlin. I searched for our family there—but didn't find anyone. Then I got myself transferred to Palestine."

He grinned, revealing that rascally expression of his. He gave her a friendly nudge.

"So, I'm here," he said.

Judith kept holding his hand tight.

"Looks like Uncle Albert brought us together after all," she said softly.

He nodded.

"What's next for you? Can I help somehow?" he asked after a while. He gazed over at the Arab village. "It's so damn dangerous here. And the way I see it, the situation will not be improving in the near future. Do not delude yourself. The Arabs are still fairly unorganized, in contrast to the Jews, but they will not tolerate more and more Jews coming to this land."

He paused a moment. "Nor will the British."

Judith didn't reply.

"One can hardly blame the Arabs," he continued. "I mean, they've been living here for centuries, and now here come the Jews and say: this is our homeland, it says so in the Bible, so you better make room for us."

Judith let go of his hand and self-consciously clutched her Hebrew book. Above them, between the kibbutz and the village, the falcon was circling again.

"I'm staying here," she said cautiously after a while. "There's no other place I can go. And besides—"

She didn't finish the sentence. She wasn't sure herself what came next. Was that the only reason she was here? Because she didn't know where else to go? She had landed here by chance. It certainly hadn't been her aim to become a shepherdess in Galilee, especially not so close to Arabs who were defending their land. But Uncle Albert was dead, and so she had returned.

Josef looked at his watch. "Sorry," he said. "It's getting late. I have to get back to Jerusalem."

He stood and helped her up. They hugged.

"Promise me you'll look after yourself," he said tenderly. "And do think it over. I can help you. I can get you out of here. This isn't for you. I can take you to England; I'll think of something. I'm sure you've heard that the British Government informed the United Nations yesterday that London does intend to give up its mandate for Palestine. Not directly, but as soon as a solution can be found."

Judith walked him to his jeep. She noticed the kibbutzniks following, all eyes directed toward the British officer at her side, who now kissed her and started up the engine.

"Please, come visit me in Jerusalem. And I'll say it again: do think it over." He revved the motor. "Before it's too late."

The jeep started moving. She waved at him as he went. Only after a while did she notice that Uri was standing next to her, his arm around Yael.

"So, your brother's with the Brits," he said coolly.

Judith didn't understand at first.

"That's just what we need—a British officer taking an interest in our kibbutz," Uri said. "As if we don't have enough problems."

Judith was shocked, speechless for a moment. Then she pulled herself together. "The British took him in after the Nazis drove him out. They gave him a homeland. He fought against the Germans with them. He liberated Bergen-Belsen."

Yael stared at her feet.

Uri continued: "He's a British officer. And the Brits are worse than the Arabs. The Arabs fight us, and many hate us, but that's because they fear for their land. But the Brits, they're just playing little games with us. First they so generously promise us a homeland with their Balfour Declaration, then they back out. And now, now all they care about is their strategic position in the Middle East, about the oil in Iraq, in Saudi Arabia, about the Suez Canal, about their empire. Jews are disrupting their plans. We're a nuisance to them."

He was working himself into a rant.

"When Rommel was closing in on the Suez Canal, suddenly they let us wear their uniforms, suddenly they formed the Jewish Brigade. And you know what? They made me an officer, just like your brother. That's right, I wore their uniform too. I was with them in Egypt, in Italy, then in Vienna, and even in Germany briefly. But no sooner had the war ended than we'd served our purpose to them, and again they turned back to the Arabs. Now they fight us, thwart us, bully us, courting the Arabs whenever possible. Most of them are worse anti-Semites than the Nazis."

He spat at the ground in disgust.

"But we're not going to accept that. When they put pressure on us, we'll put the pressure right back on them. When they shoot at our people, we'll shoot back. And it's working: now they're looking for a way to be rid of the Palestine problem. Please do. We're happy to help."

Judith turned away and slowly walked back over to the pasture, where the herd of sheep was grazing peacefully, and sat back down on the rock. She buried her face in her hands. Her body began trembling, harder and harder, until she burst out sobbing. Only some time later did she notice a hand on her shoulder. It was Yael.

"I'm sorry. It's not your brother's fault the British are making our lives really goddamn tough." She pulled her hand back. "Until Uri's left, it's best you stay with the herd. He'll calm down again soon."

May 1, 1947

The khamsin finally let up after two days, but the hot wind had driven up temperatures in Jerusalem. People sat in the outdoor cafés and enjoyed the warmth. For a few hours, the city seemed to be living in peace.

Hana wiped the sweat from her forehead and took off the smock she'd been wearing during the two-hour operation. Nurse Sarah set the telephone back on its cradle.

"Dr. Cohen would like to speak to you."

Hana jumped up, then caught herself and tried to act calm and composed. *Had Sarah noticed anything?* she asked herself, yet again. Dr. Cohen had been calling for her too much in the past few weeks, too often asking Nurse Sarah if the nurse trainee could help him with some important task.

Hana was soon standing outside the physicians' room. She paused a moment, trying to calm herself, then knocked on the door.

She waited until she heard a lively "come in," looked up and down the hall one more time, quickly opened the door, and shut it swiftly behind her. David jumped up from behind his desk piled high with medical records, reached for her shoulder with one hand, and locked the door with the other. Then he kissed her on the mouth and squeezed her tight.

"I've been waiting for this the whole morning," he said with a mischievous smile.

"Please, not here," she whispered gently.

David smiled. "Good Nurse Hana. Always so well behaved." He lowered his hands. Then he kissed her again. She granted him that.

"We're acting like teenagers," he said with a grin. "I am, anyway. You, you're—"

The telephone rang, cutting him off. His face turned serious.

"Yes, I'm coming." He put down the receiver. "Another gunshot wound." He buttoned up his doctor's coat and gave her a kiss on the forehead.

"I'm free this evening. You think we could go out, maybe to the movies?"

For one beautiful second, Hana let herself consider it. Of course, what David didn't understand was that it was totally impossible. She couldn't keep getting home so late. The situation was bad enough already. She'd exhausted all her excuses to keep Youssef at bay. Not even her own mother was willing to accept her constant evasions anymore. Hana swallowed. Then she heard herself say:

"I'd like that, David. Yes, I'd really like that."

The British police officer showed the photo around. It was a poor image, blurry, but the man was obviously young and had a noticeably bald head.

"Horowitz," the police officer said, "Abraham Horowitz. Ever seen him?" A woman shook her head. The officer turned to another passerby, but he, too, only shrugged.

The British had increased their presence in the streets after the Irgun had thrown grenades at an Arab kiosk in the Old City that afternoon, and another one at a police station. The grenade thrown at the Arabs was apparently homemade and hadn't gone off, but at the station, one British sergeant had had an arm blown off, and a second was slightly injured.

Their faces sullen, the uniformed officers now stood at intersections throughout the Jewish neighborhoods, their machine guns at the ready.

On Jaffa Road, several police jeeps had parked outside a building. A cluster of people had formed on the sidewalk.

"Move along, right now, go on, go on," the annoyed officer demanded.

But the curious onlookers didn't budge. After a while, five officers exited the building, pushing two young men in handcuffs in front of them. They roughly loaded the pair into a jeep. One of the policemen was carrying a crate with the barrel of a Bren machine gun sticking out of it.

From inside the crowd, a young man of about twenty, his bald head covered with a flat cap, screamed: "You pigs, goddamn pigs. Get out of Palestine already!"

The police officer recognized him at once, but by the time he'd fought his way through the throng, Abraham Horowitz had already disappeared around the corner.

David, who'd been standing with Hana, led her away anxiously.

"Come on, let's go. The movie starts in ten minutes."

A long line stood outside the Zion Cinema. The radio had reported the latest attacks, yet people seemed to have grown accustomed to it all.

William Wyler's *The Best Years of Our Lives* had finally come to Jerusalem. The movie told the story of three Americans returning home from war, and had recently won an Oscar. David bought two tickets. The cashier gave Hana a disapproving glance, which David tried to ignore. They made their way through the rows to two empty seats in the back.

When the lights went out, he slid closer to Hana and placed an arm around her. He felt how she leaned against him. *My God,* he thought, *what am I doing sitting here with an Arab nurse in a movie theater in a crazy city where the death toll increases by the day, where Jews and Arabs are at each other's throats? Absurd, completely absurd.* But there was no denying his feelings for Hana—they were way beyond that now. As she leaned her head on his shoulder, he thought involuntarily about Lea. In movie theaters, she'd always kept her distance from him, even though she was terrific in bed. Sex was one thing for her, feelings another.

Sex, he thought with resignation. That wasn't a priority with Hana. He knew she was engaged—she'd confided that she didn't want to marry the guy, this Youssef, but the engagement had still not been broken off. And so, she was restraining herself, at least where sex was concerned. David hadn't asked, but he was pretty certain that she was still a virgin. As educated as her family might be, she was still a young woman from a conservative, religious village. Sighing to himself, he tried concentrating on what was happening on the screen. But he could feel sweet Hana near. He leaned over and kissed her.

After the end of the film, people poured into the cafés. The evening was still warm despite the late hour. David took Hana's hand and they strolled up King George V Avenue. His small apartment was only two blocks away. He cleared his throat.

"Should we—I mean, would you want to—should we maybe go back to my place for a while?" he asked. "I won't do anything out of line, I just—"

She gave him a serious look. "I can't." She looked at her watch. "I have to go now. The last bus is leaving in fifteen minutes."

He walked her to the bus stop on Jaffa Road. She waved goodbye from her bus window.

Yes, I did want to go to his place, she thought after the bus had cleared the Jerusalem city limits. She wanted to feel him, really feel him, like a woman felt a man. She often pictured it, how it would be. David and her, a couple. Should she talk to her father? Could he possibly convince her mother to accept it? But before any of that, she had to be sure, completely sure. She loved David, but did he truly love her as well?

And first, she needed her saga with Youssef to come to an end.

Hana was relieved that Youssef wasn't waiting out on the street for her again. Through her bus window, she could see a light on in the living room of her parents' house.

When she entered, her father was sitting in his chair at the window, smoking a cigar. Her mother had lit the candles and served strongly sweetened tea. Together they were listening to a symphony orchestra on the radio, playing Tchaikovsky. Her mother's face was wrinkled in the way one would expect from a woman in her midfifties, but her black hair only showed a few gray strands. Hana always marveled at how beautiful she was.

Hana went up to her father and gave him a respectful kiss on the forehead. Her mother stood up and turned off the radio.

"It's late," her father said.

Hana remained silent.

"Youssef has been here twice already asking for you," her mother added in an accusing tone. "I told him that you still had work to do. How many more times must I tell him this?"

For a while, only the steady ticking of the wall clock could be heard, its pendulum swinging back and forth.

"You know that I cannot marry him," Hana said finally.

Her mother's expression hardened. "We promised his family. There's no other way."

Hana's father took a long puff on his cigar before setting it in his glass ashtray. "I spoke with your cousin," he said to his wife without looking at Hana. "I am prepared to pay him a large sum, to sever the engagement."

"And? How did he take it?" Hana's mother asked.

"He asked for time to consider," he said, his gaze fixed on the extinguished cigar. "Go to bed, Hana."

Hana left the living room. As she left, she could hear her mother.

"She brings shame to our family."

July 15–16, 1947

The mukhtar clapped his hands. Judith guessed he had to be around seventy years old. His tanned face was furrowed, framed by a thick gray beard. Despite the heat, he had on a kaffiyeh, that square cotton cloth tied around the head, and a long brown cloak.

A curtain parted, and a plump woman in a black, floor-length dress came in and served them tea. They were sitting on the floor, on several overlaid carpets.

The mukhtar waited awhile, until all had taken a drink. Then he said, "It truly was a terrible thunderstorm."

Judith nodded along with her two companions, Adam and Zvi. Ever since the armed attack at night, relations between the kibbutz and the neighboring Arab village Deir El Nar had been extremely tense. But the kibbutzniks had now decided to send a delegation to the village. Five sheep had escaped in a panic when lightning struck a tree in their pasture. The sheep now found themselves on one of the Arabs' fields. Judith had the assignment of getting them back.

"But this rain that came with the storm, it is good, good for us all," said the mukhtar.

Zvi, who knew Arabic, interpreted.

"Yes, that is true," Judith concurred.

"God, most Merciful and Almighty, praise be to his name, wishes that we live together," the old man continued. "But some are not ready to obey God's will."

Judith understood. By now, she had learned that most of the villagers wanted to continue living in peace with their Jewish neighbors. They'd benefited from it. Whenever a doctor came from Tel Aviv, he also treated the villagers.

"There is much hate in some people," he said. "It comes from far away."

He gestured with his head toward the east, to where the Golan Heights stood, part of Syria. "They do not want peace." Again he clapped his hands, and again the woman appeared and topped off their tea.

The mukhtar fell silent now.

Judith turned to the subject of the sheep. "We can offer you oranges. Five sacks, one for every sheep."

"Ten."

"Seven," Judith proposed.

"Eight," responded the mukhtar.

She nodded. "All right, eight."

They rose and shook hands.

"That old swindler," Zvi said with a grin once they'd left. "But we got our sheep back."

They walked down the unpaved street under the villagers' wary eyes, last night's rain puddles evaporating in the hot midday sun. It struck Judith that most of the children were barefoot. A pack of dogs accompanied them, barking, running in front of them before coming back, scuffling in the dust.

"The old man was trying to warn us," Adam said, thinking it over. "Warning us about the Syrians, that they're inciting the people in Galilee against us. The mufti is in cahoots with them, and the mukhtar can't do much to fight it."

Judith shot up, bathed in sweat. She'd had the dreams again, visions of the train with the two thousand corpses. Dachau. The dreams wouldn't go away. A few times she'd tried talking about them with Yael, with whom she now shared a room, but she gave up when she noticed that Yael wasn't really listening. They had other worries on the kibbutz. Where would they keep the weapons for repelling the Arabs' increasing attacks? And how would they hide those weapons from the British with their frequent hours-long raids? How many more new arrivals could they accept? How would they sell the harvest? Would there be enough water this summer? The young people on the kibbutz were focused on the future, not the past.

Yael groaned in her bed. Judith lit the kerosene lamp, went over, and placed a cold cloth on her forehead. Her friend had been suffering from a high fever for two days now; the kibbutzniks' malaria kicked up at regular intervals, a quarter of the residents sick at times. Malaria was one of Palestine's scourges. Judith dissolved a quinine tablet in a glass of water and fed Yael the medicine.

"Toda," Yael said—thank you—and sat up.

Judith propped a pillow behind Yael's back, to make her more comfortable, and sat on the end of her bed.

The night was oppressively hot. In the distance she could hear the dogs barking in the village, followed by the excited back-and-forth of high-pitched donkey shouts until all the animals calmed down and stillness fell over the valley again.

"How was the mukhtar?" Yael asked in a weary voice.

"Conciliatory."

"I don't think this peace is going to last long," Yael replied.

Judith set her hands in her lap. "How long has the village actually been there?"

"The village? No idea. For ages. Under the crusaders, under the Turks, now under the British. The Arabs have simply had to comply.

They get by, just barely. You saw it yourself, all poor, mostly illiterate, the way it's always been."

"But—" Judith's voice hung in the air.

"But what?"

"But it is their homeland, after all. You just said they've been living here for centuries."

"Yeah? So?"

"I mean, now here we come. No wonder they're scared we're going to take it away from them."

Yael straightened up. "Judith, they've been here all along, but Jews have too. For thousands of years. We're definitely not religious here on the kibbutz, you know that. But we are Jews, and we do intend to finally have our own homeland. Where we don't have to keep apologizing for merely existing. Where we won't be exiled or exterminated. If the Arabs can understand that, there's enough room for all of us."

"And if not?" Judith interjected.

"Then we'll defend our ground. With all available means. We built this land up, working with our hands, hard goddamn work, every day. And we don't have any intention of giving it all up again. Imagine sending all those refugees back—refugees like you, Judith. No country will take them. Where would they even go? Camps?"

For a while, only the excruciating whine of mosquitoes could be heard in the room.

"But how's that supposed to work?" Judith asked.

"It's simple: we want a state, our own state, and they should have their own too."

Judith shook her head. "But that means—if we stay here in Galilee and expand our settlements, if this part of Palestine is supposed to become part of our state, then the Arabs in the village here will have to go somewhere else."

Yael shrugged.

"They aren't going to simply accept that!" Judith said. "There's no peaceful way that's going to happen, Yael. It could only happen through violence."

Yael stubbornly kept silent.

"We Jews in Europe, we just learned firsthand what violence means," Judith blurted. "We were victims. Must we now be perpetrators? Shouldn't we be the very ones who are most committed to finding a peaceful solution?"

Yael took a deep breath. "We wish to settle here, peacefully, if possible. But that takes two." She slid under her blanket. "And, by the way, the Palmach are holding shooting practice tomorrow. I think many here would view it as a good thing if you joined in." She turned to the wall.

Judith stood and put out the lamp. She lay awake in the darkness a long time, listening to the mosquitoes.

The telephone wouldn't stop ringing.

"How far off are they, Higgins?"

Lieutenant Josef Goldsmith eyed the sergeant anxiously. Higgins had a map spread out before him, on which he'd penciled in the routes of both the *Exodus* and their British escort ships.

"Still about fifty miles from the coast, sir."

For days now, the Jerusalem headquarters of the British Armed Forces had been monitoring the course of this ship, a converted river steamer that used to cross Chesapeake Bay just outside Washington. On July 11, it had weighed anchor in Sète, France, under the name *President Warfield*.

"Must be bloody cramped on that old tub," Higgins muttered. "I certainly wouldn't like to be in their shoes. But they probably wouldn't want it any other way. They want their propaganda display, at all costs. Our boys will show them soon enough."

Under the command of the light cruiser *Ajax*, six destroyers and two minelayers were following the ship across the Mediterranean. Higgins lit another cigarette. On board the ship designed for just 600 were crammed 4,500 European refugees, among them many survivors of the concentration camps. It was meant to serve as a symbol of immigration to Palestine.

"We've told them to pack it in enough times," Higgins said. "But that captain is stubborn. Yesterday they even gave the ship a new name—now they're calling her *Exodus*. Hoisted the Jewish flag too! Well, they'll get their surprise later tonight."

Josef raised his head.

"You know the orders, sir," Higgins said. "The Mandate government doesn't want those Jews setting foot on Palestinian soil, not under any condition."

He handed Josef the written order. "Here, see for yourself. Clear instructions. The code name is Operation Oasis."

Josef parked his jeep beside the wall along the quay. A soldier saluted him.

"This way, sir."

Thousands of people stood in the port of Haifa. A long line of British soldiers, armed with wood batons, guarded the pier from the curious onlookers. It was already afternoon, and the sun had reached its hottest point. The convoy appeared in the distance. The ship was slowly towed into the harbor. It sported a hand-painted sign below the bridge that read "Haganah Ship Exodus." Josef could see damage on its side from being rammed last night by British destroyers. He knew from the *Ajax*'s radio transmissions that the battle had lasted seven hours before British soldiers seized the *Exodus* and broke the passengers' resistance by force. The desperate passengers had greeted the British with a hail of screws, cans, potatoes, bottles, and boards. The battle only ended when the British fired into the crowd, killing four and severely injuring many more.

An elderly Jew in a long black caftan with a black hat over his sidelocks and a pointy white beard stood in Josef's way and spat in front of him.

"British swine," he shrieked. "My son, my Menachem, he's up there and you won't let him off."

The elderly man waved his arms and pointed to the *Ocean Vigour*, which sat in the harbor along with the cargo ships *Runnymede Park* and *Empire Rival*. Just now, five British soldiers had hauled the last passenger off the *Exodus* and over to the *Ocean Vigour*, a young man taking violent swings at them. With that, the operation had come to an end. The soldiers had carried out their orders. Except for the dead and seriously injured, all the passengers had been transferred—4,400 people now found themselves on board the three freighters. The *Exodus* sat deserted, a battlefield cleared, the Haganah's worst defeat thus far.

"He was in Auschwitz," wailed the elderly man.

Again, he spat before Josef. He stomped his feet helplessly, started to cry.

"What camp are you taking him to this time? To Cyprus like the others?"

Josef tried to clear a path to his jeep but was met by hate-filled faces at every step. *They would hate me even more if they knew,* he thought. Under Operation Oasis, none of the passengers would be taken to neighboring Cyprus, where the illegal immigrants were normally deported. This time, the Mandate government wanted to set an especially strong example. The next morning, these three British steam freighters would put out to sea under military escort and take the passengers of the *Exodus* back where they'd come from. To camps in Europe.

Josef had finally reached his jeep. He started the engine and stepped on the gas. He took the coast road, along the Mediterranean. Inside his head, a movie was rolling in fast reverse showing the stages of his life, first as a soldier, Haifa, Jerusalem, Berlin, Bergen-Belsen, Normandy,

London, then the movie rolling on, further and further back, faster and faster, England, Holland, Germany, back to Berlin, Bahnhof Zoo, the refugee, the Jew. The movie stopped.

Josef looked down at his uniform. He suddenly felt constricted in his khaki cloth with its British decorations and insignia, trapped in someone else's skin. He'd worn the uniform with pride for many years; now he felt like he was in disguise. His foot searched for the brake, and the jeep skidded to a stop on the side of the road. The red-orange sun was sinking into the Mediterranean. *Sentimental kitsch,* he thought angrily. He fished the pack of cigarettes from his chest pocket, lit up a Dunhill, and inhaled deeply.

After a while, he went around the jeep, lifted the gas can from its holder, and filled up the tank. In the last glow of the evening twilight, he took a look at his map of Palestine and searched for a spot in Upper Galilee.

Moshe Ben Porat could see the headlights from afar. They were moving fast through the darkness, toward Yardenim. It was a starry, moonless night. Moshe, up in the watchtower, planted his eyes on his binoculars. He wasn't certain. Could there be someone from the Haganah coming this late? Or was it a British military vehicle? He couldn't take any risks, especially since Haganah commander Rabinovich was spending the night on the kibbutz. He sounded the alarm. A few moments later, figures with rifles started darting out of the kibbutz's tents and houses.

The headlights were getting closer. Moshe had positioned himself at the entrance to the kibbutz along with two other Palmach guards. Soon, he recognized the outline of a jeep heading straight for the entrance. The men blocked its way in; the jeep came to an abrupt halt. Moshe shined his flashlight on it. A British officer sat at the wheel, his face and uniform covered with sand and dust. Blinded by the light, he was shielding his eyes with one hand.

Moshe took a closer look. The Brit's face looked familiar.

"Goldsmith," the man said. "Josef Goldsmith."

Moshe waved to the others. "Let him through."

Josef started up the jeep and drove through to the middle of the kibbutz, halting right in front of the new hall that served as the center of their village. Figures slowly emerged from the shadows of the houses. They gathered around the jeep. Judith had pulled a sweater over her pajamas and joined the others swarming the military vehicle.

"Josef," she shouted when she saw the man at the wheel.

She wrapped her arms around him. Her brother hugged her and held her tight for a long moment. Then he stepped out. The others stared at him, silent, suspicious. Uri finally stepped forward.

"An odd hour to pay a visit, Mr. Goldsmith."

Josef didn't reply. Instead, he reached for the leather holster on his belt holding his service pistol. Moshe rushed up next to Uri and raised his Sten machine gun for Josef to see.

The British officer drew his pistol from its holster and held it by the barrel so that the grip faced Uri.

"Here, take it," he said. "I don't need it anymore."

It took a moment for Uri to comprehend. He took the pistol. Josef peeled off his uniform jacket now, too, and tossed it into the jeep.

And with that, the tension was broken. The kibbutzniks, many still in pajamas and underwear, clapped and hooted. Ben Zvi had run into his tent and come back with his accordion. Moshe grabbed a can of kerosene and poured it over the pile of wood lying out in front of the mess hall. He tossed on a burning match. The flames shot up. Ben Zvi tried out a few bars on his accordion. The kibbutzniks cheered. They grabbed the hesitant Britisher, lining up to embrace him or shake his hand.

Judith ran into the kitchen and came back with a basket full of bottles. She handed out the wine along with some glasses. Uri filled a glass and handed it to Josef.

"*L'chaim*, to life," he said. "Welcome home."

After breakfast together in the large hall of the kibbutz, Uri took Josef by the arm. "Let's take a little walk." He led Josef to one of the fields across from the Arab village. "It won't be long before they attack us," Uri said. "And we must be prepared for that." He pulled Josef's service pistol out of his jacket.

"Here," he said, "take it back."

Josef stared at him, confused.

"It's very simple: of course we're happy about anyone who finds their way to us. We need every man. Every last one. But each in their right place. And I can't think of anything better for us than having an officer right inside the headquarters of the British Armed Forces."

Josef stopped. "You mean, I'm simply supposed to carry on as before? To carry out their orders, keep arresting Jews and having them deported? I can't do it anymore, not after seeing what they did to those people from the *Exodus*."

"You won't be carrying on as before. Sure, they'll see you that way, the good officer of His Majesty the King. But you'll really be working for us, inside their center of power."

Uri pointed at the kibbutzniks digging an irrigation ditch.

"You can be infinitely more helpful to us there than by picking up a shovel here." He led Josef back to the jeep. "What we need is information, tips about raids on us, the movements of the British forces, weapons depots and, when it comes to it, their exact plans for withdrawal."

Josef hesitated. "I'm not cut out to be a traitor. And besides, I owe the British a lot."

"What do you think they'll make of you if you stay here, if we have to keep hiding you from them—you, the deserter? No, you've crossed the line. You're one of us, and you know it."

Uri was still holding the pistol. "Here, just take it already. And put your uniform back on. Report for duty, tell them that your jeep broke down."

Josef took the pistol. "Very well," he said softly.

August 1, 1947

"Bye, David," Hana said, trying to sound American.

David took her in his arms and kissed her. "Bye, my darling. See you this evening?"

Hana flushed. Of course she wanted to see him this evening, tonight and every night. But she needed to speak with her parents again. For a moment she was tempted to say: *Just come with me. Why shouldn't I introduce you to my parents?* But she knew it was impossible.

"I'm sorry," she said, "but I really can't tonight."

She stood on her tiptoes and kissed him again. All around them, the nurses and doctors from the day shift were streaming to the waiting buses. David held her by the arm.

"I'm going to miss you, darling, very much," he said, smiling. "Till tomorrow, then."

"Till tomorrow. I'll be thinking of you."

As she went to step onto the bus, she felt another hand on her arm. She turned around and stared into the face of her father.

Mohammed Khalidy wore a suit and a dark felt hat despite the August heat. His face was tense and gray. From the other side of the valley, they could hear bells ringing in the Christian churches of the Old City of Jerusalem, calling people to evening prayers.

"Hello, Father," she said, and kissed his cheek.

Her father said nothing, just took her by the arm and led her to his car. He opened the rear door and shoved her inside. Then he climbed in next to her and nodded at Ali, who sat at the wheel. Ali started the engine.

"Where are we going?" Hana asked, shifting nervously in her seat.

"To your new apartment."

Hana looked at him in disbelief. Ali piloted the Chevrolet down the narrow street, maneuvering dangerously close to a bus.

A little later, the big car stopped in the Jerusalem district of Sheikh Jarrah, in front of a building of light sandstone with a flat roof and six apartments inside. Sheikh Jarrah was overwhelmingly populated by Arabs, people who belonged to the city's middle class and mostly worked in the city. Ali stepped out and hauled several large suitcases from the trunk. He opened the building's front door and carried in the suitcases. Hana remained in the car with her father.

"This building belongs to me, you know. And I'd like for you to move in. At once."

Hana swallowed. Her father seemed to want to put his arm around her, but he held back.

"You do not wish to marry Youssef, and I do not wish to force you. But you can't live in Deir Yassin any longer. It's hard enough for the family, for your mother above all." He cleared his throat. "By the way, who was that man you kissed in public?"

Hana stared at the floor. "A—friend."

"He didn't look like an Arab."

"Uh, no. He is—" *a Jew,* she wanted to say, but she stopped herself. "He's an American."

"An American?"

"Yes. One of the doctors." Hana knew that this had to be a shock for him. "What are you going to tell Mother?"

"Nothing," he replied stiffly. "She and I have already discussed the rest. That was hard enough for her, accepting the dissolution of your engagement."

"You broke off the engagement?"

"Yes, I paid his family a great sum."

Hana threw her arms around him, but her father pulled away.

"Be careful. Listen to me. Be very careful. You must promise me that."

Then he leaned down and kissed her on the forehead. His hat slipped back in the process. He straightened it. His hands were shaking. Hana saw tears in his eyes.

"Now get going," he said. "I'll come visit you soon."

She hugged him tight one more time, then jumped out of the car and ran into the building.

Youssef kicked the garbage can so hard it fell over with a crash. He pulled the old revolver from his pocket and fired into the air until the cylinder was empty. Lights came on in the windows of Deir Yassin. Youssef didn't care. Let them stare down on him. *They're all cowardly traitors*—he thought—*the mukhtar, all of them. They want their peace and quiet. They think they can live alongside the invaders from Europe without problems. They've obviously forgotten they are Arabs and followers of the Prophet. Fools!*

He heard dogs barking, from all sides. One had started, and the others joined in. Youssef marched down the village road, the angry clamor following him, and kept on going until he'd left Deir Yassin behind. Beyond the hills, he could see the lights of Jerusalem.

The night was warm and cloudless. The rocks still radiated the summer heat they'd absorbed during the day. He searched for a large rock and sat down. He stared blindly into the darkness.

She had brought shame to him, that much was clear. Everyone in the village knew it. What was he supposed to do now? Simply accept it and hope they would forget at some point? What girl would now be prepared to become his wife? The wife of a loser.

He weighed the revolver in his hand. Should he lie in wait for Hana somehow, avenge the shame with blood? He twirled the revolver with his finger in the trigger guard. On the other hand, his father had taken the money from old Khalidy, a lot of money. Shouldn't he be obeying his father's decision?

Even worse than that broken promise of marriage was the fact that she was now entering the Jews' world for good. The Jews! They wanted more every day. They were building their fortified villages everywhere, spreading out, occupying ancient Arabic land, acting like their new masters. They wanted their own state, with Jerusalem as their capital. Jerusalem, the third-holiest Muslim city. Al-Quds! What madness! God would not allow it. Never!

Despite the darkness, he could make out the road that wound high through the mountains toward Jerusalem. He knew what everyone knew: this was the city's lifeline—provisions from the coast ran through it. It wasn't easy to defend, and Arabs were always shooting down on Jewish supply convoys from up in the hills. In the distance, Youssef could see a small light. Lights from a car, making its way up the rise.

Youssef flipped open the cylinder of his revolver and dumped out the empty cartridges. He hurriedly searched his pocket for more. He found two left, quickly filled the cylinder, and locked it back into place.

He knew the terrain. Youssef ran, jumped, fell down, picked himself back up. The car came closer. He found a spot behind a boulder, about twenty yards above a stretch of road that climbed a little less steeply for a few hundred yards.

He raised his right arm and felt how heavy the old revolver was. His hand shook a little. He used his left hand to help support it. Once the car was directly below him, he pulled the trigger. The first shot missed the target by a few inches, ricocheted off a boulder, and landed in the gravel at the side of the road. Youssef fired again. He heard glass shattering and saw the car swerve, then speed away with its engine howling. Again he fired, but the hammer struck nothing.

Josef Goldsmith stepped hard on the gas pedal. The jeep picked up speed slowly, far too slowly. The rear window was shattered. British Command in Jaffa had warned him about driving back to Jerusalem at night. Too unsafe these last few weeks. But Josef had insisted, since General McMillan had summoned his officers to an important meeting the next morning. It concerned a large-scale operation against Jewish self-defense groups, primarily the Irgun but also the Palmach. Josef didn't want to miss it, not on any account. The Haganah was waiting for his report. He'd been in contact with them regularly of late. He'd frequently been able to warn them before the British struck again.

He glanced at his sergeant next to him. Jonathan Higgins had drawn his service pistol and was peering behind them.

"You all right, Sergeant?"

"Bloody Arabs," cursed Higgins. "Only thing worse are the Jews."

Josef raised an eyebrow.

"Uh, sorry, sir, I mean—of course there's also your friendly Jews, right? You know what I mean."

Josef opted to remain silent and concentrate on the road.

Higgins lit a cigarette. The embers lit his angular face. "They're all barmy here," he muttered. "About time we finally clear out of this god-awful country."

November 29–30, 1947

They were standing on the street in front of her apartment building. Hana gave David a kiss on the mouth. He took her in his arms.

Ever since Hana had moved into her own apartment, they'd been playing a game. A game whose rules she'd laid down. It was the we're-not-married game. And David had accepted it, though sometimes reluctantly.

Down here on the street, said the rules, their evenings together ended. Hana wanted it this way—at least, that was what she told him.

And, of course, he complied. For him, the situation was frustrating sometimes. Especially since he was the heartthrob of many pretty nurses at the hospital, not just Hana.

He'd been tempted to indulge their obvious advances once or twice, but he'd always been able to control himself. Sometimes he asked himself why; after all, Hana herself was the one who kept reminding him that it wasn't as if they were married. On his fifteen-minute walk home alone, he'd often ask himself what exactly was making him so patient. And then he would acknowledge something he really would've preferred not to. He was, he told himself, simply not ready. Not yet. But ultimately, he had to be honest, at least with himself. It was simple. He loved Hana.

This evening after their usual trip to the movies, she held him tighter and longer than usual.

"I—" she began, hesitating. "I have a radio in my apartment. Today's the day, you know."

She let go of David and fished her keys from her purse. She pushed the door open and took his hand with a timid smile.

"Come."

He followed her into the stairwell, tentatively, climbing the two flights of stairs up to her apartment door. She smiled again when she opened it and, pulling him by the hand, stepped inside. She waited for him to help her out of her coat, and then invited him into the living room.

"Have a seat," she told him.

David awkwardly took a seat on the sofa, surprised at how self-conscious he was.

"I'll make us some tea," she said, and disappeared behind a door.

As he listened to the water running and dishes clanking, he took a look around. The living room was impressively appointed, with thick, handwoven carpets, solid oak furniture, and a large oil painting displaying the Jerusalem cityscape with the Dome of the Rock and its golden cupola—much like the view they had from the hospital. Heavy velvet drapes blocked the bright streetlamps. On a sideboard stood a large photo of an older man with an earnest look. Next to it, David spotted a smaller picture frame with a group photo from the hospital, with himself in it, laughing, Hana right next to him, also smiling. At the other end of the long sideboard was the radio, a Philips model.

After a while, Hana brought out a tray with a teapot and two cups. She set it on the coffee table and sat on the sofa with him, keeping a formal distance, as though they were meeting today for the first time. Hana poured some tea and handed him the cup.

"Please."

He took the cup and drank. The mint tea was sweet and refreshing. It was silent for a while in the room. Then David couldn't take it any longer. He moved over to her, took her in his arms, and kissed her passionately. She didn't resist. But after a while, she freed herself from his embrace and looked at her watch.

"The broadcast from New York is about to start," she panted. She went over to the sideboard and turned on the radio.

The fire burned higher than usual, the kibbutzniks constantly tossing more wood on the blaze. Night had fallen quickly over Upper Galilee on this November evening. Judith had eaten with the others in the communal hall like she did every evening, but she didn't have any appetite.

Today's supposed to be the day, she thought, and felt equally tense and unsure. If the United Nations agreed to it, their dream of their own country would become a reality—but would it truly be hers?

Yael sat down next to her. She, too, was unusually quiet. The day had passed like every other day on the kibbutz, with hard work in the fields, but the tension was palpable. Everyone knew that the event taking place some six thousand miles from here would change their lives, one way or another.

Uri, who'd arrived around noon from Tel Aviv, tired out, his face ashen, was the only one who'd withdrawn to his room.

"Wake me when it's time," he'd told Yael.

Ben Zvi had grabbed his accordion and played a few bars, but then quickly saw that no one was in the mood, so he closed his instrument again. He stared helplessly at the others, some of whom had positioned themselves at the fire or kept sitting on their benches, their empty plates before them.

"I heard the Americans were putting pressure on the Latin Americans and the Filipinos," Yael said, turning to Judith. "It's going to be close, real close."

Judith didn't respond.

"Doesn't matter. We're not going to let some bureaucrats put us down," Yael said, purposely louder now. "Even if they say no, we're not leaving."

Most of the others raised their heads.

"Yes, you're exactly right," Ben Zvi said. "We're not just going to let the Arabs have all this, are we?" His voice carried a hint of uncertainty. "What do you all think?"

Yael spoke up again. "No, no, never. We can't let it be for nothing, all this work, all this danger."

Moshe Ben Porat, the oldest on the kibbutz at thirty-five, had kept silent until now.

"There will be war, no matter what they decide. The Arabs have already declared they won't accept a partition of Palestine under any condition. So, if we win in New York, they're not going to accept the result. And if we lose—" He paused a long time. "If we lose, we're not going to surrender either. That would surely mean we'd go on forever without our own state, a persecuted minority inside Arab Palestine. Or does someone here see things differently?"

Judith stared at her fingernails. *Violence,* she thought, *always more violence.* Would it ever end? Could her brother possibly be right? Should she just give up and go away, to England, if he could get her in? Or even to America? But hadn't he himself decided to fight for a Jewish state? Didn't refugees like her need a place where they belonged? Did the Jews always have to be a people with no right to their own homeland? Oppressed forever?

Three hundred delegates of the United Nations sitting together in Flushing Meadows, New York, were about to decide this very question. Should Palestine be divided into a Jewish and an Arab state, with the city of Jerusalem under international control? This was what the UN partition plan proposed. The idea was to create an independent homeland for about 650,000 Jews and about 1.2 million Arabs. Two-thirds of the fifty-six UN member states had to agree to the plan—a goal that was by no means certain.

There'd been extensive discussions behind the scenes over the past few days. Most notably, US President Truman had instructed his chief delegate in New York to employ any means possible to secure a majority. The Soviet Union had also announced their support for partition. Now, the eyes of the world were on that gray concrete UN building where New Yorkers had once glided around on ice skates.

"Go wake Uri," Judith told Yael. "It'll be any moment now."

Yael ran over to the wood house where her room was. After a few minutes, she came back with Uri. They all sat around that battery-driven radio on the long table in the hall. Moshe Ben Porat turned it on. The Palestine Broadcasting Corporation was playing classical music. Almost immediately, the program was interrupted. Uri stared at the ground, his face stony, forbidding. Ben Zvi clutched his accordion. Moshe nervously sucked on his cigarette and drummed his fingertips on the tabletop.

It was midnight in Palestine, ten in the evening on November 29 in London, as the president of the United Nations, Brazilian Osvaldo Aranha, announced the result.

"The United Nations General Assembly," they heard over the speaker, "in a vote of thirty-three in favor, thirteen against, and ten abstentions, has decided to partition Palestine."

For a moment, Uri didn't move. Then he raised his head and shouted: "We did it! Yes, we did it!"

Yael flung her arms around him.

"We did it, we did it!" the kibbutzniks shouted to each other. "We have a country, we have our own country!"

Yael turned to Judith and hugged her. "Soon you'll be an Israeli, you hear me?"

Moshe came out of the kitchen carrying a basket of wine bottles. He didn't bother looking for glasses. He handed the bottle to the first man next to him, who took a big chug and then passed it on.

"L'chaim," he shouted. "To life!"

Everyone then directed their attention to Uri, as if this one Haganah officer had achieved their victory in New York all on his own. They clapped him on the shoulders, shook his hand. Judith, too, approached, somewhat timidly, and hugged him. Uri pulled her close to him, laughing.

"Mazal tov," he said into her ear.

Judith found herself holding him tight. An unfamiliar feeling ran through her, making her dizzy. This body in her arms was both emitting great strength and conveying a sense of security, a combination she'd never before experienced. She let go, stumbled backward, and took a deep breath. "Congratulations, Uri."

But he'd already turned back to Yael.

Ben Zvi struck up a few notes. The others set their bottles on the table, stood up, and took each other's hands. Yael dragged Judith into the circle. Soon, everyone recognized the melody. They loudly sang the Zionist anthem, "Hatikvah," the song of hope.

Hana sat frozen on the sofa. Her face was pale. After a while, she stood up and turned off the radio. Then she returned to David. She didn't look at him. He moved closer and carefully took her hand, holding it without a word.

A piercing tone sliced through the night, growing louder, appearing to rise, then to proliferate. Louder and louder came the sounds from Mea Shearim, the Orthodox Jewish quarter. Men with sidelocks had pulled out their shofars and were blowing with all their might into the ram's-horn trumpets, a tradition that the Israelites had used in battles for their Promised Land for thousands of years.

Hana squeezed his hand tighter and leaned close to him. She trembled and kept her eyes closed, but she appeared to want to say something.

The Arab Quarter of Sheikh Jarrah was silent, but the sounds of Jewish inhabitants in the urban areas southwest of Jaffa Road drifted over as they boisterously danced in the streets. It was as if all the nearly one hundred thousand Jews in the city had streamed outside.

David felt uneasy. He would've liked to have been on Ben Yehuda Street, taking part in the celebrations. Israel would, it was clear to him now, be his country as well. He was a Jew, and that mattered to him, even if he wasn't observant. But he was sitting next to an Arab—next to the woman he loved.

He kept holding her hand tight. Hana's face was hard and motionless. Then tears began running down her cheeks. Her upper body started trembling, and she threw her arms around him.

"David, I'm scared," she sobbed. "So scared." Hana pulled away and looked him in the eyes. "Tell me, what's going to happen to us now?"

The question caught him by surprise. All at once, he realized that he had to decide, here and now. The time for flirtations was passed. He couldn't avoid the issue of how he imagined his future with this young Arab woman. He had to give her an answer, and himself one as well.

He took both her hands and held them tight in his. "I love you," he heard himself say, "and I'd like for us to be together."

She stood up, without letting go, and pulled him up. As if in a daze, he followed her to the bedroom.

Inside the doorway, she kissed him.

"You want us to be together? Forever?"

"Forever," he said without hesitation.

From the bed, they could hear the din of cars honking, the howl of speeding engines. Only in the early morning hours did quiet slowly return to the city, which from now on would be two cities, divided in the lives and minds of its roughly 165,000 residents.

The delegates in Flushing Meadows had deemed it so, and there was no going back now.

December 2, 1947

Jonathan Higgins sprang up from behind his desk and snapped to attention. "Good morning, sir."

General Gordon McMillan nodded curtly and strode into his office, his chest puffed out. He removed his uniform cap and placed it on the desk beside him, along with his gloves. Then he smoothed out his khaki-colored tunic.

"The report, Sergeant," he shouted.

Higgins grabbed the slim folder and ran in to plant himself before the general. He clicked his heels.

"Well?"

"Rather lively night, sir."

The general eyed him impatiently. "Details?"

Higgins flipped open the folder. "Yesterday, some Arabs, coming from Jaffa Gate, made their way across the Jewish commercial center on the other side of the Old City. Rather disorderly, if you ask me."

McMillan lit a cigarette. "Continue."

"Well, first the Arabs began looting, and then they started fires. There were said to have been British police in the area when it happened." He cleared his throat. "Some of them were said to have helped tear the bars off shops."

The general's expression didn't change.

"Rather large fires, heavy smoke, lots of injured. The Haganah boys then fired over the Arabs' heads. They're getting more and more brazen that way, practically showing off."

"Then what?"

The sergeant glanced at the densely written pages before him.

"Then the Jews struck back. Apparently, it was that lot from the Irgun. In any case, they forced their way into an Arab cinema, the Rex, and set it on fire. It's completely burned down. In addition, there were grenades thrown at cafés, a synagogue set on fire in retaliation, pedestrians stabbed. Some people have even abandoned their apartments, having now found themselves on the wrong side of the partition."

McMillan stubbed out his cigarette in an ashtray. "And the rest of the country?"

The sergeant flipped through his documents.

"The same picture. Attacks everywhere, on buses, in markets. Several dead. It's really getting started now, if you ask me. The UN plan didn't exactly have many supporters among the Arabs, to put it mildly, and the Jews would feel justified, of course, in striking back in the proper manner."

"Looks that way," McMillan replied. "See to it that there's a two-day evening curfew. That'll cool their heads." He lit up another cigarette. "And tell Goldsmith to get in here."

Higgins clicked his heels again. "Yes, sir. A curfew. I'll see to it directly."

When Lieutenant Goldsmith entered, General McMillan was standing at the window, staring at the barbed wire surrounding the British headquarters.

"Just a few months more, Goldsmith. We ruled this place for thirty years, and soon it'll all be over." The general turned around. "But until then, we still must maintain order, somehow. Or at least act as if we have done."

He fixed his stare on the lieutenant. "So that we do not misunderstand one another: for me, this is not about those lunatics out there. This is about our boys. We're sustaining dead or injured nearly every day now. I don't have the slightest desire to put our soldiers at any more risk, so we'll keep out of their squabbles as best we can. Beyond that, the orders from London are clear: crack down hard when we're attacked. Is that understood, Lieutenant?"

Josef shifted uneasily. "With all due respect, sir, aren't the Jews just angry because we usually take the Arabs' side? And how are they supposed to establish a state when we don't allow them into the country?"

McMillan watched him with cold eyes. "Perhaps you didn't hear me. Our orders are clear. We're not to alter our immigration policies. Britain will still have powerful interests in the Middle East after we've left this dreadful country. Oil, energy, the Suez Canal. I really don't need to explain that all to you. We were not for this Jewish state nonsense, and we see no reason to view things any differently now. Besides, are you suggesting we show leniency even when those Jewish terrorists in the Irgun are killing our boys, throwing grenades at them, stealing our weapons? You know as well as I that those bastards are proud of every Brit they kill. So, Goldsmith, we're going to crack down hard. Over the next few weeks, we'll be hanging as many of them as possible in Acre Prison. I owe it to our troops' morale."

Josef didn't let his shock show.

McMillan continued: "I know, Goldsmith. You have a rather complicated past. But I demand loyalty from all my officers. Is that clear, Lieutenant?"

Josef waited a moment too long before answering. "Yes, sir. Naturally, sir."

McMillan gave him a penetrating stare.

"Dismissed."

December 15, 1947

In Yardenim, they had wavered a moment when it came to the question of who was best suited for the mission. Yet all eyes of the kibbutzniks had turned Judith's way, and so now she was riding in a truck on the way to Jerusalem. It was loaded with vegetables now but was to return with completely different cargo.

Ben Zvi was behind the wheel. He hadn't said a word since the trip began. Every time a group of Arabs appeared on the side of the road, he nervously touched the Sten gun next to his seat. Judith, too, had a revolver, under her own seat. In the truck bed were two boys from the Palmach, with Stens on them as well.

Every mile closer to Jerusalem brought memories that Judith resisted. Memories of Uncle Albert, of death, of disillusionment, of her attempt to put an end to her life. *But was that fair?* she wondered. Didn't the city also represent compassion and hope for her? What about Nurse Hana and Tamar Schiff? She had lost her uncle, but hadn't she also found her brother?

And why did Jews and Arabs alike have to create so many myths and such outcry over Jerusalem?

No one on the kibbutz was very religious, but when it came to the historic capital, not one of them was willing to give it all up. One evening, as they sat around the fire, discussing how much the city meant for the future Jewish state, Moshe had even pulled out the Torah and flipped to Psalm 137:5, where the children of Israel bemoan their suffering in Babylonian captivity: "If I forget you, Jerusalem, let my right hand wither away"—it was the Zionists' battle cry.

"Here, it says it right here." Moshe continued quoting: "May my tongue stick to the roof of my mouth if I do not remember you, if I do not make Jerusalem my chief joy."

Curious, Judith read the psalm later, and was startled by what followed: "Daughter of Babylon, you destroyer, blessed shall be the one who repays you for what you have done to us! Blessed shall be the one who takes your small children and smashes them against the rocks!"

All of this spun through her head as the truck made its way through the Jordan Valley. Eye for an eye, tooth for a tooth—that's what the Torah said. But did Jews have the right to make this the doctrine for their struggle to found a new state? *They do,* she thought. They should finally free themselves from their Babylonian captivity, finally have their own land for themselves. But how high a price would they have to pay?

After they'd passed through the river valley, the truck climbed the steep hills toward Jerusalem. When they reached the top, the city spread out before them.

"Please turn toward Mount Scopus," Judith told Ben. At Hadassah Hospital, she asked him to make a stop.

Judith had brought Hana a large bouquet of the roses they'd been cultivating on the kibbutz, despite any good economic sense.

"I wanted to properly thank you, finally," she said.

Both hesitated a brief moment, then they hugged. Hana began to cry.

"My God, what's wrong?" asked Judith.

Hana, wiping away her tears with a handkerchief, only shook her head. "It's—it's nothing. I'm just—Oh, it's nothing, believe me."

She tried a smile. Judith noticed that her eyes looked tired, with dark rings under them.

For a while, they tried to make small talk. But Hana seemed distant, inhibited, uncertain. And Judith felt self-conscious, thinking about the strained relationship between Jews and Arabs that Hana was confronted with at the hospital day in, day out. She looked at the time.

"Oh, it's late," she said. "I have to go."

Hana nodded. But then she wrapped her arms around Judith again and held her tight.

Hana started to cry again. "I'm sorry. I really don't know what's wrong with me," she whispered into Judith's ear. "Thank you, thank you for coming here."

Judith carefully released herself. "Whenever you need me, you let me know, please. Promise me that."

Yet she wondered how she could help Hana, whether she truly was capable.

On Jaffa Road in the city center, Judith jumped out of the truck and carried her heavy basket up Ben Yehuda Street to the building where the Schiffs lived.

She looked around, hoping Shimon was playing somewhere nearby so he could help her with the basket, but she didn't spot him. So, she schlepped it up the stairs and rang the bell, a little out of breath.

Tamar Schiff opened the door. "It's you." She beamed. "What a surprise!"

Judith set the basket of fresh vegetables down in front of her. "For you, for the children," she said. "Straight from Yardenim."

Tamar waved her inside. "That was a dangerous trip you made to get here."

"I don't think it's any more dangerous than life around here," Judith said.

"You're right, I'm afraid," Tamar replied. "I barely dare to let the kids play outside by themselves. And Shimon doesn't want to believe any of it, of course. All he can think about is soccer." She looked Judith in the eyes. "And you? How are you doing?"

"To be honest, I'm not really sure how I'm doing," she admitted. "Yardenim is making progress, despite the Arabs' attacks. We keep building. I guess I belong there, but sometimes I don't feel like I do."

"Well, do you want to belong there?" Tamar tried.

"Yes, my head tells me to want it, but I often think that can't be any future, always living amid such conflict, surrounded by such hate."

Judith heard impatient honks from the street. "Oh, excuse me, I really need to go. They're waiting for me out there."

Tamar walked her to the door.

"I hope we'll see each other again," Judith said. "Give the kids a kiss from me."

Darkness had fallen fast. Six miles east of the city, on the road to Jericho, a jeep bearing British Army markings was parked. As the truck neared, the driver of the jeep flashed its headlights. Ben Zvi pulled up next to it.

A man in British uniform climbed out. Judith jumped down from the truck's cab and hugged him.

"Oh, Josef, it's so good to see you."

He stroked her hair. "You're so brave. Out there all the time. I worry about you a lot."

Judith did her best to sound normal. "Please, it's nothing. I'll be fine."

They could see lights in the distance, a car approaching.

"Hurry up," Josef urged, and yanked back the tarp covering the back seat of the jeep. Ben and the two boys from the Palmach reached down and hauled twenty rifles and three wooden boxes of ammo into their truck, all straight from British Army stocks.

Judith kissed her brother on the cheek. He tried holding her there, but she freed herself and jumped back into the cab. Its wheels spinning, the truck took off down the road.

December 29, 1947

Hana didn't leave the grand entrance of Hadassah Hospital for a long time. She kept standing right before that six-pointed star set into the marble floor. She'd never thought about it, had never looked at this symbol at all when showing up for work each morning. But she was aware of it now, very aware. It was the Star of David, the Jewish star.

Nurse Sarah passed by, still wearing her coat. "Good morning, Hana."

Hana didn't respond.

The nurse stopped. "Are you not well, Hana?" she asked, touching her gently on the shoulder.

Hana looked at her, startled. "I'm fine, fine, thanks. I'm doing fine."

Nurse Sarah walked on, shaking her head.

Hana wondered how many of her Arab coworkers were staying home again today. First it had only been two, then more stopped showing up for work every week. Now only a few dared make their way up Mount Scopus. The access roads passed through Arab neighborhoods, and the cars driving from there up the steep hill to Hadassah Hospital kept getting fired upon. The number of Arab patients had severely decreased as well.

Hana felt dizzy. She considered how far it was to the nearest toilet. She'd already thrown up once at home. She considered whether to take Nurse Sarah into her confidence but decided against it. So far, she'd kept it a secret from David as well. In the beginning she wasn't sure, but now she knew for certain. She had gone over the symptoms so many times in her training; she had advised countless Bedouin women when they'd come into the clinic with the same signs.

She would never be able to go back now, not to Muslim Deir Yassin. How was she supposed to tell her mother? After all, she was the one who'd always been against her getting trained in the Jewish hospital, who'd always warned her about getting involved in such work. And about having daily contact with Jewish doctors.

Hana left her spot at the Star of David and leaned against the wall. She closed her eyes and tried to fight the nausea. She took a deep breath and considered what she should do. Should she go to him now and tell him? But how would he react? Still dizzy, she felt her way along the wall. She labored to climb the low stairway connecting the wide entrance hall to the rest of the hospital. He was probably in the operating room already. She decided to wait until the evening. He'd told her he'd come over once he was able to get off work. Work these days mostly meant dressing gunshot wounds, removing bullets, amputating shredded limbs. The nausea waned a little, and she continued on to the nurses' room.

She wore a colorfully embroidered Arabic gown. Her black hair, which she usually wore pinned up, fell loose over her shoulders. Hana tried a smile as David stepped through her apartment door. She immediately saw how tired he was. He leaned down and gave her a kiss.

"You probably heard they had to shut down Hebrew University," he said with resignation in his voice. "And that's located right next to the hospital. It's simply become too dangerous for the students. There are shoot-outs on the way there nearly every day now."

He paused a moment. "And victims, of course."

He set down his briefcase and followed her into the living room. She had lit candles, and a meal of chicken and rice was waiting on the dining table, a bowl of dates to go with it.

David took Hana in his arms. "You almost make me forget the conditions we're living in."

He noticed she was tense, not returning his hug. "Hana, what is it?"

"I'm not feeling well," she said faintly. "I keep getting queasy; it's been going on awhile now."

David took her hand and felt her pulse. He placed a hand on her forehead. "You have a fever? Maybe it's a virus?"

"No, Dr. Cohen. I'm actually quite healthy."

David gave her a bewildered look.

"I haven't had my period, my breasts feel tight and achy, and I keep having to throw up."

David took her right hand in his. "You're . . . ?"

"Yes, David, I'm pregnant. There's no doubt about it."

He stood there in silence for a moment. He needed to make sure that he really was here, in her living room, that he'd heard it right, understood correctly. He wanted to ask again if she really was certain but stopped himself. Hana was gazing at the floor, and he was still holding her hand.

After a while, he realized how much the silence in the room was weighing on them.

He pulled her close to him. He could feel her tears soaking his shirt.

"You don't have to cry," he whispered. "It's just that—this comes as such a surprise."

She stopped crying. Her gaze rested firmly on him. "David, I've been asking myself for days: What's going to happen now? With you, with me, with us?"

He hesitated. "I—"

Let me think about it, he wanted to say. *I have no idea myself. Right outside, everyone's attacking each other, the violence deadlier and deadlier, the future more uncertain, and here we are, a Jew and an Arab, in the heart of Jerusalem, and we're about to be parents.* The situation was completely absurd. Could anyone justify bringing a child into this city full of hate? Should he ask Hana if she really wanted that?

Instead, he took her in his arms again. "I love you," he said, and pushed the strands of hair from her face. "We will manage, somehow we will."

January 12, 1948

Youssef Hamoud stood on the side of the road, brimming with expectation like the others.

"He'll be here soon," whispered the little boy next to him. "Abbu Moussa is finally coming back!"

The boy had never seen him. Youssef never had either. But thousands had crowded the small village of Beit Surif, southwest of Jerusalem: fellahs from the villages in shabby robes; young Arabs from the cities in dark suits, fezzes on their heads; women in long, dark dresses. They needed to see him, to be there, to experience his return to Palestine.

A car appeared on the edge of the village. Youssef felt the boy grasp his arm and tug on it with excitement.

"That must be him, that must be him!" he cried.

The women released sharp, shrill screams. The car came to a stop. A man in a dark suit and a kaffiyeh on his head stepped out. The throng set in motion.

"Abbu Moussa is here!"

Abdul Qader al-Husseini took the jubilation in stride. He stood in one spot, allowing the people to touch him. Youssef held out a hand, and al-Husseini took it and held it tight. *Finally,* Youssef thought, *finally. He should be our leader—he's proven himself often enough.*

The man they called Abbu Moussa was a prominent member of the Husseini clan, the most important Arab family in Jerusalem, to which his cousin Mufti Hadj Amin al-Husseini also belonged. Like his cousin, Abbu Moussa had led the Arab uprisings in Palestine a decade earlier. And like his cousin, he'd also spent time in Nazi Germany. The British had locked him up for years, and now he was secretly returning to Palestine. Now his enemies were no longer the British. Now he had only one goal: preventing the Jews from founding their state on Palestinian land.

Abdul Qader al-Husseini went up to the house where the mukhtars from all the villages around Jerusalem were waiting. It was to be a long meeting, with an extravagant welcome dinner to start things off.

Youssef waited patiently outside. Like all the excited people around him, he instinctively felt that he was witnessing a decisive moment in the battle for the Holy City. For now a man had come who possessed the one crucial ability that most other Arab leaders lacked: not only could he inspire the masses—he could unite them.

Hours later, after Abdul Qader al-Husseini had finally come back out and raced off in his car, Youssef fought his way over to one of the guests from the dinner, a man he knew from the neighboring village of Kastel.

"What did he say?" Youssef asked.

"He said we're going to block the road to Jerusalem. We're going to starve the Jews out."

January 25, 1948

Yael had given him a photo, a small black-and-white picture of her from Yardenim. He noticed she'd gone out of her way to put on a nice blouse and skirt instead of her usual khaki shirt and shorts. She was smiling—a provocative, inviting smile, self-assured and uninhibited.

Uri set the photo on the dashboard. He steered the Ford toward Allenby Street. The latest news from Qantara was alarming: the Syrians were on the move. He bit his lip. This was a direct threat to Galilee, to Yardenim. It was time for the German.

He parked the Ford and climbed out. He was pleased to find Fritz Paulsen already sitting out in front of the café with Ephraim Rosenstein. As always, Ephraim was wearing that old tweed jacket over his scrawny frame, and that flat black cap, his wiry gray hair sticking out from under it. He was one of the first refugees to arrive in the country after the war, having somehow survived the Warsaw Ghetto and then Treblinka.

Uri knew Fritz and Ephraim met here regularly. Ephraim had the chessboard out between them and was waiting for the German to make the next move.

Fritz advanced a white bishop, and Ephraim quickly parried. Within a few minutes, the first of Fritz's figures were lying off the board, and now he focused on protecting his king.

Uri had positioned himself next to the table unnoticed, a cigarette between his lips, considering the board. Then he grabbed a rook from Ephraim and placed it before Fritz's king.

"Check," he said, grinning.

Fritz looked up in surprise.

"Excuse us for a moment," Uri told Ephraim.

Fritz nodded at Ephraim and stood. "See you tomorrow."

"See you tomorrow," Ephraim said, already standing the chess figures back up again.

"They're starting to organize a proper army to attack us—calling it the Jaysh al-Inqadh al-Arabi, the Arab Liberation Army," Uri told Fritz as they walked down the sidewalk. "In Qantara, a military camp south of Damascus. Our man there reports that it's quite a mess. Syrians, Turks, Palestinians, Iraqis, Lebanese, and—now comes the interesting part—men from the Balkans and even Germans. Of course, the Germans and the guys from the Balkans are your old SS friends and Wehrmacht soldiers who escaped from POW camps. They're the best trained, many of them experts in explosives, in weapons of all kinds. And the ones we're most interested in."

He stopped walking and looked right at the German. "It's time, Fritz."

Fritz looked past him, at the display window of the shop in front of them. The glass reflected the image of a tanned face with black hair and a black mustache.

Uri followed his gaze. "Enough with the hide-and-seek."

"When?"

"Tonight. I'll take you as far as the border. Our man will escort you from there, right to the Syrian camp."

He drove Fritz to his apartment.

"We'll meet here in three hours," Uri said.

Fritz disappeared inside.

At the arranged time, Uri pulled up at the front door of Fritz's building and nervously checked his watch. The German was late. Uri took his photo of Yael off the dash and caressed it gently. "I'm looking out for you," he muttered. But he wondered just how much he could actually do. Finally, the front door opened. A blond man came out. It took Uri a moment to grasp that it was Fritz Paulsen. He looked like something out of a Nazi propaganda film, all blue eyes and thick blond hair.

Uri quickly put away the photo and pushed open the passenger door.

"Let's go," he said as he started up the engine.

An old man wore a kaffiyeh on his head and the fellahs' traditional long robe. He had a curved dagger tucked into his belt and held an ancient rifle in his right hand. He spoke the simple Arabic of the countryside. He looked around hesitantly before joining the hundreds waiting in line to volunteer in the fight against the Jews.

Fritz leaned against the barracks and observed the men streaming in. It was mostly young Arabs wanting to sign up, many of them wearing old British, Turkish, or Syrian tunics and military boots. They also brought a no-less-motley mix of weapons, mostly outmoded carbines from the days of Turkish occupation, though a few clutched British machine guns, which were available in the souks of Damascus.

A Syrian colonel stepped out of the barracks, accompanied by a blond, German-looking man in a medium-gray uniform, black jackboots, and a belt bearing the inscription *"Gott mit uns"* ("God with us") on the buckle. His tunic sported an eagle above the breast pocket, its claws holding a swastika, and Fritz instantly recognized the shoulder insignia of a first lieutenant in the Wehrmacht.

Their eyes met. Fritz stepped up and stretched out his hand. "SS Hauptsturmführer Paulsen," he said.

The Wehrmacht lieutenant stood to attention for the higher-ranking SS officer, clicking his heels.

"First Lieutenant Müller, Hauptsturmführer."

They shook hands.

"Just arrived," Fritz said. "By way of Rome, then Beirut. Wasn't exactly easy making my way here. But I'm here now."

"You've come at just the right time, Hauptsturmführer," Müller replied. "The war against the Jews is about to start in a big way. And here in Qantara, you'll meet some men who used to fight alongside us. We Germans are in great demand as instructors. As you can see, there's plenty to be done."

He pointed at the men crowding around the entrance.

"I myself bolted from a British POW camp in Palestine, Latrun, just a few miles outside Tel Aviv. I was with Rommel at Tobruk—that's where they nabbed me." He added a grin. "But a sympathetic British sergeant turned a blind eye and I was out before anyone knew it."

He pointed at the barracks where volunteers were gathering. "We have British deserters here, plus Muslims from all over, even some from the Balkans. They're totally fanatical, and no wonder; some of them are ours, from the SS Handschar Division, the unit comprised entirely of Muslims. Lots of them are experts we can rely on for sabotage, bomb attacks, and what have you. Very effective."

Fritz knew former SS Muslims. They were especially strong adherents of Mufti Hadj Amin al-Husseini, who had spent the war in Berlin. Hitler and Himmler had enabled the mufti to hound Palestinian Jews all the way from Germany.

"I'm familiar with them," he said. "I was one of their instructors."

In the long line of willing warriors, a young, unshaven man wearing a red-and-white checked kaffiyeh used the waiting time to clean his carbine. Aaron Mehulem had no trouble making conversation with the others in line. His Arabic was better than his Hebrew. He had grown up in a suburb of Baghdad, the son of Jewish parents, and his family later emigrated to Palestine. He ignored Fritz, and Fritz did the same, as if both were invisible. But Aaron had an important mission. He wasn't only the Jewish spy in this training camp—he was also the liaison between Fritz and the Haganah.

February 9, 1948

"Here we go," Sergeant Higgins said. His face flushed, the sergeant stood before Lieutenant Goldsmith's desk. Looking almost jubilant, Higgins showed Goldsmith the folder containing the report from British Military Intelligence.

"The Arabs are attacking. Things are getting lively now."

Josef took the report from his hands.

> *Heavy units of the Yarmuk Battalion are preparing for a massive assault in Upper Galilee. They've already deployed units of the Arab Liberation Army across the Syrian border.*

He buried himself in the numbers, in the armaments described. His gaze then fixed on one line:

> *One of the probable targets for attack is Kibbutz Yardenim, which is strategically located on a road connecting the border with Lower Galilee.*

Josef sat up. "Does the general know about this report?"

"Of course, sir," Higgins said.

"So how do we plan to respond?"

The sergeant's face revealed his delight. "We are to 'observe' the situation, sir."

Josef glanced at his watch. It was already past midnight. If he left now, he could be there in five hours.

The light of the full moon recast the rectangular window as a diagonal glow on the floor. It was enough for Judith to make out the hands of the old alarm clock on her nightstand. In an hour and a half, the sun would come up.

She pulled the covers over her shoulders to fight off the February night's cold. She'd been lying awake for hours. Her nightmares had faded for a while, but then returned in the past few weeks. Again and again, the barking of the SS execution squads' machine guns invaded her dreams, assaulting her with images of violence and death, mixing with memories of the vast churning sea, ships bouncing up and down, faces, Esther drowning, a blond man, a tombstone bearing the name Albert Wertheimer. Finally, she'd jolted awake, lying in her cold sweat.

Ever since the United Nations decided on partition, tensions with the Arabs had increased considerably. In the first few weeks, they'd still had contact with Deir El Nar, then nobody dared to cross over anymore. At dinner in the communal hall, Moshe Ben Porat had reported that trucks kept appearing near the Arab village. The next kibbutz over, about six miles to the north, had survived an intense shoot-out with Arab attackers two days ago. Two Jewish settlers were killed, five injured. How many deaths the Arabs had suffered wasn't clear, but the kibbutzniks had captured one—an Iraqi, another sign that the conflict was no longer local.

Judith tried closing her eyes, but she was afraid of falling asleep again. She didn't want to return to that other world, the world of her nightmares.

The road through the Jordan Valley was riddled with potholes. Josef was grateful for the full moon, but the sandstorm from the south kept driving sand across the windshield, leaving him with nearly no visibility as he drove on. *Judith,* he thought. Why hadn't he insisted that she leave Yardenim? It was absolute madness what was happening in this part of the world. His sister had survived Germany. How could he let her end up in danger again? He needed to warn her, he needed to make sure that she left Palestine immediately. Because a decisive battle between Jews and Arabs was imminent, and it would be a bloody one.

He glanced again at his watch and stepped even harder on the gas pedal. The Arab attack would likely come at first light of day. It was still darkest night for now, but he had a little over thirty miles to go yet.

Josef had to slam on the brakes to avoid a chunk of rock in the road, then he accelerated again, and the jeep raced along, bucking like a horse over the potholes. He kept passing Arab villages. Soon he would be in Yardenim, soon. Still nine, maybe only six miles to go.

Again the jeep smashed against a deep pothole. Josef had trouble keeping the vehicle straight. It suddenly started lurching. He clamped the wheel but soon realized there was no point giving it more gas. He slowed to a stop, scared now. *No, no.* The jeep had a flat.

For a while Josef sat there in silence, his head lowered over the steering wheel. He wiped the sand out of his eyes, considering whether he should simply continue on foot. But he couldn't possibly walk fast enough. He rose from the driver's seat and went around back to find the spare tire. He looked for the wrench. Then he paused.

From a distance, he heard a rattle, then a sharp bang that kept repeating, over and over in short intervals. He knew that sound. He'd heard it all too often during the war in Europe. It was mortars firing, interspersed with machine guns.

Josef felt faint. He went back and collapsed into the driver's seat. *My God,* he thought. *It's too late.*

Yael lay in bed, facing the wall. Her breathing was regular and deep. She seemed unaffected by the tensions of the past few weeks. She had that self-confidence of the sabra, born in Palestine, familiar with the land, also familiar with the dangers. She only became anxious when she was waiting for Uri, but he rarely came to Yardenim now, mostly with new weapons hidden under the seats of his Ford.

The noise of dogs barking reached them from Deir El Nar, becoming louder, wilder. Judith sat up and listened nervously. Outside their small wooden house, she heard fragments of words exchanged in Hebrew, whispers of the night watch. Their numbers had been enhanced in the past week: the lookout tower was now occupied by two guards, and two extra kibbutzniks were now patrolling Yardenim's buildings with their machine guns.

The dogs didn't settle down. Judith threw back her covers, pulled a thick sweater over her nightshirt, and reached for her khaki pants.

The explosion caught her off guard. Window glass shards dug into her upper arm and shoulder, the wood of the window frame crashing against her temple. She tried bracing herself against something but couldn't, and she dropped to the floor unconscious.

"Judith, wake up. Judith."

Someone was shaking her by the shoulder. She tried to ignore it, to remain in limbo. But the shaking would not cease. The voice became clearer.

"Judith, can you hear me? Wake up."

She opened her eyes and saw the face of Ben Zvi.

"Thank God," Ben said. He handed her a canteen. "Here, drink."

It was hot coffee. She swallowed it, coughed. She suddenly felt the pain radiating from her upper left arm and left shoulder. She looked down and realized her arm and torso were bandaged, the blood seeping through.

"You got lucky," Ben said. "Just shallow wounds—they'll heal quick."

Judith stared at him in amazement. "What happened?"

"The Arabs attacked." Ben pointed at the splintered window frame. "One of their grenades exploded right in front of this window. We beat them back, but it was close. Damn close."

He pulled a pack of cigarettes from his breast pocket and held it out for Judith. She declined. He lit one and inhaled deeply.

"What about the others?" Judith asked.

"Five dead, three severely wounded, and four mildly," Ben said. "We hardly had any ammo left—one hour more and they would've overrun us. But they lost their nerve and took off. We must've hit one of their commanders."

He smiled sadly, staring into space.

"You rest. We'll come get her in a bit."

Judith stared at him blankly. Ben nodded toward the other side of the room. On the floor lay a stretcher, a lifeless body on it, a large puddle of blood all around.

"Yael," Ben said, shamefaced. "The shrapnel tore through her carotid artery. She bled to death."

The falcon made a wide circle over the stony fields between Yardenim and Deir El Nar, as if it couldn't decide. Eventually it descended to grab its prey. Then it veered off and flew away.

Judith watched its flight. From here, Deir El Nar appeared completely unaffected by the horrors of the past twenty-four hours. A light easterly wind carried over the muezzin's voice, calling the believers to midday prayers from the small minaret.

The mood on the kibbutz was gloomy. They had buried the dead right after sunrise, the first graves since Yardenim was built. Uri, who'd arrived late in the night, had stood stone-faced while they laid Yael in the shallow grave. Later, he retreated to one of the wooden benches in the communal hall and stared at the floor. Judith gathered all her courage and sat down next to him.

"I—I'm so sorry," she said awkwardly.

But Uri didn't respond. He looked right through her. As if he'd enclosed himself in some impenetrable armor, words unable to reach him. In his hands was a small photo of Yael.

Judith could feel a flush filling her face, and she couldn't do a thing to prevent it. She didn't know what to do, what to say.

"She—she was—" she stuttered. "Yael really was a good friend." The flush in her face intensified. She shifted on the bench uneasily. "We'll miss her, we all will," she suddenly blurted. She stood up. "If there's anything I can do."

Uri stood partway, but then sat back down. "Thanks," he said finally. "Thanks very much." He put his head in his hands. Judith went to the kitchen, leaving him there, not letting herself look back.

Reinforcements for the Palmach arrived late in the evening. Fifty fighters from the Levanoni Brigade leaped off the trucks and unloaded a heavy machine gun, twenty Bren submachine guns, and thirty rifles, plus several cases of ammunition.

Avi Gutmann, their commander, a dark-haired Pole with an unruly beard, shook Uri's hand in silence. They'd known each other a long time.

"Tomorrow morning at five," he said.

Uri nodded. The Palmach troops and the kibbutzniks had gathered in a half circle around them.

"We've received intelligence from their camp in Qantara that they'll soon be sending more troops across the Syrian border. Here's what it comes down to: either we hit them as hard as we can, or they hit us. Let's not fool ourselves—there is no peaceful solution now. It's high time we showed them they cannot destroy us. Those gangs from the Arab Liberation Army are becoming increasingly aggressive, especially here in Galilee."

Murmurs of agreement.

"We are going to drive the gangs out of Deir El Nar and the residents along with them."

"The residents?" Ben asked.

"You heard me, drive them right out," Gutmann answered.

"What about the families, the children?"

"They go, too, all of them, we have clear orders. Nothing is to be surrendered, not one square foot of land, not one settlement."

Ben spoke up again. "What if they resist?"

Gutmann lifted his machine gun. "This will make them get a move on. And none of you better get sentimental. The time for that is over."

He turned to the men standing around him. "Any other questions?"

No one spoke.

"In that case, apart from the sentries, we should all get some sleep," Gutmann said, ending the meeting.

February 10, 1948

Tamar held both of her children tight by their hands. They kept trying to wriggle free.

"He'll be here soon," she told them again. She was standing at the Jerusalem bus station on the western edge of the city, waiting for the bus from Tel Aviv.

Tamar Schiff leaned down to Ayelith. "Pull your scarf tighter."

"And you," she said to her son, "you keep your hat on."

Tamar had Judith's letter in her pocket. It had come on the last convoy. She hadn't said a thing to the children about it. In it, Judith had announced that a gift was coming for Ayelith's birthday. She'd asked that Tamar have her husband, Yossi, pick it up from someone in Tel Aviv, a woman named Hilda. *Awfully secretive,* Tamar thought—*Haganah likely had a hand in this. Pretty crazy way to deliver a birthday present, but then again, these are crazy times.*

The people waiting for the Tel Aviv bus shivered in the February rain. An ambulance bearing the words "Magen David Adom" was waiting with its motor running. In the past few weeks, the ambulance had become part of the usual welcoming committee for the buses. Two medics pulled out a stretcher and set it on the sidewalk.

"You think Abba will bring us something?" Ayelith said. "I really want a new doll."

Shimon yanked his hand free from his mother. "Look, look, the convoy's coming!" he shouted.

An armored truck turned onto the street leading to the bus station, followed by a line of more trucks and a regular bus with several windows shattered. It stopped and the door opened. The two medics jumped inside and came right back out with a bleeding man they laid on the stretcher. Ayelith and Shimon looked up at their mother with fright.

"Where's Abba?" Ayelith asked.

Tamar bit her lip. *Where was Yossi?* The medics helped a woman wearing a heavy, bloody bandage around her head, then the other passengers stepped out. Tamar held her breath. Finally, she saw him. He had a package clamped under his left arm, wrapped in newspaper. Ayelith ran to him.

"Abba, Abba!" she shouted.

Yossi held her tight with one arm, hiding the package behind his back with the other. Then he leaned down to Shimon and kissed him on the forehead. He took his wife in his arms.

"Let's get out of here quick. There's two more dead in the back of the bus," he whispered. "Right after we entered the mountains, near Bab el-Wad, the Arabs shot off more of their fireworks."

"You have to wait until Ima's back," Yossi said, trying to calm his daughter. "She's out getting a few things real quick. We want to make you such a nice feast, princess, seeing as how you're seven today."

"Please, please, Abba," Ayelith insisted. "I wish I could see my present now."

"You'll get it soon. Promise."

Shimon was the first to hear the sound of the door and ran down the hallway. He pulled the door open to reveal Tamar, her key in her hand. She put on a strained smile and stepped into the living room, setting down her shopping basket: bread, a can of sardines, a package of margarine, and two eggs.

"I'm sorry," she said gently. "This is all they had in the shop. They're saying things are going to get even tougher if more convoys don't get through."

Shimon stared at her. "What's that mean, Ima? We're going to starve?"

Yossi stroked his head tenderly. "Come on, there's no way it's going to get that bad," he said. "So, Ayelith, let's see about that present Aunt Judith got for you."

He handed it to his daughter. She quickly unwrapped it, smiling at Judith's hand-drawn card.

"Thank you, Abba," she cheered, petting her new doll.

The gunfire finally ceased. A herd of cows was moving toward Yardenim. Judith figured it had to be early afternoon. A thick plume of smoke rose in the bright blue sky over Deir El Nar. The cows were getting close, driven along by men from the Palmach.

"Juicy spoils, literally." Avi Gutmann grinned as he led his group onto the kibbutz. "I think we've earned ourselves a barbecue today. Meat, real meat. Been so long since I've had any." He pointed at one of the fifteen cows. "Don't you think?"

Moshe Ben Porat, the village elder, nodded with hesitation. "All right, it's fine as far as I'm concerned. Bring her around behind the building. And get a good fire going."

"Look what I found." Gutmann held up a tattered booklet for all to see. "This is German, am I right?"

"Give it here," Moshe said. His parents came from Lodz, where people spoke Yiddish and German along with Polish. He whistled through his teeth. "A paybook from the German Wehrmacht. Where on earth did you get it?"

Gutmann took back the booklet.

"It was lying next to one of the dead, obviously a European."

He attempted to decipher the name. *"Müller,"* he read. *"Oberleutnant Klaus Müller.* A German lieutenant serving with the Arab Liberation Army. They never give up, do they? Always some German wanting to kill us Jews."

Ben Zvi came up to the main square, his machine gun slung on his back, and sat on the grass before the firepit. Judith joined him. Ben Zvi stared off into space.

"She was staring at me," he said to himself.

"Who?" Judith asked.

"The mukhtar's wife. The one who'd served us tea that time. She was lying there, in a corner of the house, staring right at me as if she could see me." He swallowed. "She'd been dead awhile."

Judith winced. She remembered the woman well, her dark robe.

"They shot her, the people from the Palmach just shot her."

Judith stared at him, her eyes wide. "And the mukhtar? What about the mukhtar?"

"They shot him first."

Judith placed a hand on his arm. "My God."

"God has no part in this," Ben said.

Avi Gutmann came and sat down with them. "Man, am I hungry," he declared.

Judith jumped up and went over to the water station. Uri was there, washing his right leg. Judith saw the blood. She felt a sting run through her chest. *He's wounded,* she thought. *Uri.*

"It's nothing, really," Uri said, seeing her reaction. "We were lucky: only a few wounded, no dead. The Arabs were fighting us like crazy. The liberation army troops had holed up in the village—we literally had to smoke them out. Then they fled, at least those who still could. In any case, Deir El Nar won't be a threat to us anymore. We've taken it."

"And what about the mukhtar? And his wife?" Judith asked, her voice straining.

Uri hesitated a moment. "The people from that village were supposed to go, those were our orders. And since they didn't, the Palmach helped them along. It worked. They're gone, all of them."

Judith could feel every part of herself resisting. "No," she said. "We can't be doing this. Not us, of all people. Jews." She sank onto a bench. "Tell me how you could do this? How could you? Tell me!"

Uri straightened up, at attention. "They attack us, we strike back. We must fight this battle. It's now or never. It's our only chance, we must take it."

"But—but fighting back can't mean killing innocent people, driving them from their homes, taking their land. Uri, we can't do that, especially not us."

Uri glared at her. "Don't be so naive. And stop playing the victim. The Holocaust is over, you hear me? When they try to kill us, we have to defend ourselves. You know what their leader says: 'We must drive the Jews into the sea.' That's exactly what they're trying to do right now. It's only going to get worse once the British are really gone."

His shoulders fell, and he sat down next to Judith. He buried his head in his hands. After a long moment of silence, he said, scarcely audible, "Yael is dead. This was her only homeland. They killed her."

Judith thought she heard him release a heavy sigh. He held his head in his hands again. Then he looked up and wiped his eyes with the back of his hand.

"Excuse me," he said. "It's just—I always wanted to build a future, for Yael, for us, a secure future."

To Judith, Uri had always seemed so strong, someone the darker side of life bounced right off. To see him vulnerable now—for a moment she was tempted to move closer, to touch him, take his hand. But she suppressed the urge.

Uri stood up. "Excuse me," he said again, his voice raw. "I need to go."

As he left, she had to exercise all her restraint not to run after him.

February 20, 1948

The man wore a traditional fez, an eagle with a swastika prominently displayed on the front. His skin was dark, his hair black. On the collar patches of his tunic were two runes, the insignia of the SS. Everyone in Qantara knew him as Mustafa. He came from Kosovo. In 1944, they had picked him from the Muslim Handschar Division of the SS to be sent to Germany for special training. Few knew their way around explosives better than he. He was now the bomb maker in the camp. And the next target was a special one: the heart of the Jewish Quarter of Jerusalem. Mustafa would build the bombs. British deserters would deliver them to the target.

Fritz Paulsen watched from his barrack as Mustafa loaded the explosives onto the stolen British truck. Here in Qantara, word of his own arrival had spread quickly—another SS officer joining the Arabs! They treated him with great respect everywhere. The camp commander had asked him to select the best of the volunteers and to form a special unit. Fritz had agreed, but he requested a little time. Right now, he needed to find out the exact destination for the bomb attack in Jerusalem. Then he would send Aaron Mehulem to warn the Haganah.

As Fritz stepped out in front of his barrack, Mustafa came up and planted himself before him.

"You're the traitor," he proclaimed. "The deserter they sent to Dachau. You're him. Paulsen. I was there. Our SS commanders had us fall in and watch when they took you away, as a deterrence to us."

Fritz felt a hard blow to his head. Everything went dark.

February 22, 1948

It was a clear night. With the first stars, Shabbat had ended, and the people had stayed out late at the cafés on Ben Yehuda Street, enjoying the unseasonably mild temperature.

Tamar Schiff stood at the window of her apartment and looked down on the now-deserted street. She'd been unable to sleep so many times in the past few weeks. In the morning, Yossi was going to Tel Aviv for two days, on one of the convoys that was getting hit ever harder by the Arab gangs.

She was going to give him a letter for Judith, an invitation to Passover. Tamar just hoped he'd be able to make it home safely. Jerusalem was now experiencing daily shootings and explosions. Just three weeks ago, a bomb had devastated the building housing the *Palestine Post*.

This morning she would go to Chaim Grünbaum's little shop and try to get a sliver of meat and some milk for the children. She wondered how much more she'd have to pay to get him to make another exception. On his last stay in Tel Aviv, Yossi had scared up a sack of grain. But she was keeping that as a last resort, in case the food supplies turned even worse.

Shouldn't she just go with him, take the children, get on the bus, and leave Jerusalem behind, like so many had recently? Why couldn't she live in Tel Aviv, on the sea, in a city that was practically all Jews, where things were relatively safe? Of course, the people from the Jewish

Agency, just a few hundred yards away on King George V Avenue, would be against that. Jews weren't allowed to leave Jerusalem, not right now, so soon before the British pulled out. But how could she keep exposing her children to such danger? She sighed. Yossi was against moving too. His family had lived in Jerusalem since the end of the nineteenth century, and he would never agree to abandon his city.

But Tamar's family came from Poland. None of her relatives were still living. They'd died in the Warsaw Ghetto, starved to death. Wasn't she, too, now living in a ghetto, cut off from the regular world? Couldn't her own family come to the same end? She decided to broach the subject with Yossi in the morning.

Tamar looked up at the dark, star-filled sky. In a few hours, the sun would rise again in Jerusalem. In the distance, from Jaffa Road, she could hear the drone of large motors. *British troops again,* she thought. She quietly opened the door to the children's bedroom. Ayelith and Shimon were sleeping soundly. She sat on her son's bed and gently stroked his hair.

Fritz Paulsen had given up pulling on his restraints. They were so tight around his arms they were cutting off his blood flow. The blow to his head from that rifle had resulted in a severe concussion. He'd only been awake occasionally since. Somewhere in his consciousness, it had registered that he was lying on the bed of a truck. He had heard voices. They sounded like English ones. He heard the driver changing gears a lot. They were obviously driving through a mountainous area. Inside his aching head, indifference had set in. The truck seemed to be going slower now. Then it came to a stop. Fritz tried to concentrate.

"Go, quick, get moving," he heard someone say in English. Footsteps, moving away. From the cab he heard a soft hiss, combined with the strong smell of something burning. The hissing came closer and Fritz's consciousness sharpened again. He remembered that smell from an SS sabotage course. It was the smell of a burning fuse. He shut his eyes, and bitter tears streamed down his face.

The children's room faced the back, away from Ben Yehuda Street. The explosions of three British military trucks, each filled with a ton of TNT, sent window shards hurtling through the living room. A large shard tore into the door to the kids' room, flinging it open. Tamar was thrown onto Shimon, who started crying. Ayelith lay speechless on her bed, clutching her doll.

Tamar heard a sound from the living room. Then he was standing in the doorway. Yossi. Blood was streaming down his face. Several shards had struck him. But he was alive. Tamar sized up the situation in a flash. There had been a massive explosion on Ben Yehuda Street. But her family, both kids, her husband, she herself, had survived.

She jumped up and yanked a towel out of one of the cabinets, bounded over to Yossi, and started wiping the blood from his face.

He grabbed her hands. "I'm all right. Just a few cuts, not as bad as it looks."

Yossi sat next to his son on the bed and held him tight until he started to quiet down. Then he went into the living room and peered through the blown-out window.

"Look at this!"

About thirty yards away, toward Jaffa Road, was a crater in the street. The buildings on both sides had crumbled. Hotel Amdursky was a ruin, the six-story Vilenchick Building totally collapsed. People in pajamas wandered the street, over which thick billows of smoke gathered. Bodies could be seen. This was the worst attack yet.

"What madness." Yossi turned to Tamar. "If they think they're going to drive us from this city this way, they're wrong. Jerusalem belongs to us, just as it has for three thousand years."

March 1, 1948

The last snow atop Mount Hermon glittered in the sun, high above the Golan Heights. In the valley below, spring spread slowly, a little more every day. Judith watched the sheep make their way over to her on the meadows' fresh new greenery. She sat on a rock and set down her Sten machine gun. Even though the meadowlands were in clear view of the watchtower, Moshe Ben Porat now insisted that everyone carried weapons when leaving the kibbutz. Despite their capture of Deir El Nar, nighttime skirmishes had increased significantly in the past few weeks as Arab Liberation Army gangs attacked Jewish settlements.

Judith set her head on her arms and closed her eyes. *Just for a moment, one moment,* she thought. She could feel the weariness in her body, leaden, ever present. Ever since Yael had died, she lay awake for hours at night, startled by every sound, repeatedly changing her sweat-soaked nightshirt, falling asleep only at sunrise, exhausted.

Why fight? she thought. *For what? For a piece of land?* A piece of land that was still half stones and thornbushes even after months of hard work? And was it supposed to just go on like this forever—fighting the Arabs, fighting for survival? Her Hebrew had improved, but she noticed she was still thinking in German. Recently, Moshe had snapped at her for speaking German, a language many kibbutzniks understood better than Hebrew.

"Will you stop that?" he'd said. "That's Hitler's language."

She'd defended herself without thinking, unleashing her fury for the first time. "Yes, it sure is. I'm well aware. But it's also the language of my parents and grandparents, and even though you might not like it, of Theodor Herzl. He didn't know any Hebrew."

With her eyes closed, she listened to the sparrows chirping excitedly. She could feel rays of sunlight tickling her neck. Memories filled her head, memories of warm summer days. It was summer 1932, she was nine, lying blissfully next to her mother on the beach beside Lake Wannsee in Berlin. That last carefree summer. It surprised her to be recalling this of all things. She wondered what Berlin looked like now. Was it all just rubble everywhere, or did something like normal life exist? Was her building in Dahlem still standing? Who lived there? Would she ever see it again? She stopped herself. Was she homesick for Germany? For her language, her culture, her roots?

She tried to switch off her mind, but another thought crept in, slowly blanketing all the old images. For days now, she kept catching herself asking the same question: What was he doing right now? Was he in danger? Sometimes she felt ashamed when she passed the graves of Yael and the others. But she couldn't stop. She kept thinking about him. Uri.

The clacking of horse hooves startled her. She looked up. Ben Zvi climbed down from a white horse and tied it to a tree. He was wearing a sort of uniform—khaki pants, a khaki shirt with epaulets, and a wool cap from American military stocks. A rifle hung from his shoulder. He took it off, placed it next to the rock, and slid down to the ground next to Judith.

"It's finally getting warmer," he said.

"It is, finally."

"Am I disturbing you?"

"What? No, not at all," she replied. "I'm just a little tired. You know how it is, these short nights."

They fell silent. Ben moved closer to her. He reached for her hand, somewhat awkwardly.

"You always seem so sad. Is there something wrong?"

She shook her head. "No, it's just—Maybe it's just that this is a little too much all at once. You know, first everything that happened before, then the ship, my uncle dying, then Yael—" She wanted to add: *along with the constant death and dying all around us, which we ourselves have a hand in.* But she kept quiet.

"If there's anything I can do." He caressed her hand.

Judith pulled it away. "Thank you, Ben. But I think not. I'll be fine."

He flushed, shifting back and forth. "Excuse me, really, I—I didn't mean to get too close. Really, I didn't. I just thought—Anyway, like I said, if you ever need any help—"

He stood and shouldered his rifle. Then he untied the horse and swung himself up into the saddle. With a nod, he rode off. Judith watched him go, then laid her head back on her arms. After a while, she fell asleep.

Judith opened her eyes and saw a pair of dust-covered military boots. Startled, she looked up. Uri Rabinovich. He was standing before her, alone. He clearly hadn't shaved in days. His face looked tired, only his eyes lively.

"I just wanted to tell you goodbye."

Judith stared in surprise. "Say goodbye? But you only just got here."

"We're pulling out of the villages. We're looking for volunteers," he explained. "All of Jerusalem is at stake. The Arabs are systematically sealing off the city. If we don't break their siege, they'll starve out some hundred thousand Jews. Then the city will fall. And you know what that means: a Jewish state without Jerusalem—it's unthinkable."

Judith rose from her rock and stood up. Only a few inches separated them. She could feel his physical presence, and she instinctively wanted to press up close to him, to hold him tight.

"I need to go," Uri said.

Judith hesitated. "Are you looking for more volunteers?" she said finally. "Are you taking women too?"

"We're taking any volunteers who are truly prepared to use a weapon when it comes down to it. It will be tough, really tough. The roads into Jerusalem are now the main battle zone."

Judith understood. They were looking for fighters, not angels of peace. No one plagued by scruples. No one afraid of killing. No one, she realized, like her.

She gathered all her courage, stood on her tiptoes, and gave him a kiss on the cheek. "Take care of yourself," she said softly. "Promise me that."

He placed a hand on her shoulder and held her tight, a moment too long. Then he turned away without another word.

The truck was waiting with its motor running. Five volunteers from Yardenim had climbed onto the bed and were greeted with pats on their shoulders by their fellow recruits from other kibbutzim. Uri Rabinovich climbed up into the cab of the first truck and gave the driver the signal. The column set in motion for the steeply rising road.

The first two trucks had already disappeared over the hill when it happened. The third vehicle lurched slightly, then stopped. The driver jumped out and took a look at the left rear wheel. He angrily kicked at the flat tire.

"Everyone down, help me change it," he shouted.

The Haganah recruits leaped out and started unscrewing the spare tire.

The first shot came once they'd unmounted the wheel. A bullet whistled past the driver's head. The Haganah troops scrambled to get the weapons they'd left on the truck. The Arabs came running down from one of the hills full of olive trees, screaming battle cries, rifles trained, some brandishing curved daggers.

Judith had been watching the trucks depart. The attack, a good hundred yards away, seemed to transpire before her as if in a movie. It took her a moment to grasp the reality of it, right before her eyes: Arab Liberation Army guerrillas assaulting a Jewish convoy.

Ben Zvi ran past her, followed by Moshe Ben Porat. Ben Zvi fired his machine gun at the attackers, but he wasn't close enough.

Judith immediately went into motion, as if by instinct. For a moment, she forgot which truck Uri was in, whether it really had been the first one, already safe behind the hill. She only had one thought: *the Arabs are attacking the convoy,* his *convoy.* She stumbled, pulled herself back up, kept running, following Ben Zvi, who kept on firing.

Right before reaching the remaining truck, Ben Zvi collapsed. Blood pumped from his chest. Judith spotted his attacker, a young Arab, about Ben Zvi's age. His gun must have been empty—the man stopped and frantically started searching his pockets for ammo. He found some and shoved the first cartridge into the barrel. Judith reached for the Sten gun Ben Zvi was still grasping and ripped it from his hands. She raised the gun, aimed at the young Arab, and pulled the trigger. The Arab stood still a moment, then collapsed. His rifle thudded on the ground next to him.

Judith clutched the gun in both hands, staring at it in amazement. She had killed a human being.

From the rise came the staccato of machine guns, interspersed with the cracks of rifle fire. The two other trucks had returned and the Haganah recruits were now firing on the attackers. After about fifteen minutes, the firing ceased. The surviving Arabs withdrew beyond the olive grove.

Judith lay behind the cover of the big spare tire, still holding the machine gun. Uri ran over and sat on the tire. He took the gun from her and pulled her up to him, placing an arm around her. They sat in silence for a long time.

"Well done," he said finally, his voice hoarse. He gave her a timid kiss on the forehead.

The truck driver cleared his throat. "Hate to disturb you, but we need that tire."

They stood up, looking around awkwardly. No one was watching them. Everyone was too busy replacing the tire.

"Finished," the driver shouted after a few minutes.

Uri leaned over to Judith once more and kissed her again on the forehead. Then he climbed up onto the truck bed. The others followed. Uri waved to her from above.

"See you soon," he shouted.

Judith was standing right behind the truck, looking up at him. Then she raised her hands. She stood like that for a moment, her arms stretched high. Uri seemed to hesitate, her gesture taking him by surprise. Then he reached for her hands and pulled her up onto the truck. The others clapped wildly.

"Drive on!" Uri shouted. "To Jerusalem!"

March 2, 1948

Hana's nausea had eased. She had gained weight, but she was wearing baggy clothes, and no one apart from David knew that she was three months pregnant.

She kept wondering whether it would be a boy or a girl. *A boy,* she hoped.

Every morning, she tried taking the short bus ride from Sheikh Jarrah up to Hadassah Hospital, but the bus increasingly failed to show because of the snipers firing on it from the Arab Quarter. At the hospital, only a few Arab employees still remained on duty, and the Arab patients had stopped coming altogether. Hana could feel the tension that had built up between the Arabs and the Jews in the hospital. Her own relationship with a certain Jewish doctor definitely played a role. It started out as whispers, then came the nurses' first remarks. David had eventually confirmed the rumors to his colleagues. "Yes, it's true," he'd said. "Hana Khalidy and I are a couple."

Her apartment doorbell rang, making her start. That could mean danger now, here in Sheikh Jarrah. Could it be the Haganah fighters who'd been breaking into buildings to drive out Arab residents? Arab guerrillas seeking an apartment to use to keep watch on the street? The British searching for any and all intruders in their desperation to keep the road to Ramallah clear—this being their own line of retreat once they got the signal?

She took a cautious look through the peephole and saw a trusted face, one she hadn't seen for a long time: her father's. She let him in and quickly shut the door. He took her in his arms and held her tight for a long time.

"Come in, I'll make us tea," she said.

Her father settled onto the living room sofa with some effort and waited for her to bring the tea. They drank in silence.

Finally, he said, "It's time for you to come home."

Hana's eyes widened. *Home, to her village, now? In her condition, away from David?*

"It's quiet in Deir Yassin," he said. "We have an arrangement with the Haganah. They leave us alone, and we make sure there's no trouble with those guerillas from Syria and Iraq."

He took a drink.

"Come with me, before it's too late," he asked in a soft voice. "Your mother would also like you to come home."

Hana hadn't seen her mother for months. She had never gotten over her daughter besmirching the family's honor by not marrying Youssef Hamoud. *So now,* Hana wondered, *was my mother forgiving me? Or was she merely obeying her husband's wishes?*

She poured her father more tea, to buy time. He looked at her expectantly. Hana kept all her focus on stirring the sugar in her cup.

"I can't," she said eventually. "I simply can't."

Hana had always been amazed by her father's strength. He was a dignified man, a man who knew what he wanted. Yet now he sat slumped on the sofa, his face pale.

The sound of a key turning in the door startled them both. A moment later, David stood in the doorway to the living room, staring at them in surprise. Hana leaped up and kissed him. She stood next to him.

"Father, let me introduce you to Dr. David Cohen," she said.

David moved toward Hana's father, his right hand outstretched.

But Mohammed Khalidy remained sitting.

"David is the father of my child," Hana said. "I'm due in six months."

Her father still did not move to shake David's outstretched hand.

David cleared his throat. "I understand your being surprised, sir," he said. "It's certainly not the best time for a development like this." He took a step back and placed an arm around Hana.

"But Hana and I belong together, in spite of it all. And I very much hope that you'll approve of our relationship—and that we'll get to know each other better."

Hana's father didn't respond. He only sat there and stared into space, his hands pressed to his thighs. He looked aged, a beaten man.

"Please, Father," Hana said into the silence of the room.

Then, Mohammed Khalidy seemed to return from some other world. He stood, without looking at either of them, and walked to the door with his shoulders drooping, down the stairs to the street, where Ali was waiting for him in the car.

March 10–11, 1948

"No, no, a thousand times no!" the man screamed in Yiddish. "I'm not driving there. Not to those murderers out on the streets. They're just waiting for us."

Uri pulled his revolver from his belt and pressed it to Yaacov Gernstein's temple. "That's enough, you hear? You are going to drive there, just like the others."

Gernstein whimpered. "I have children, three of them, a wife. Think of them. I have to provide for them. They need to eat—every day. If I'm dead, are you going to care for them?"

Uri lowered the revolver.

"Stop your crying. Up there, in Jerusalem? Women and children are dying, you hear me? Starving to death, dying of thirst because of cowards like you. That's what you want to tell your children? *I was too much of a coward?*"

Gernstein removed his flat cap and turned it in his hands. Then he kicked at the truck's tire. "Aw, shit. All right, I'll drive."

Uri grinned. For the past few hours, the Haganah had been using the threat of arms at Tel Aviv intersections to conscript the trucks and drivers they so urgently needed. These they directed to a field next to the warehouse on the outskirts of the city. The drivers were angry, not wanting to be forced into a convoy that was to drive right through the dead zone of Bab el-Wad the next morning. Uri turned to Judith, who'd been observing the scene.

"We have no other choice. Either we finally get a convoy through with food, or Jerusalem falls. It's as simple as that."

The warehouse looked like a huge bazaar. Stacked all over were sacks of flour, barrels of oil, crates of oranges, milk powder, canned sardines.

"Move, get to work, it all goes on the trucks!" Uri ordered the drivers, who were still wavering over in a corner of the warehouse. Then he turned back to Judith.

"You see how I have to keep an eye on things. On top of that—" He paused. "On top of that, I have to say goodbye. I mean, I have to leave early tomorrow morning. So, um, see you soon."

Judith kept a firm hold on his arm. "Why goodbye? I heard from Adina that there are at least ten women on the Haganah convoy, and they're armed."

"So?"

"I'm coming with you to Jerusalem."

"You?"

"Yes, me. You yourself were just telling that driver the only ones not going are cowards."

Uri looked thrown off balance. He clumsily leaned over, as if wanting to touch her. A hot sensation rushed through her body. Then he evidently regained control.

"We'll see," he muttered, and turned away.

The night was rainy and cold. Everyone had been loading supplies on the trucks until well after midnight. Judith was now sitting together with Adina and two other girls in a corner of the warehouse, drinking tea.

"Tomorrow morning, around ten, we'll be in Jerusalem," Adina said. "The convoy can only travel very slowly, what with those trucks so overloaded and the road so steep."

Adina took a brush from her bag and ran it through her hair. "God, I'm so tired," she said.

"Then why are you doing that?" asked one of the girls. "Why brush your hair in the middle of the night?"

"Who knows when else I'll have time?" Adina said, and gave a mischievous laugh. "I'm meeting up with someone tomorrow afternoon, in Jerusalem. Yitzhak."

Judith suddenly realized that she hadn't seen Uri for hours. She anxiously looked around.

"Have you seen Uri anywhere?" she asked Adina.

"You mean Uri Rabinovich? Uri the Great, the big boss? That Uri?" She grinned. "You mean—you and Uri are . . . ?"

Judith turned red. *No,* she wanted to say, *you got it wrong. I couldn't do that to Yael.* But Adina had it exactly right.

"Listen, it's completely fine," Adina said. "You don't have to bullshit me. Go see him, right now. Life is short, understand? Super short. Don't miss out or you'll regret it in the morning."

Adina was right. He could be dead tomorrow. Or she could. So, didn't different rules apply? Shouldn't she just say to hell with convention and follow her heart? On the other hand, could she simply go to him, right now? When he was still mourning Yael? And what was she supposed to tell him? The truth? That she loved him? That she wanted to feel his mouth on hers, his skin on hers? Just like that? Just throw her arms around him, right here in front of everyone? *No,* she decided, *it wasn't going to happen that way.*

She looked for the dark-green, British-issue military tent, where she'd been told she could sleep. A large puddle had formed around the tent from the rain. She opened it tentatively, trying to adjust to the darkness. Five figures lay on the floor. She slipped under an old wool blanket as quietly as possible. She thought of Uri, trying to picture his face, his eyes, his smile. Then weariness overcame her. She pulled the blanket over her head and was asleep within seconds.

Judith jolted awake from a wild and confused dream, then fell back into an unruly half-sleep, a world between waking and dreaming. Eventually she opened her eyes, and in the darkness saw a figure kneeling over her.

"Shh," said a gentle voice. "It's me, Uri."

Judith sat bolt upright.

"Shh, sorry, I didn't mean to scare you," he whispered.

They could hear the other sleepers' steady breathing around them. One was snoring.

He searched for her hand and held it tight.

"I just wanted to tell you that—" He squeezed tighter. "I think it's very brave of you, how you're handling yourself. I mean, do you really want to come on the convoy to Jerusalem? You know how dangerous it is."

She took a deep breath. "I do, Uri. I'm sure of it."

He leaned down to her, searching for her lips. He kissed her, first hesitantly, then harder. Judith, caught by surprise, let it happen. He suddenly let go and moved to stand. But Judith held him tight.

"Stay, Uri, please," she whispered. "Don't go, not now."

"I can't, I really can't. The convoy's leaving in two hours, and I have to make sure the trucks get filled up with gas."

He kissed her, and this time she returned his kiss.

"We'll make up for it, I promise," he said softly. "In Jerusalem."

Then he crawled out of the low tent, out into the rain that didn't want to stop.

Youssef hugged his rifle and tried to keep his teeth from chattering. The storm coming in from the Mediterranean pushed heavy clouds into the mountains of Judaea, and the rain pattered against the rocky cliffs. Youssef tried to shelter against a boulder and hoped that young Nadir didn't notice how much the cold was getting to him. Nadir was only fourteen, a distant cousin from the neighboring village. The boy had pulled his wool cap over his head and nodded off despite the rain. Youssef decided to let him sleep.

Youssef was proud that Abdul Qader al-Husseini had personally given him this mission. He was to keep watch on the road to Jerusalem. If the convoy came, Nadir was supposed to run into the village to alert al-Husseini's fighters. So many conquerors had come down this road to take control of Jerusalem. The Romans, the Crusaders, the Turks, the English.

Since al-Husseini's return, the Arabs' will to fight had intensified. He'd given them courage and a clear goal: encircle the Holy City and starve the Jews. If only the British would finally clear out! Still, their withdrawal was only a question of weeks. The hour would arrive, the hour of vengeance. Palestine would belong to the Arabs—only the Arabs.

He thought of Hana. What might she be doing now? Was she back at her hospital, with her Jewish doctors? He would never overcome the disgrace she'd brought him. *May God punish her,* he thought. *Or better yet: May God give him the chance to carry out the punishment himself.*

The rain started forming little streams that ran past Youssef down the slopes, burrowing channels in the reddish-brown clay. *Were they coming today?* he wondered. The convoys only traveled at irregular intervals now; al-Husseini's plan to block the access roads to Jerusalem had been a huge success.

Yet the road below Youssef lay empty. He resigned himself to the fact that there was nothing for him to do at the moment but wait.

The cargo of flour sacks made the rear of the truck sag down low. Yaacov Gernstein gave Uri an aggravated look.

"We'll make it," Uri assured him. "You'll be back with your family the day after tomorrow."

Gernstein shook his head. He climbed up into the cab without a word and started the engine.

The trucks formed a line a hundred yards long. Uri strode down the line, waving to the drivers. Some waved back, others stared past him. He eventually reached the armored car at the front.

Ezer Landauer had a cigarette between his lips, his cap pulled down low over his face. Uri placed an arm around his shoulder.

"How you feeling?"

Landauer gave him a tortured smile. "I'm looking forward to a coffee at Atara; it always was my favorite spot in Jerusalem," he said. "And their cheesecake!"

Uri clapped Landauer on the shoulder. "The cheesecake is on me," he said, then walked back to the armored car he was to drive.

He looked at his watch. It was time. Maybe she'd reconsidered? He knew he should be ashamed, so soon after Yael's death, but the way things were now, he just had to keep living as best he could. Maybe Judith thought less of him for it?

He couldn't go looking for her, anyway, not in front of everyone. Impossible, simply impossible. He took another uneasy look at his watch. Then he jerked open the armored car's heavy door. She was sitting in the passenger seat, a Sten machine gun between her knees.

"I'm ready to go," Judith said.

"They're coming."

Youssef gave Nadir a sharp nudge in the ribs. The morning light had taken its time creeping over the mountains and opened up a clear view to the west, onto the broad plain leading down to the sea. There, on the horizon, Youssef thought he could make out the first few vehicles of a long column.

"Go, run, as fast as you can, tell al-Husseini's fighters that they're coming. The Jews are coming!"

Nadir ran for the village.

Youssef chambered a round even though the convoy was nowhere near within firing range yet. The nighttime cold that had made his limbs stiff and hard seemed to have vanished. He felt his head throb a little, his pulse racing. A fever seemed to have seized him. He felt for the handle of the curved dagger he kept stuffed in his belt. He hoped he'd get close enough to them to use it.

At twenty-five years old, Uri was the oldest member of the Haganah escort team safeguarding the convoy. He sat with Judith in the second armored car, a converted truck with armor plating mounted on its cab. The lead armored car had been fitted with a dozer blade.

Behind him, Uri had heard the young people singing ever since they'd left the warehouse, trying to outdo one another in volume. But now, with Latrun behind them, all singing ceased. The terrain sloped upward before them. On both sides of the road, hills rose into the morning sky. The Arabs called this Bab el-Wad, the Gate of the Valley, but they were firmly determined to make it a Gate to Hell for the Jews. The narrow route led right into the middle of it, and whoever controlled it during these few weeks would decide the fate of all in Jerusalem.

Youssef slid down the steep mountain slope. He was delighted to see hundreds of fellahs come running out of their villages, their red-and-white kaffiyehs fluttering in the wind. Abdul Qader al-Husseini had promised them abundant loot, and now his promise would be fulfilled. The fellahs hauled out everything they had in the way of weapons—old hunting rifles, homemade explosives, hand grenades from British deserters, knives, axes.

"Start breaking up the road!" Youssef shouted at them.

Some men began smashing up the surface with their axes while others rolled rocks into the roadway and piled them up as a barricade.

Suddenly, they stopped. All eyes turned to the man walking down the path from one of the villages, his stride forceful yet measured. He wore the traditional kaffiyeh and two bullet belts crossed sideways around his broad chest, a modern rifle slung on one shoulder. When he reached the roadway, Abdul Qader al-Husseini raised a hand.

"The day of decision has come. Fight for Al-Quds, the city of the Prophet Mohammed. You are the Jihad Muqaddas, the muftis' warriors. *Allahu Akbar!*"

For a brief moment, there was reverent silence, then the men started screaming, shaking their rifles and axes. *"Allahu Akbar!"* sounded the cry from deep in their throats, again and again. "God is great!"

The road rose steeply now. The convoy trucks crawled forward at only nine miles an hour. After a mile came the first curve. Beyond it stood a barricade.

"There they are, dammit."

Ezer Landauer, driver of the lead armored car, stepped on the gas. Its broad front dozer blade crashed into the piled-up stones, eating away at them. Some boulders tumbled off to the side, but then the truck came to a halt. Landauer stepped on the gas again. The engine howled, then stalled. Landauer frantically grabbed at the key, turned the ignition. The engine started again. His trembling hands threw it in reverse, the heavy vehicle started moving. Landauer shifted into first gear and stomped on the gas pedal as hard as he could. The armored car rammed the stone barricade. To no avail.

At this moment came the first shots from the hills. Soon the Arabs' excited cries combined with the whistling of bullets, then the first men jumped out from behind rocks and ran toward the convoy, waving their rifles. One tossed a Molotov cocktail, then more came flying through the air. Their cries grew into penetrating howls.

Youssef's eyes gleamed. He saw little Nadir striking the armored car's door with an ax, to no effect, and took the ax from him.

"Step aside, quick." Nadir gave him a quizzical look, then jumped behind a rock when he saw the grenade in Youssef's hand. Youssef set it on the armored car's gas tank, pulled the handle, and threw himself behind the rock next to Nadir. The explosion tore the tank open, and flames engulfed the car within seconds. The fellahs erupted in howls of victory.

The narrow slit in their armored car's side windows gave the Bren gun a limited field of fire. Uri kept firing again and again, made contact multiple times, saw attackers collapsing or retreating behind the rocks.

"Look, more of them, coming from all sides," he gasped between bursts of fire. "Quick, give me another magazine." Judith handed him one. "Oh, God, look!" She followed his gaze to the armored car blazing up ahead. He hesitated a moment, then grasped his Bren gun even tighter.

"Cover me!" he shouted.

He pressed the handle down, threw himself against the armored door with all his might, and shoved it open. He fell to the ground, pulled himself back up, and ran toward the burning lead armored car. A slight boy, practically a kid, planted himself in his way, holding an ax. Uri fired. The boy collapsed. Uri heard a salvo at his back, the bullets striking right behind him, dropping two more Arabs to the ground. He looked around and thought he made out Judith's face in the viewing slit behind the barrel of a machine gun, its barrel flashing. Then he reached the burning lead car. He jumped for the door and tore it open. Thick smoke rolled out of the cab. Ezer Landauer fell onto him, Uri unable to stop his lifeless body from tumbling out. The passenger was leaning against the right-side door, not moving either. There was no one left to save here.

Uri turned and looked down the road. Several of the trucks were in flames. Some of the fellahs had stopped firing. They'd jumped onto the truck beds, to cash in on Qader al-Husseini's promise. They plundered the cargo, heaving sacks and cans onto the roadway.

Uri released a burst of fire but realized it was pointless. The convoy was stuck.

"Turn around, turn around!" he shouted and frantically waved back down the road. He leaped onto the running board of the third truck.

"You need to turn around!" he shouted at the driver.

The driver put it in gear but could hardly steer—at least one tire must've been shot up. The driver moved forward and back multiple times before managing to steer it around.

But the truck in front of him was on fire. It was blocking the road, loaded to the top with sacks of flour. On the running board sat a man, his hands clamped around his left thigh. Blood seeped through his shredded pants. Uri ran up to him.

"Shit," groaned Yaacov Gernstein, his face contorted. "I'm hit."

Uri pulled him up. Gernstein stood, gritted his teeth, and threw an arm around Uri. He limped along on his right leg next to Uri, who pushed him toward their second armored car. Judith leaned out of the cab and pulled him inside. Uri jumped in too. Through the viewing slit, he saw an imposing figure with crossed ammo belts on his chest, emerging from between two fellahs. He seemed to be trying to goad his men to keep on fighting—many were squabbling over the flour sacks.

Uri blanched. He'd seen that face in a photo in the *Palestine Post*. Before him, only a few yards away, stood Abdul Qader al-Husseini, leader of the Arab resistance in and around Jerusalem.

Uri fired, but the shots landed next to Qader al-Husseini. Uri took aim again, this time more precisely, and squeezed the trigger. But the Bren gun jammed. Qader al-Husseini leaped to safety behind a truck.

"Crap!" Uri shouted. He now had to focus all he had on getting the convoy to safety. He started turning his armored car around.

"What are you waiting for?" he shouted at the driver in front of him. "You need to push it off the road!"

The driver accelerated and slammed his truck right into the side of the burning wreck. It slowly lurched to the side, then tipped over. Uri could hear Gernstein groaning. He'd just lost his truck on the road to Jerusalem.

March 13, 1948

Tamar Schiff pulled out her food ration card and showed it to Chaim Grünbaum at the counter of his little shop. Grünbaum didn't bother looking at it.

"I don't have anything," he said. "Look around here—my shelves are empty. Fifteen minutes after I opened, it was all gone."

"Don't you worry," Ayelith told her doll. "I still have some bread that I hid under the bed. I'll share it with you."

Grünbaum leaned down to her. "Come back this afternoon. We might be getting another delivery then—they've told us there'll at least be bread."

He turned back to Tamar Schiff. "For the children, we're allowed to provide an extra ration of milk. Apart from that? There's still some flour left, but of course no fresh vegetables, meat, fish."

He sighed. "It's been such misery." He patted Ayelith's head. "So, come back this afternoon with your mommy, and we'll get your doll's tummy full somehow."

An older woman standing behind them in line chimed in: "You hear what the Jewish Agency has come up with now? They want us to grow vegetables ourselves, on roofs, in yards, fields, anywhere we can. They got hold of seeds from British depots. And on top of that, now we're supposed to eat mallow!"

Tamar Schiff nodded. "I'm glad we have it. It's just a weed, but with a little extra effort, you can substitute it for spinach. And it has vitamins."

But the woman didn't want to calm down. "And we're supposed to ration water too! And kerosene. And cook only with wood if we can. And not heat our homes. Where will it end?"

She looked around, seeking approval. "It gets worse every day. Just take a good look outside at this street. Still just rubble everywhere from that bomb. We're lucky we're even alive. And what happens when the British really do pull out? Everyone's so happy they're finally going. Not me, I tell you. What happens then? The Arabs will overrun us. First they starve us out, then they butcher us."

"Oh, just stop," Grünbaum said. "The Haganah will find a way to protect us."

"Really? The Haganah? They're just kids! So few weapons, it's all improvised. And here we are without food. Where will it end? I have a brother in America, in Florida, and from the sound of his letters, he's living the good life. And you know something? Soon as I can, I'm going, too, to America."

Grünbaum was red with anger. "Great, just go. Go as soon as possible. We don't need cowards like you in Jerusalem."

Tamar Schiff took Ayelith by the hand, the girl nervously clasping her doll, and pulled her over to the door. "Come on," she said, "quick."

She opened her still-damp umbrella. Outside it was raining again, pouring. This winter, the rain had been unusually heavy. *That was something at least,* she thought. *It made the mallow grow.*

March 15, 1948

Uri sat in his old Ford, his head on the steering wheel. His body trembled. Judith took his hand and gently caressed it.

"There was nothing you could do," she said gently.

He didn't respond, his head low.

Judith tried again: "Uri, listen to me, please. It's not your fault."

He didn't move, except that his body trembled even more. She squeezed his hand tighter.

"Please, Uri, there's no need to cry. No one's blaming you. You did everything you could."

But Uri kept sobbing. She stroked his hair. She only now realized how hard he was taking the convoy fiasco. They had seven dead to mourn and twenty-two injured and had lost fifteen trucks and two armored cars. And even worse: the road to Jerusalem was still impassable.

He wasn't responsible for the Arab raid. There were simply more of the attackers, and the Haganah, seeing no other way to get supplies into Jerusalem, had knowingly taken the risk. Yet he still blamed himself.

That afternoon, Uri had taken Judith with him to the hospital to look for Yaacov Gernstein. The bullet had cleanly passed through Gernstein's thigh and he had a good chance at a full recovery. But his most important possession was now a wreck on the road to Jerusalem. Uri had put all the money he had on him on the nightstand. Gernstein wouldn't look at him, but his wife, sitting on the edge of the bed, had taken the money in silence.

"Uri, please, look at me, please," Judith said now.

He slowly raised his head. She wiped the tears from his eyes.

"No matter what happens, you have me. You hear me? And I love you."

The bed was small, the room in the little hotel on Allenby Street just a narrow rectangle. Smoke from half a pack of cigarettes hung in the room. An empty wine bottle had rolled under the bed, and two glasses stood on the night table. Uri had slept fitfully, his mouth and limbs twitching.

Judith could still feel his skin on hers, the strength of his body. To her, it was as if he'd put all his pent-up feelings into that one moment, into their wild embrace—all his disappointment, his anger at himself, his frustration, his need to somehow boost his ego after the defeat. He had been passionate, unrestrained, nearly insatiable. She herself had surrendered to the onslaught, following his rhythms, reveling in the breathless ecstasy of the moment, which left her giddy, so helpless yet strong all at once. For the first time since she'd arrived in Palestine—no, for the first time ever—she had really felt like a woman. Perhaps it was only temporary, but on this one night, she had put her past behind her.

Judith stood up, pushed back the faded curtain, and looked down onto the street. A cat crossed the empty road and disappeared behind two overturned trash cans.

She had started smoking after leaving the kibbutz, since everyone around them was doing it. Now she took a cigarette from Uri's pack and lit up, inhaling deeply. Freezing, she crawled back into bed. She stared at the ceiling for a long time. So that was it. Her first night with Uri.

It had been his unswerving strength that had lured her from the start, that had enthralled her so.

She watched him sleep. He had lost some of his magic with his defeat, and she was almost glad of it. Now she was certain she really loved him.

Her thoughts went back to that morning in the valley. She was certain she had gunned down several Arabs at Bab el-Wad. She was astonished to discover that the thought didn't bother her now. She had been attacked, she had returned fire, her attackers had fallen by the wayside. *Could a person really become dulled to it all so quickly?* she wondered. Was there such a thing as a just war—and if so, was she on the right side? Or was it really like in the Torah, an eye for an eye, a tooth for a tooth? Was everything just a matter of survival?

Judith heard a noise in the hallway, then a light knock on the door.

She heard a restrained voice, the voice of a woman. "Uri? Hello, Uri?"

Judith stood and searched her clothes for her revolver. She pulled on her khaki shirt, grabbed the gun, and tiptoed over. She turned the key and opened the door a crack. She saw a familiar face. It was Adina. Adina stared a second at the gun, then recovered.

"The Haganah sent me. Uri needs to come, right away. He's supposed to fly to Jerusalem. The plane's taking off at dawn. A car's waiting downstairs."

Judith lowered the revolver. She'd heard that the Haganah had bought a few small military planes as scrap in Europe over the past few weeks. Manning them were pilots who'd flown for the British in the Royal Air Force. At the moment, they were the only way of getting to Jerusalem.

"I'm going with him," she told Adina.

"Not possible. They only have two seats, for pilot and passenger."

Judith wanted to protest, wanted to find some way, but then she grasped that she needed to control herself. "All right, I'll wake him up."

"I'm sorry, really," Adina said. "To interrupt your night together."

She rummaged around in her pocket and pulled out an envelope. She said, somewhat bashfully, "Here, a letter. Can you give it to Uri? It's for Yitzhak."

Judith took it.

"The car's waiting," Adina urged.

Judith went back over to the bed and shook Uri by the shoulder. He opened his eyes and sat up in shock. Judith turned on the bedside lamp.

"The Haganah wants you to leave for Jerusalem. Now. By plane."

Uri jumped out of bed and began searching for his clothes. Next to the nightstand was a bowl with water.

"I'd like to come, too, but there's no room on the plane," Judith said while he washed his face.

He abruptly turned to her. "You'd like to do what?"

"Go to Jerusalem, soon as I can. Somehow."

"No, you won't," he replied as he dried his face with a towel.

"And why not?"

"Because—because I don't want you to," he said, but then he saw he'd gone too far. "Because it's not good for you. You yourself have seen how dangerous it is."

Uri buttoned up his khaki shirt. "I don't want anything to happen to you," he said. He took her in his arms and held her tight. "I simply couldn't bear it." He took his revolver, stuffed it into his belt, pulled on his jacket, and walked to the door. He turned around one last time and pulled her to him. "Maybe you're right," he said. "Maybe this all had to happen, for me to find you."

Judith lay back on the bed and realized that Uri had left his cigarettes there. She lit up a new one and thought back to those few days she'd spent in Jerusalem one year ago, her first time to the city. She wondered what her brother was doing. He would finally be leaving with the British in a few weeks after the mandate expired. She thought about

Tamar Schiff and her family. How were they doing now that no more food was getting delivered? And about Hana, whose blood was running through her own veins. Was she now Hana's enemy, just because Hana was an Arab?

Judith took a long drag of her cigarette. She wanted to know for certain. She wanted to see for herself. And she would follow Uri, no matter what.

April 1, 1948

"They're here!"

The men around the table broke into spontaneous applause. Uri saw the relief in the face of David Shaltiel, commander of the Haganah in Jerusalem.

"Finally," Shaltiel said. "Make sure that weapons reach the units as soon as possible."

Hours before, the *Nora* had arrived in the port of Tel Aviv, bearing the valuable cargo the Haganah had been yearning for. Concealed under a load of onions in the hold were four thousand, five hundred rifles, two hundred light machine guns, and five million rounds, a shipment from the Czech Republic that covert emissaries of the Jewish Agency had secured months before in Prague at a price of twelve million dollars.

Uri knew just how long Shaltiel had been waiting for this moment. Like all in the room here in the Jewish Agency headquarters, he followed along as the commander ran a finger over the map on the table before him.

"Now we're getting somewhere," he said. "Time to launch Operation Nachshon. This will enable us to break the Arabs' stranglehold on Jerusalem. The villages along the road to Jerusalem are to be taken and cleared of invaders. And one of the most important targets is this right here."

He pointed at a spot about six miles west of Jerusalem. "This is Kastel. It goes far back. The Crusaders even built a fortress there for controlling the road to the city. Kastel must be taken, no matter how. And right away."

The Haganah commanders applauded again. It caught Uri off guard, and he realized he hadn't been fully paying attention. He'd been thinking of that night, the one that now seemed such a long, long time ago. He caught himself, once again, thinking about her. About Judith.

April 3, 1948

Officially, Sherut Avir was a small private airline that was supposed to be operating shuttle flights over Palestine. The *Piper Cub*, a light, single-engine military plane, was parked at the edge of the runway at Sde Dov, north of Tel Aviv.

It was still early morning, and a stiff breeze blew in from the Mediterranean. Judith was freezing. She'd been sitting for an hour on an old wooden box next to the plane. The *Piper Cub* and its pilot were her only hope.

Joshua Weinberger finally came out to his plane. Without asking, he pulled off his old brown, fur-collared leather jacket and placed it around her shoulders. Judith smiled in thanks. She thought Weinberger looked like little more than a boy—*a big, handsome boy,* she thought, and briefly felt guilty. She considered returning his warm jacket as a way of punishing herself, but then found comfort in the thought that she needed him to get to Uri.

"How are things going up there?" she asked, looking up to the mountains. Atop them lay Jerusalem.

"Not too well, if you ask me. So little to eat, and there's shoot-outs every day. One thing's clear: it's starting any second now. The real battle begins the moment the British pull out."

He gave her a searching look. "It's none of my business, but can I ask you something? What could a young woman like you want in Jerusalem right now anyway?"

"I—" She searched for the words.

Weinberger looked at his watch. "What a load of crap. Is this guy ever gonna get here?" he muttered. He'd wanted to be in the air an hour ago, at the first morning light, so as not to attract too much attention.

The sun now bathed the airfield in a warm and increasingly brilliant light. Weinberger went around the *Piper Cub* once more, turning the small propeller, checking the flaps and rudder. He had flown Spitfires for the Royal Air Force during the war, escorting British bombers over Nazi Germany. He was a Canadian from the Machal, one of the roughly three thousand foreigners recruited by the Haganah, most of them experienced veterans of the war, Jews and non-Jews, idealists, adventurers, regular soldiers. Weinberger was now one of the pilots assigned to create something like an air force for the Haganah. He was waiting for a man from the Jewish Agency, an important official who'd been at a meeting in Tel Aviv with Ben Gurion to discuss the volatile supply situation. His two-seater plane was loaded down with rifles and ammunition that people in Jerusalem needed just as desperately as they did that important passenger who hadn't yet arrived.

The sound of an engine caught their attention. A jeep approached at high speed and came to a stop next to the *Piper Cub*. A Haganah courier climbed out.

"He's not coming. Had to go to the hospital. His appendix."

Weinberger nodded at Judith. "Well, climb on in for all I care. Off we go."

He watched her hesitantly climb up into the cockpit behind him.

"Ever flown before?"

She shook her head.

"Don't worry, they always come back down."

Joshua Weinberger took off into the wind that kept gusting in from the Mediterranean. He turned the *Piper Cub* into a sharp left curve and set a course for the east, toward the mountains of Judaea.

Judith got a queasy feeling in her stomach, but soon the plane was gliding along smoothly, the propeller before her a disc shimmering with light, the engine humming reliably, and she was able to enjoy their vast view of the mountains, their flight right into the sun. Never before in her life, apart from her early childhood in Berlin, had she felt so carefree.

They soon left the green plains behind them. The jagged hills rose, became mountains. Winding through the middle of it all was a narrow gray strip. It was hard to believe this was the same road that, a few weeks earlier, was still echoing with the screams of dead and wounded, of gunfire, of exploding hand grenades.

Judith felt a lightness of being, as if she'd emerged in some newfound reality once she'd left the earth, one that had nothing to do with her life thus far. His question entered her head: *What did she actually want in Jerusalem?* Yet the answer didn't seem important to her at that moment. Up here on this bright morning, more than three thousand feet above the soil of Palestine, all she wanted was to live.

A sudden tremor passed through the plane. The westerly wind was driving air up over the mountain valleys, and it tugged at the light craft. Judith frantically searched for a handle to grasp. She pressed her back tight against the seat, fighting the wave of nausea.

"It's nothing, just a little turbulence!" shouted Weinberger. He pressed the control stick forward, speeding up. They descended so steeply that Judith's stomach seemed to rise to her chest.

"There, there they are!" she heard him shout. She made herself look out the window. The mountaintops were now at eye level, the *Piper Cub* snaking its way through the canyon.

Rushing by below them were the burned-out wrecks of the convoy. Judith spotted a dead donkey lying next to one of the trucks.

Weinberger pulled the stick toward his gut, and the plane climbed into the sky. Soon, the road was only a narrow strip again, far below them.

Villages now became visible on both sides of the road, nestled against the mountain slopes. Above one village rose a dense plume of smoke.

"Down there!" Weinberger shouted in excitement. "Those are our troops! They're smoking out the Arabs."

The question resounded again in her head. *What did she want in Jerusalem?* Such a straightforward question and yet so complicated.

There was a very simple answer. She needed to see Uri, even if she'd never tell Weinberger that. But her reason went beyond her feelings for Uri.

The closer the *Piper Cub* got to Jerusalem, the clearer it became: there was no going back to her previous life. She had left Berlin behind. She had left Dachau behind, and that British camp on Cyprus. She had left Judith Wertheimer behind. She would, once the new Jewish state was founded, need a new name. Her Hebrew name.

On the horizon, in the east, they could make out the outline of Jerusalem. Weinberger started his descent.

"Kastel," shouted Weinberger. "High above the road there, on top of that mountain, that old fortress. Now an Arab village. We have to take it no matter what."

He pressed his foot on the rudder pedal, pulling the control stick to the right. The *Piper Cub* flew at a slant, giving Judith a direct view of Kastel. She thought she could make out flashes of gunfire. Weinberger made another steep ascent.

"Better play it safe," he said. "One wing has bullet holes from the last flight."

He looked forward, focusing. Now began the most dangerous part of the flight, the approach to the temporary airfield in Jerusalem. He

159

kept the craft high in the air, then at the last moment, after a sharp left curve, switched to nearly a nosedive and only got the plane under control right before the gravelly airstrip began. The *Piper Cub* finally touched down, jolting along.

Joshua Weinberger turned to Judith. He grinned. "Welcome, my lady. Welcome to Jerusalem. I have to head right back, but if you've ever got nothing better to do than have coffee with a pilot—you think of good old Josh."

A jeep was waiting next to the airstrip. Some Haganah men started hauling the guns off the plane and into the jeep. Judith kept to the side. Her legs were still shaking a little. She turned to a young woman trying to lift a heavy crate.

"I'm looking for Uri. Uri Rabinovich."

The woman shot her a wary look.

"He—he's a friend, a good friend," Judith added with hesitation.

"Give me a hand," the woman replied.

Together they hoisted a crate of weapons onto the jeep.

"You ever hear of a place called Kastel?" the woman asked.

Judith nodded.

"You didn't hear it from me, but your Uri? I bet he's there."

April 6, 1948

Abraham Horowitz finally wiped off the razor blade on an old hand towel. Satisfied, he looked at himself in the dim mirror standing on a crate in the glow of candlelight.

"Are you done?"

Nahum Jaffe impatiently spun his revolver by the trigger guard like a hero in some Western. He rubbed at his stubble.

"I get a kick out of how obsessed you are with your looks. Were you like that on the kibbutz too? Or did you bolt before they made you pick up a shovel?"

"I left because I was sick of talk," Horowitz said. "Because I wanted to do something for the cause, for our cause."

There was a knock on the door to the cellar that the Irgun men had made their headquarters. They were in a building near Jaffa Road, about the same elevation as Mea Shearim, the Orthodox quarter. Horowitz approached the door, revolver in his hand. He carefully looked out the cracked door, then threw it open.

"Come in," he said.

"Supplies," explained Shaul Avriel. "Straight from His Majesty's weapons depot." He pushed an ammo crate into the room with his foot. "Got this yesterday, from British stocks. Unfortunately cost two dead Englishmen."

Avriel shut the door behind him. He passed around a pack of cigarettes.

"Dunhill, the finest. Also from British stocks. We're going to miss them, the Brits. All their lovely depots," he quipped, "filled with all your heart's desires: weapons, ammo, cigarettes, whiskey even."

"Two dead Brits?" Horowitz said. "A small fucking price to pay considering how many of our dead they have on their conscience."

"You remember Josef, the Pole? And Moshe Mirkowitz? And Shmuel, the Iraqi? Two months ago. All our people, all hanged, in that goddamn prison of theirs in Acre."

Horowitz caressed the ammo case. "Good, then let's get to the point. I think it's time we attempt something big. We have to set an example, show that the Irgun can take the lead. Show the Haganah too. The Brits will be gone soon. Now, it's all about showing who's the man of the house. Jerusalem belongs to the Jews, period. So, there can be no more discussing it, not with any of those weaklings proposing internationalization. And Judaea and Samaria belong to us, too, all the ancient Jewish lands. We fought the British long enough that they finally left. Too many of us have died to give up now. It's time to deal with the Arabs in a way that they can comprehend once and for all."

He grabbed a map and spread it out on the floor.

"You know Deir Yassin, on the western edge of Jerusalem. That's our goal." Avriel rubbed at his nose, took a drag on his cigarette, then cleared his throat. "Deir Yassin is known as especially peaceful," he said. "That could make trouble with the Jewish Agency and Ben Gurion's people, not to mention the international community, and with the Brits, of course."

Horowitz flushed red. "Since when do we care what those idiots think? To hell with Ben Gurion, to hell with his crew in Jerusalem, to hell with the Haganah! The Irgun doesn't care what works for the Brits or any of those scaredy-cat peacenik Jews. Those fine gentlemen in Tel Aviv, with their constant griping about us—where would they be now if we hadn't been so ruthless in taking the fight to the Brits? They brand us as terrorists, but the truth is, we were the ones who brought the Brits to their knees. We'll strike hard just like we always have."

Horowitz glanced around, daring them.

"I say Deir Yassin is a fine target," he continued. "We increase the element of surprise even greater by attacking just this kind of village. We don't want the Arabs to reach the gates of Jerusalem. We can't afford sentimentality. Any questions?"

The others kept silent.

"Deir Yassin needs to go. And we are going to make sure that it does."

April 7, 1948

Youssef, his eyes gleaming, held the new rifle that Abdul Qader al-Husseini had thrust into his hands. He didn't know that it was one of only a few that Qader al-Husseini had brought back with him from Damascus.

The day before, Qader al-Husseini had been in Syria to try to win support in his battle for Jerusalem. But to no avail. The military committee leading the ALA, the Arab Liberation Army, had fobbed him off with only a few weapons, which he carried in the trunk of his car.

"You're all traitors to the Arab cause," he screamed in their direction as he left Damascus, "and history will show that you were the ones who lost Palestine!"

It had finally become clear to Qader al-Husseini that the idea of Arabs uniting in the struggle for Palestine was a myth, that everyone only thought of their own interests. The ALA didn't want to cede the field to the Jihad Muqaddas. It feared that the Jerusalem muftis from the Husseini clan would end up wielding too much influence.

This was why Abdul Qader al-Husseini himself was conducting the attack on Kastel, which the Jews had recently taken. He could rely on the fighters from the villages. The Husseinis were the most powerful clan in and around Jerusalem, and the men showed him true loyalty.

Youssef Hamoud didn't know any of that. All he heard was his leader shouting: "Defeat the Jews! Drive them from their homeland! *Allahu Akbar!*"

And Youssef, ecstatic, cheered him on.

Uri sat cowering on the floor, pressing his head between his knees. A bullet passing through the shot-out window slammed into the opposite wall, bounced off, ricocheted across the room, and banged against the floor a few inches from him. Uri was too exhausted to react. He didn't even feel hunger anymore; all he had was thirst.

The battles for Kastel had been going on for days, house by house, hill by hill. The Haganah hadn't given up yet, but the Arabs were constantly bringing in hundreds more irregular troops and sending them into battle. They kept up their attacks, even tonight, even fiercer than before.

A Haganah man came crawling into the room on his stomach. It was Mordechai, an old friend of Uri's. A second man Uri didn't know followed him in. He rose up and released a burst from his Sten gun into the darkness.

"I think I got one," he said.

Mordechai patted him on the shoulder.

Uri got a nudge to his ribs. It jolted him from his fatigue.

"Cover me," Mordechai told him. Uri took position with his machine gun and fired into the dark night. Mordechai ran over to the dead Arab in a crouch, quickly frisked his pockets, and found his papers. Then he ran back.

April 8, 1948

"We drove them out. We drove the Jews from Kastel." Youssef's eyes glistened. He cleaned his weapon with satisfaction, standing it between his feet. Then he took a drink of sweet mint tea.

"God, praise be to his name, all thanks to God, and of course to Abdul Qader al-Husseini. Where would we be without him?"

Youssef was sitting with a group of Arab irregulars at a campfire on the edge of Kastel. Flames illuminated his face. That morning, the number of Arab attackers had risen to over a thousand. The Haganah couldn't withstand their incessant hail of bullets.

"Did you see how they took off? How they retreated down the mountain? They're all gone!"

A boy came running up, out of breath, his face pale despite his exertion. "Hurry, come on, come up the hill."

Youssef jumped up and followed, together with the others. They soon found a group of men, most in the traditional long robes, weapons in their hands. They stood with their shoulders drooping, staring at the ground. Youssef squeezed in between them. Then he saw. Before them lay Abdul Qader al-Husseini. Above his crossed ammo belts was a large stain of blood.

"He's dead. The Jews shot him," whispered a man. "He is a martyr."

April 9, 1948

Sergeant Jonathan Higgins had opened the window to his office.

"Listen to that, sir," he said. "What fireworks!"

The cracks of gunfire from the eastern part of Jerusalem carried all the way to Bevingrad, the British headquarters east of Jaffa Road enclosed by dense barbed wire. Josef stood and went over to the window. He clasped his hands behind his back and closed his eyes. *Just like during the war,* he thought. For the Muslims, Friday was actually their holy day, their day of pious prayer, but in this city of three religions, today was not to be one of contemplation.

The Damascus Gate, the northern portal in the medieval wall to the city, couldn't take in all the masses. A knot of people had been forming there for hours, seeking entry, turning down the narrow lanes, pushing and shoving, their state of hysteria mounting the closer they got to the Temple Mount. At its peak—and on this one point, at least, the Jews and Muslims could agree—Abraham had nearly sacrificed his son, only to be prevented from doing so at the last moment by God. Now, the crowd kept firing off their shotguns, shooting into the sky, venting their emotions.

Thirty thousand mourners elbowed their way through, all wanting to get close to the spot where Abdul Qader al-Husseini would be buried in the Dome of the Rock, where according to Muslim belief, the Prophet Mohammed had risen to heaven on his mare.

Youssef was out among them, trying to touch the coffin as it was passed hand by hand over the heads of mourners. Vengeance filled him. Abdul Qader al-Husseini could not be allowed to die in vain.

The phone rang in Sergeant Higgins's office. He picked up and listened attentively a moment. Then he shouted to Lieutenant Goldsmith: "Interesting report from our Arab informant. Imagine this: the Arabs have all gone to the burial, even the fighters from Kastel. The Haganah got word of it—so they've just retaken Kastel, with no resistance. I think you Jews call that *chutzpah*."

Higgins arranged the latest reports on the desk before Josef. "The latest statistics, sir, for the general. Just take a look. It's a disgrace that so many of our boys had to kick the bucket for this. What for? That's what I'd like to know."

Josef paged through the report. Between December 1 and April 3, 6,187 people were killed or injured in combat, including 430 British soldiers.

He also knew another number. Hundreds of British had deserted, most of them now serving with the Arabs. But not all.

The phone rang again. Higgins picked up. "For you, sir."

Josef listened with an indifferent air to the excited voice on the line, and then he turned to Sergeant Higgins. "Where is the general? I need to speak to him, on orders of the High Commissioner. There's been an attack on the Arab village of Deir Yassin, a horrible affair, evidently. He wants our troops to intervene."

Higgins pointed at the large door. "He's in his office, came in a half hour ago."

Josef rushed out. Five minutes later, he was back. Outrage was etched on his face.

"General McMillan doesn't have the least intention of following the High Commissioner's orders. He doesn't wish to endanger British soldiers in any way, not this close to withdrawal."

"I can't say I blame him, sir."

Hana held David's hand tight as they walked down King George V Avenue. Her eyes were bloodshot and were lined with dark rings. News of the Irgun's attack on Deir Yassin had spread like wildfire through the city, electrifying residents of the Jewish and Arab neighborhoods alike. Rumors made the rounds, unconfirmed accounts, casualty figures, and although people in Jerusalem didn't know the exact details, one thing did seem clear: something horrible must have happened to the village of Deir Yassin and its seven hundred souls.

Hana pressed up against David.

"Listen, we—I," he stuttered helplessly and placed an arm around her. "I'll try to find out exactly what's happened, as fast as I can."

The trucks came down the street from the west. On their open beds stood people with their hands raised, guarded by Irgun, their machine guns trained. On the first truck, Hana spotted a child she knew—Ali, ten years old, her neighbors' boy. Ali's face was frozen, his trembling arms raised in the spring air.

A woman turned their way. Hana gasped. It was Miriam, her cousin. "Miriam, over here! It's me!" Hana shouted.

Miriam's long robe was torn and smeared with blood. She tried to move, to lower her arms, to stretch them out to Hana. But one of the guards gave her a brutal blow to the ribs with the butt of his machine gun.

Hana dug her nails into David's arm. She recognized faces on the second truck as well—old neighbors. Then the third truck rolled by.

Hana's breath caught in her throat. She saw an old man leaning on the truck's cab. He was having trouble standing upright.

"Father!" she shouted. "Father! Father!"

She broke free from David's arm and ran toward the truck. David hesitated a moment, then bounded after Hana and held her back when he saw an Irgun man aim his machine gun at her.

Judith would've loved to sit in some café and enjoy the warm sun spreading over her bare skin so soothingly. But she was in a hurry. She needed to get to a Haganah meeting in the Jewish Agency headquarters. She was about to cross the broad avenue when she saw the column coming, three trucks moving slowly down the road.

She stopped to let them pass. A small group of onlookers had gathered along the street, and Judith could hear them murmuring. They kept whispering a name: Deir Yassin. On the trucks, she saw the men and women with machine guns, saw their prisoners.

As the third truck rolled by her, she heard the screaming. It was coming from the other side of the street. A young woman, apparently an Arab, was trying to run up to the truck and a man was preventing her from doing so. Her screams pierced Judith's heart.

Judith frowned. She thought she'd seen that face before. Then suddenly she knew. Hana, Hana Khalidy, the nurse from Hadassah Hospital. And Dr. Cohen.

She watched Hana, crying, cling to the doctor as the trucks disappeared down the street. Judith crossed the street and touched Hana's shoulder.

"It's me, Judith."

Hana didn't respond.

"Hana, please, listen, it's me, Judith. Don't you remember?"

Hana slowly let go and turned to Judith. Her eyes told Judith that she recognized her, but she remained silent.

"It's her father," Dr. Cohen explained. "He's on one of the trucks from Deir Yassin. She's terrified for her mother and the rest of her family."

Judith put her arms around Hana and whispered in her ear: "Don't worry, please. I'm with the Haganah, and I'm going to take care of this."

The upper main facade of the U-shaped Jewish Agency building was still in ruins. Three weeks before, a car carrying the American consul general had pulled into the courtyard. The consul general wasn't inside the car—only his driver was, an Arab. When the bomb went off, thirteen people lost their lives.

Judith ran up the stairs to the offices where David Shaltiel had set up his headquarters. She flung the door open. Shaltiel was holding a two-way radio receiver to his ear and gestured for her to take a seat. The top Haganah commanders had assembled here. She bit her lip and sat next to Uri.

After a while, Shaltiel placed the receiver back on the radio set.

"Our man is reporting that the Irgun and Lehi have inflicted a horrific massacre in Deir Yassin," he said in a low voice. "And apparently it's still going on."

Judith couldn't hold back any longer. "So? What are we doing about it? Have any of you taken a look out the window? They're proudly parading their prisoners by out there. Unbelievable. It only provokes people."

Shaltiel looked at the faces in the room. "Uri, take a few men. Go there and stop this madness. By force of arms, if you need to."

Uri stood to go.

Judith followed him into the hallway. "Uri, there's a man I need to help, Mohammed Khalidy. He's the father of Hana, the nurse I told you about." She held out her wrists. "Look at these veins. Her blood flows through them. Without her, I would not be here today."

Uri stood on the square outside the house belonging to the mukhtar of Deir Yassin. Sporadic gunshots could still be heard from inside some buildings. He kept taking deep breaths, in and out, in and out. He dug around in his pockets for a pack of cigarettes but couldn't find any. At that moment, Abraham Horowitz exited one of the houses across from the mukhtar's with a pistol in his hand. Uri instinctively chambered a round.

"Halt, stay where you are!" he shouted at Horowitz and trained his machine gun on him. He held out his left hand. "Hand over the pistol."

Horowitz stood still, hesitating. "What's wrong with you, Haganah?" he shouted. "You completely insane?"

"Us? If anyone's insane, it's you—you and your people. You're murderers, nothing more than brutal murderers."

Horowitz spat at him. "What do you know about it? They fired on us when we entered the village. Four of us are dead, dead as doornails. What, we're just supposed to let that go unpunished?"

Uri was tempted to knock his face in.

"You're telling me that justifies what I've see here? Women, children, old men—slaughtered like pigs! These houses are full of their corpses. There must be fifty, a hundred, two hundred!"

"What's any of this got to do with you anyway?" Horowitz said. "This operation is run by the Irgun and the Lehi. This is our concern and ours alone. And don't go acting as if all you in the Haganah have a monopoly on morality, Uri, just don't. What, no one ever died in any of your operations?"

He spat toward Uri again. "You make me want to puke. Get the hell out of here."

Uri pointed his Sten right at Horowitz's stomach. "Give me your weapon. And tell the others to hand theirs over as well. That's a direct order from David Shaltiel."

"That so?" Horowitz sneered. "The noble Mr. Shaltiel. You want to know what he told us? We were to take this village and hold it at all costs. He wants to build a landing strip nearby, see, which can only work with us in control of Deir Yassin."

Blood rushed to Uri's face. "So did he also tell you to slaughter everyone? Taking a village is one thing. Turning it into a massacre is quite another. Give me your pistol, now!"

Horowitz curled his finger around the trigger of his gun. "Why don't you come over here and get it?" he said, grinning.

They squared off.

"Shoot already, you coward," Horowitz sneered. "Show the world how the Jews kill each other. The Arabs would love it, and the Brits will slap their thighs with laughter. Go on, do it already."

Uri lowered his Sten. He couldn't bring himself to do it. He had felt such rage, such violent rage, but now he only felt emptiness.

"I need one of the prisoners," he said in a low voice. "An elderly man, Mohammed Khalidy."

"Suit yourself, sir." Horowitz stuffed his pistol in his belt. "We'll send him over. As for the rest, leave me in peace."

That was the last Uri ever saw of Abraham Horowitz. The Irgun man was soon reported missing in the battle for Jaffa.

Youssef smashed the radio against the wall. The Jews' radio station, which was also broadcasting in Arabic, had just announced that they'd taken Deir Yassin. First the death of Abdul Qader al-Husseini—and now this, only a few hours after the great man's burial. God had decided to test them.

For a moment, he'd forgotten that his cousin Ahmed was sitting before him. He opened the window, which looked out over one of the narrowest old lanes in Jerusalem, and fired his gun into the air. He kept emptying rounds, again and again, until his ammo was spent.

Ahmed cowered on the small bed and cried. His left eye twitched uncontrollably. Ahmed had made his way to Jerusalem. He was one of the few villagers to escape the massacre. He held the Koran in his hands.

"Here, from your parents' home," he said, and handed Youssef the book. "They are dead. Your oldest sister too." He sobbed. "Just like— my mother."

Youssef took the Koran and pressed it to his chest.

He had sworn to the Almighty that he'd take vengeance, and on his life and the honor of his mother, he would keep his word.

"Where are the others?" he asked Ahmed.

"Gone, long gone. They headed for the Jordan River, to cross over into Transjordan."

Hatred shot through Youssef like a bolt of lightning. By taking Deir Yassin, the Jews had achieved their goal: panicked Arabs were leaving their villages by the thousands.

The jeep stopped in front of a building in Sheikh Jarrah. Mohammed Khalidy hadn't spoken a word the whole trip over and now remained slumped in the back seat.

Judith glanced at Uri, who had his hands clamped around the wheel, and climbed out. She looked for the doorbell with the name Khalidy, pressed it. A window opened above her, and she saw Hana's face. A few moments later, Hana came running out of the building, crying, and threw her arms around her father.

Eventually Mohammed Khalidy rose from the jeep's bench seat with difficulty and clambered onto the sidewalk. Hana propped him up. She led him to the front door of the building, but then halted before the entrance.

"What about Mother?" she asked.

Her father teetered, as if about to collapse. Judith, who'd escorted them to the door, grabbed him below the arms until he'd steadied himself again.

He didn't respond. He just stared into space.

Hana, at a loss, looked to Uri. Uri could have told her. He had seen her mother. But he couldn't bring himself to tell Hana how her corpse had looked.

He shook his head helplessly.

David Cohen appeared at the door and opened it wide, to let Hana and her father in. When Judith started following them, David stood between her and the door, his face like stone. He eyed her up and down, her khaki uniform, the pistol on her belt.

"I think it's best that you go now," he said in a toneless voice.

"But, I—" she began. *I'm not one of them at all,* she wanted to say. *I didn't do it, not me, not me of all people.* But the words got stuck in her throat.

David stepped back and shut the door.

Hana's blood flows in my veins, Judith thought. But was it the blood of her enemy?

She slowly went back and climbed into the jeep next to Uri.

"Drive away. Goddamn it, just drive away already."

April 13, 1948

David woke her with a whisper. "I have to go."

Hana sat up in bed. "No, stay with me. You can't go, please stay."

"Don't be afraid. We're well guarded."

"No! It's too dangerous! Those gangs have been roaming the streets for days. You know they want to cut off Mount Scopus from Jewish Jerusalem once and for all."

"Which is exactly why I need to go," he replied. "We can't let them force the hospital to close. We do have a responsibility to our patients."

He reached into his jacket pocket and placed an envelope on the nightstand. It had American stamps. She gave him a quizzical look.

"A letter from my parents in New York. They told me they'll come over whenever we want them to—for our wedding."

Hana's eyes suddenly widened. "For our wedding?"

He hugged her. "Please forgive me—I know it is somewhat unorthodox, telling you this way, but these times we're living in, they're more than unorthodox, and I wanted to make sure my parents were going to be here before I surprised you with it. Yes, Hana, I would like us to get married. Finally."

He kept hugging her tight. "Please, Hana, please say yes. I know, these are terrible times, for you, for all of us. But I love you, and there's only one thing I want: for us to be together, as man and wife."

He carefully caressed her belly. It had started growing rounder. "And, of course, I'd like for our child to have a whole family."

She started to cry. "David, I—I don't know what to say."

"Just say yes, please, Hana. Just say yes."

She flung her arms around his neck. "Yes, David, yes."

They sat together like this for a long moment, holding each other tight. Then he gingerly tried freeing himself from her embrace. But she wouldn't let go of him.

"David, don't go. Stay with me." She gave him a pleading look.

"I have to. I can't let the others down."

"Then I'm coming," she said firmly. "I do work there after all."

"Please, be reasonable. That's not possible anymore. Not in your condition, and on top of that—" He fell silent. On top of that, it was exceedingly dangerous for an Arab to still be working in the Jewish hospital. "You have to keep an eye on your father," he said instead. "He needs you."

He stood up, kissed her, and took his jacket off the back of a chair. Quietly, so as not to wake her father sleeping on the sofa in the next room, he left her apartment.

"Over there, those are the British." Youssef could clearly make them out, on the other side of the road, where the Antonius House stood. Several soldiers from the Highland Light Infantry were sitting in the sun atop an armored car.

"They don't look very interested in what happens around here," said the Iraqi lying next to him on a wall, his rifle ready. "Did you hide the mine real good?"

Youssef nodded. He lay between Ahmed and the Iraqi. Ahmed looked pale, his left eye still twitching. But Youssef had insisted that he come along.

"Think of your mother," he'd said. "Today is the day of revenge."

The narrow street between the Antonius House and the Nashashibi Bend was surrounded by stone walls. It rose steeply for several hundred yards. Beyond the bend, the road led up to Hadassah Hospital. *Good,* Youssef thought. *Very good. They can't escape us here.*

He turned onto his back and looked up into the blue sky over Judaea. The sun reflected off the golden cupola of the Dome of the Rock. It promised to be a warm spring day.

The buses were already waiting with engines running at the rendezvous point on Hasolel Street. David looked at his watch. It was a few minutes before nine. He'd just made it.

Hadassah Hospital urgently needed supplies if it was going to keep providing medical care. Haganah guards had been escorting the supply trucks for weeks now. Because of its strategic location in East Jerusalem, the hospital had to be held no matter what happened.

"It's nice to see you keeping the faith, David."

He felt a hand on his shoulder. It was Dr. Haim Yassky, the head of Hadassah.

"We have to rely on every single person," Yassky said. "The population of Jerusalem needs a functioning hospital. But I'm not certain whether we'll be able to keep functioning up there on the hill—cut off from the rest of the city, in the middle of an Arab area. I'm afraid we'll have to start looking for an alternative."

Yassky looked depressed. Hadassah was his life, and now the future of the hospital was in danger.

He patted David on the shoulder again. "We have to hang on, David. We simply have to."

Yassky took his wife, Fanny, by the hand and climbed into an armored ambulance with a large Star of David on the side. David followed them, but then got on one of the buses.

"We should go," Yassky said in a weary voice to the Haganah man at the wheel.

The convoy started rolling east: two buses with patients, doctors, and nurses; three trucks; two ambulances; and two Haganah escort vehicles.

"Keep still, real still." Youssef was trying to keep his cousin from jumping off the wall. Ahmed's whole body was now trembling, beads of sweat covering his forehead.

"Don't be afraid. Take a look around. Our fighters are everywhere here. And we're prepared, not like in Deir Yassin. This time we will attack, and we will prevail. You can count on it."

Yet he, too, felt the tension rising inside him. They had carefully selected the target. They would deal the Jews a massive blow, along with all those who believed in understanding between Jews and Arabs. There was no better target than the staff of Hadassah Hospital.

Dreamers and fantasists, all of them, he thought. How much more proof did they need to understand it? What more had to happen for it to be clear to everyone that Jews and Arabs could never, ever coexist equally. Not in Palestine. Not in Jerusalem.

He gritted his teeth in anger. Hana. She counted among them, among those lunatics. He wondered what she was doing now. He'd heard that she'd shown up in the Arab section of Jerusalem somewhere. He would find her, as soon as this operation was complete.

Thinking of Hana sent blood rushing to his head. She had allied herself with the Jews. She had gone over to their side. She'd betrayed the Arabs—and she'd trampled all over their engagement. He would get even with her. It was God's will.

He looked down the street. A few hundred yards away, he saw an armored Ford driving up the steep road, behind it a convoy of trucks and buses.

Youssef nudged Ahmed. "There they are," he whispered. "Jews. Think of your mother."

David was sitting on the bus next to Sally, a nurse. She kept glancing out the window warily. He smiled at her.

"It'll be all right," he assured her. But he was anything but certain himself. The convoys had been drawing fire all too often.

They had just passed through the last Haganah checkpoint, at the Tipat Halav family clinic. He closed his eyes and tried to imagine them soon becoming a family. Hana, he, and the child. Their child.

It was the only thing that felt certain in a city where almost nothing did anymore. What would happen when the British left? The Arabs, it was clear, would simply not allow the Jews to establish their own state like the United Nations had envisaged it in its partition plan. And the Jews, they would do anything to ensure their new state. A state surrounded by hostile Arab nations.

That could only mean one thing: war. Even more war, even more violence.

And what would that mean for his little family? A Jewish-Arab marriage, at now of all times? Didn't he have a responsibility to them now? Sure, he had decided that he wanted to live in the Jews' new state. But that was before. Now, with a child coming, wouldn't it be better to take his family to safety, to America?

He opened his eyes. They were just then driving by Sheikh Jarrah. He could make out Hana's apartment building. He tried chasing away his bleak thoughts. *No*, he thought, *Yassky was right—we have to hang on, somehow. The most important thing at the moment is keeping the hospital open. It has to be a model for the future*, he told himself—*a hospital for all, for Jews and for Arabs.* His job was here, with his patients.

He watched the truck in front of them travel up the hill along the narrow road. In a few minutes they would reach Mount Scopus. Nurse

Sally was still staring out the window. Silence reigned inside the bus. The heavy vehicle crept along in first gear. David glanced at his watch. It was 9:45 a.m.

The mine exploded, blowing a crater in the road about a yard deep. One front wheel of the Ford carrying the Haganah team drove into it. And then the shooting started.

"Bloody hell! Do they take us for the fire brigade? Every time there's fireworks somewhere, we're the ones who have to sort it out!"

Sergeant Higgins had gone red in the face. His phone had been ringing for hours.

"I'll pass the message to him, sir . . . yes, sir. No, the general hasn't issued any orders. I know that the situation is serious," he said into the receiver one more time.

Higgins sprang up as Lieutenant Goldsmith entered the commanding general's outer office.

"Good of you to come. All hell's broken loose. People from the Jewish Agency calling every few minutes. They want us to intervene. And our boys at the Antonius House are constantly on the wireless, wanting to know what they're to do. The Arabs are firing on that Jewish convoy heading to Hadassah with all they have. There's more and more of them, coming in from everywhere. The general does not wish to intervene. He feels that everything will calm down again soon."

Josef stared at him in disbelief. "He *does not wish* to intervene? That means we simply watch while those people out there are massacred?"

"Looks that way, sir."

"I have to speak with him."

Josef straightened up, smoothed out his uniform, and knocked on the door to the general's office. He didn't wait for the reply, just stormed in. McMillan looked up from his files.

"Didn't the sergeant tell you I don't wish to be disturbed, Goldsmith? You do understand I have a withdrawal to coordinate?" He gave Josef an impatient stare. "Anything else, Goldsmith?"

"With all due respect, General, sir, you cannot be serious. There's a massacre taking place, literally before our eyes, and we're just letting it happen. As the mandate power, we have a responsibility to maintain order, which means for as long as we are still here."

McMillan looked at his files again. "You know something, Goldsmith? They fired at me this morning. The Jews could think of nothing better than to open fire on me as my car happened to pass by that convoy. They're shooting at us, Goldsmith. Go outside and take a look at my car. Bodywork full of bullet holes, with best regards from the Haganah. Now, if you'll excuse me? As I say, I have much to do."

Hana couldn't stand it anymore. She paced the apartment, back and forth. She was certain David was out there, in the middle of all that violence. David, the father of her child. She needed to do something, anything. She pulled her shoes on and went down to the door.

In her way stood Mohammed Khalidy. Her father wore a fez, his feet in street shoes. For the first time since the massacre at Deir Yassin, he had shaved and put on a suit. It hung off him, since he'd been refusing to eat.

"Stay here, don't get involved," he said and spread out his arms, blocking the door.

"They've been shooting for hours. David is in that convoy. Please, Father. What if he's in danger? I have to find him, you know I do!"

"Be reasonable," her father said, trying to sound strict. "I cannot allow it. You're staying here."

"Reasonable? What does that even mean? You still think there's anything like reason left? All I ever see now are dead, wounded, violence everywhere you look. What has it done for you, your reason? There's no one left who wants a reasonable solution, no one."

She gave him a defiant look.

He lowered his head. "Think of your mother, think of all the others. I don't want to lose you as well," he said softly. "Let's go away from here. They might have taken all we had in Deir Yassin, but I still have money in the bank in Amman. Let's go away, before it's too late."

"But I can't go, I can't! I belong with David, you know that."

She kissed him on the cheek and simultaneously pushed him gently to the side, away from the door.

"Forgive me, Father, but I can't abandon him."

The Haganah was only able to send a single armored car to help. It raced by the buses. The driver sped up and tried clearing the crater the mine had left in the road. He failed. The car got stuck next to the Ford.

Youssef clapped his hands. *"Ya Allah, ya Allah!"* he shouted.

This time, God was on their side.

"Ya Allah!" the others shouted too. *"Ya Allah!"*

Youssef clapped again, then he raised his rifle high in the air. *"Minshan Deir Yassin*, for Deir Yassin!" he shouted.

"Minshan Deir Yassin, minshan Deir Yassin!" came the cry from their many throats.

"To the buses! Burn the buses!" Youssef shouted.

They picked up his battle cry. "Burn the buses!" And again: *"Minshan Deir Yassin!"*

From his observation post inside the Antonius House on the other side of the street, a sergeant in the Highland Light Infantry grabbed the microphone of his radio set.

"The situation here is getting rather out of control. Request instructions."

A crackling voice replied: "Continue observing, over."

Hana ran, stumbled, fell down, lay there a moment, exhausted, then pulled herself up, running onward, toward the gunfire.

As she reached the Nashashibi Bend, she saw the buses riddled with bullets. A group of men came running down the steep road, screaming, at their head a man who seemed familiar. He held a bottle with a burning rag sticking out of its neck.

Hana intercepted him right before the first bus. He raised the bottle to throw it. Hana tried to pull down his arm.

"No, don't!" she screamed frantically. "Youssef, don't do it!"

Youssef struck her in the face with his free hand and pushed her to the ground. Then he threw the Molotov cocktail with all his might.

"Minshan Deir Yassin!" he howled.

The bottle exploded against the side of the bus. The others now threw their bottle bombs too. Both buses were in flames within moments.

Youssef turned to Hana, who lay on the ground, and kicked her. His eyes gleamed. Then he pulled out his curved dagger and stabbed her in the chest.

"For Deir Yassin!"

The Highland Light Infantry radioman inside the Antonius House grabbed his mic again.

"Headquarters, the buses are on fire. Someone needs to be raising the white flag. Request permission to intervene."

The crackling voice on the receiver remained cool. "Reinforcements are on the way. Everyone maintain position."

The sergeant looked to his officer, a major. The major lit himself a cigarette.

"Headquarters is taking their time," the sergeant said. "Meanwhile, they're burning them alive up there."

Thick smoke rose over the buses. The attackers ran around what remained, howling for joy. The major took a drag of his cigarette and slowly smoked it to the end, watching the buses completely burn themselves out. It was four o'clock in the afternoon.

"Very well," he said finally. "Fire at will. Let's stop those Arabs, put an end to this here and now."

Judith climbed out of the jeep. She caught her breath. Before her stood the burned-out ruins of the convoy: two buses, an ambulance, and farther up, near the Antonius House, the two destroyed Haganah cars.

"Look at this," she said to Uri. "It's complete madness."

The Arabs had disappeared, driven off by British fire. Fifteen of the attackers lost their lives along the way.

A few yards from the first bus lay a woman in a pool of blood. Judith leaned down to her.

"Oh my God, Uri!" she screamed as she fell to her knees. "It's Hana!"

"Horrible," said Uri, who'd also knelt next to her. "We should bury her with the others."

Judith took Hana's hand. It was still warm. She quickly felt for a pulse. It was faint but detectable. "She's alive, Uri, she's alive!" she shouted and looked around. "Where's the jeep? Go get it, Uri, quick!"

Uri drove the jeep up to where Hana lay. Together they carefully lifted her unconscious body onto the rear bench seat.

Uri started the engine.

"Where do you think we should take her?"

"Hadassah Hospital, it's the closest. The road is clear now."

The jeep wound its way past the convoy wreckage, up Mount Scopus.

A British sergeant, his Bren machine gun at the ready, stood alongside the street next to the major. He saw the general's car coming.

"He's back," he told the major.

General McMillan stepped out. He was appearing at the scene of the massacre for the second time today. The major stood to attention. McMillan looked around.

"Bloody mess here, Major," he said. "Were there any survivors?"

"Only one from the buses, sir. Almost all the others were burned to death."

"How many dead?"

"We don't know exactly yet, sir. Around eighty, I'd gather. Among them were Dr. Yassky and many of his doctors, unfortunately."

The general turned away. "See to it that this is all cleared away. Our withdrawal route will be through Sheikh Jarrah here on the way to Haifa. I want no further problems. Do you understand?"

The major saluted. "Yes, sir, we'll do our best."

Uri raced the jeep up the hill. Then he turned left and drove onto the grounds of Hadassah Hospital. Right past the traffic circle, left past the main entrance, then to the emergency department.

"A stretcher, bring a stretcher," he shouted at an orderly.

Judith held Hana's hand. Hana hadn't moved, not even when the orderlies lifted her onto the stretcher and carried her inside. A young man with a stethoscope around his neck came up to them. The name badge on his doctor's coat read: "Moshe Reubenstein."

"What's happened to the convoy?" he asked. "And to my colleagues?" His uneasy gaze shifted back and forth between Judith and Uri. "A nurse was with them, her name is Sally. Have you heard anything about her? We—she's a good friend."

Uri shook his head. "I'm sorry, I'm afraid that most are—" He searched for the right words, then decided just to tell the truth. "I'm afraid that most of them are dead."

The young doctor leaned his head against the wall and closed his eyes. Judith saw the tears run down his face. She placed a hand on his arm.

"It's horrible, I know." She cleared her throat. "But we have an emergency here, and I'm afraid it cannot wait."

Reubenstein started. Embarrassed, he wiped the tears from his face. He leaned over Hana. "This looks bad, likely a stab wound. I'll have to see if it's struck the lungs," he said after a quick examination. "I think the most serious issue right now is her heavy blood loss."

A nurse, her own coat smeared with blood, came running up. "I need more bandages!" she shouted. "Quick, more bandages!"

Reubenstein waved her over. "Nurse Sarah, help me out here, please. This is urgent. First thing to do is remove the dress."

The nurse reached for scissors and cut open the long Arab garment Hana wore. She halted a moment. "Doctor, look, the patient is pregnant. Fifth month, I'd say."

Then she took another look, into the patient's face. She raised a hand to her mouth in horror. "My God, it's Hana, Nurse Hana."

Reubenstein stared at her, not comprehending. He'd just arrived from London a few weeks ago.

"She's one of our Arab staff," Sarah explained. "She's been staying home for a while now because it's become too dangerous for her here." She paused. "She's carrying Dr. Cohen's child."

"Cohen? David Cohen?" Reubenstein asked.

Sarah nodded.

"Where is he? We should inform him at once."

Sarah turned ashen. "He was supposed to arrive with the others, with the convoy."

Reubenstein, about to listen to Hana's lungs, lowered his stethoscope. Then he pulled himself together.

"We need blood, at once," he said in a sober voice. "But first the blood type."

Nurse Sarah went over to the cabinet where the blood bags were stored. She opened it. It was nearly empty.

"The convoy was supposed to bring new ones, medicine, bandages. We have almost nothing left," she said, then paused. "Wait a second. I remember Hana saying—Hana was blood type AB. We have none of that left at all."

Judith had been standing next to the stretcher the whole time, but her thoughts were far, far away. She was surprised by it herself, but all she could think of was her flight to Jerusalem. Of that feeling of freedom, of that distance that she'd suddenly felt from all the troubles below her on the earth, of that lightness. The words "blood type AB" promptly brought her back to reality. She turned to Nurse Sarah.

"Do you remember me from a year ago?"

The nurse squinted doubtfully.

"It's me, Judith Wertheimer. I'm AB," Judith said, and started to roll up the left sleeve of her shirt.

April 24, 1948

"No, it's not possible." Judith stroked Shimon Schiff's hair. "You can't go out in the street right now, you just can't."

Shimon wouldn't give up. "But I'll be careful, I will. I only want to see my friend again, Menachem, you know. And besides, you yourself came to see us from all the way across the city," he crowed. "And no one did anything to you, did they?"

For a moment, Judith didn't know how to respond to that argument. The truth was, she had come to visit the Schiffs because she was worried, especially about the children. The shelling had been going on for two weeks. The Arab Liberation Army had positioned artillery on the mountains north of the city and started firing on Jewish Jerusalem.

The people had gotten used to making their way along building walls as closely as possible so as to avoid the shrapnel. Judith repeatedly had to take cover herself on the way to Ben Yehuda Street.

Tamar came out of the kitchen. She was holding a pot with powdered milk in it.

"Ugh, the water pipes don't have any pressure. Either the Arabs have detonated the pipes up in the mountains again or the company doesn't have oil for the pumps. Hopefully the water comes back soon," she told Judith. "Just imagine, now they're giving courses on cooking without electricity or kerosene, and on how to build wood stoves for cooking outside. How can we go on like this?"

She withdrew back into the kitchen.

Her husband, Yossi, who had kept silent so far, turned to his son. "Listen, Shimon. This afternoon, the truck with the big water tank is coming, you know the one. I'll be heading down with the can to get us some. And you get to come along, down to the front door, to help me carry it upstairs. But don't spill any, promise?"

Shimon beamed. "Yes, Abba, promise. Does that mean I have to start brushing my teeth again?"

"Yes, you'll get to brush your teeth again." Yossi tried a smile.

Judith wasn't quite sure what to say. She knew from experience how tough it was for children to be cooped up all day.

"You know what?" she said to Shimon. "Once the shooting stops, we'll go to the soccer field together and I'll see how well you really play."

Shimon ran into his room and grabbed his ball. "Fine, as soon as the Arabs are gone." He beamed again. "Then it's showtime."

They heard a knock at the door. Shimon ran over and opened it. A boy of about eleven was standing in the hallway. It was Menachem, his friend. Menachem handed him a note.

"For your father," he said, and ran upstairs to the next apartment.

Shimon brought the note into the living room and gave it to his father. Tamar had come out of the kitchen.

"It's time. My call-up orders. All now must help defend the city," Yossi said. "Either in the Haganah, the military, or a labor assignment." He tried playing down the seriousness of the situation for his son: "Oh, well, it's not like they're needing me at the bank right now anyway."

Shimon looked up at him, his eyes sparkling. "Abba, you know what? I heard that boys are now allowed to be messengers for the Haganah, just like Menachem. Can I do it too?"

Judith shifted uneasily on her chair, back and forth. She watched Tamar turn pale and place a hand on her son's shoulder.

"Absolutely not," she said in a sharp tone. "You're barely eight, so get that notion right out of your head. You're staying at home, with me."

Uri sat with his head nearly against the table. Images of the doctors being massacred kept running through his mind, over and over. He realized he was grinding his teeth. He looked around, startled, wondering if the others had noticed.

But the other Haganah commanders were listening to reports from Dov Yosef, the military governor of Jerusalem. The supply situation for the Jewish part of the city was growing desperate—three more convoys had made it through in April, but now they were cut off again. Operation Nachshon had indeed conquered important villages along the road leading in, but at Bab el-Wad, the Arabs continued asserting their control over the city's lifeline.

We're sitting in a trap, Uri thought. *And I brought her here. Admit it, just finally admit it: you're responsible; it's your fault Judith is here in Jerusalem.* He could see the eyes of those dead nurses sitting in that bus. What if Judith had been killed? He ran a hand across his face. Why did he have to think of her right now? Why did he have to think about her all the time?

"There's no more fuel deliveries coming," Uri heard Dov Yosef state soberly. "That means we'll need to stop all traffic in Jerusalem within a few days. No more buses, no personal cars under any condition, only what's most crucial: ambulances, vehicles from the Haganah, hospitals, bakeries, printers, cold storage. Though there isn't much food left to keep cool."

Dov Yosef looked right at all the Haganah officers. "We'll need to maintain strict rationing on foodstuff, water, fuel, all of it."

Uri raised his head. "How long will we be able to hold out like this?"

"Calculating based on current rations, and those are already more than tight, about four weeks. If we stretch them out even more, perhaps a little longer. We need to break the blockade of Jerusalem any way we can."

You need to get Judith out of here, out of Jerusalem, Uri thought, *any way you can.* Then he pulled himself together. *Nonsense,* he thought, *nonsense.* She wouldn't allow it, and he had no right to demand it of her. It was an absurd notion, completely absurd.

David Shaltiel turned to the document that the Haganah leaders had hammered out. "It's just as crucial that we're able to keep Jerusalem, no matter what. And in the period after the British withdrawal, we'll need to make sure we finally resolve this ethnic patchwork we have in this city and create clear and defensible lines. The attack on the Hadassah convoy has taught us a bitter lesson."

He flipped through the pages.

"This is Plan Dalet. It provides the basis for how we'll proceed. I'll read you some key points:

> *Operations to be conducted against any hostile popula-*
> *tion centers inside or near our defensive system, to prevent*
> *these from being used as bases by any active armed forces.*
> *These operations include the following categories:*
> *Destruction of villages (by setting fires, detonations,*
> *mines in the ruins), especially those population centers*
> *that are difficult to control over the long term . . .*
> *The following directives apply for search operations*
> *and checkpoints:*
> *Villages are to be surrounded and the houses searched.*
> *If there is resistance, the armed force must be destroyed.*
> *The population must be expelled beyond the borders of*
> *our state.*

"This is the military plan for creating a viable state. It also applies to Jerusalem, of course." Shaltiel paused.

A tense silence filled the room.

"There are still Arabs living in many areas," he continued. "In the next few days, we will start dealing with certain parts of the city. If we want to keep Mount Scopus, we'll have to take Sheikh Jarrah."

Uri nodded. There really was only one way. They had to free the city by combat. And he would do it, for Judith.

April 27, 1948

Nurse Sarah accompanied Hana down the stairs leading into the marble-covered entry hall of Hadassah Hospital. Hana was still wearing a bandage, but her wound was healing well. A young man came up to her. He wore an old Canadian battle jacket and a Bren machine gun on one shoulder. His left arm was in a cast, resting in a sling.

"One of our guards, from the Haganah," Nurse Sarah said in near apology. "It's the only way now. We're in the middle of a battle zone, and no one's more careful." Her worry was written on her face. "With so many of our doctors dead, I'm afraid we won't be able to hold out for much longer now."

They exited near the traffic circle leading into the hospital grounds. Nurse Sarah glanced at her watch. "She really should be here by now," she said.

A jeep sped up the hill and stopped directly before them. Judith jumped from the passenger seat.

"I'm sorry, the British put up a roadblock. We had to talk them into letting us through."

Nurse Sarah gave Hana a long hug. *"Mazal tov,"* she said. "Take care of yourself, and the baby, of course. We were really lucky; I don't think it was harmed in any way. When it's time, let me know. I'd be happy to help."

She started to let go, but then hugged Hana again.

"I'm so sorry, so deeply sorry, you know, about what happened with David. It's—I don't know what to say. It's simply awful. I still can't believe that he—" She broke down in tears.

Hana let go of her gently. "Be well, Sarah," she said. "And thank you for everything."

Judith took Hana by the hand and attempted to help her into the jeep, but Hana pulled back her hand and climbed in on her own. Judith climbed in as well. She wasn't quite sure how to act.

"Nurse Sarah was right," Judith said finally. "It's so hard to believe he's not here anymore."

Hana said nothing. Uri had his hand on the ignition key, unsure whether he should drive away.

Judith turned to Hana, who sat on the rear seat, her face frozen. "I know it sounds so trivial, so inadequate. I just can't find the right words for what I want to say. I know there's no way for me to console you."

Hana avoided her gaze. "You saved my life with your blood. I thank you."

"Forget it," Judith said. "I only did what you yourself did for me a year ago. That's all."

They could hear a few shots fired during the short drive down from Mount Scopus to Sheikh Jarrah. Black smoke billowed into the sky above a few buildings. Parked in the streets were trucks that young people, most wearing military shirts and with guns slung on their shoulders, loaded with furniture and household contents from buildings where Arabs lived.

At Hana's building, the front door was hanging from its hinges, evidently blown open by a grenade. A young Haganah fighter, a pistol in his right hand, was forcing an old man down the stairs.

Hana cried out: "Father, my God, Father!"

Judith leaped from the jeep and planted herself in the way. "What's going on here?" she demanded.

The Haganah man lowered his pistol, giving Judith a defiant stare. "What do you think's going on? As you can see, we're clearing the neighborhood. Those are our orders."

Judith pointed at Mohammed Khalidy. "Leave this man in peace. We'll take care of him."

The Haganah man shrugged. "As you wish. One less to give us trouble."

Hana had risen from the jeep's back seat and was running up to her father. She pressed up against him, hugging him silently. Judith took a step back. Behind her, she could suddenly hear the loud drone of engines. She'd recently learned to differentiate such sounds. This was the noise of heavy diesel engines and tank tracks on asphalt.

She looked around and saw three British armored personnel carriers coming around the corner, headed right for them. A machine gun loomed from above the cab of the first vehicle, its barrel aimed right at the group in front of the building. A major jumped down, followed by two corporals pointing Bren guns.

"Who's in charge here?" asked the major.

His gaze landed on Uri, who was standing next to the jeep with one hand propped next to the holster on his belt.

"You there, let's not get any foolish ideas," the major said. "Come over here, and be quick about it. I have neither the time nor the desire for any discussion. On order of British headquarters, I advise you of the following: the district of Sheikh Jarrah is to be cleared of all Haganah at once. We've given the Haganah a six-hour ultimatum. Five hours have already passed. You have one hour to withdraw your people. Do you understand me?"

Uri kept his hand on his holster.

"Evidently I haven't made myself clear," said the major. "If you're thinking of putting up resistance, you best take a good look around.

We have armored support positioned everywhere, as well as sufficient mortars. And believe me, we will use them."

Uri flushed red with anger. "So where were you when they were massacring the passengers of that convoy, right next door to here? Where was your armored support then, where were your troops?"

The major's voice turned colder. "Don't get smart with me. I've told you what our orders are, and we will implement them."

He pointed at the armored vehicles behind him. "This street through Sheikh Jarrah holds strategic importance for us, so you'd damn-well better believe we're going to protect it. What you do with this neighborhood after we withdraw makes no difference to me."

He turned to Hana and her father. "You're Arabs?" He didn't wait for their response. "Go back inside your apartment. This neighborhood is under British control from this moment on."

Uri went over to Judith and gently tugged at her arm. "Come on, it's better if we go."

Judith wanted to give Hana a hug, but Hana turned away. Judith thought she could see hate in her eyes. She stretched out her hand.

"Please, Hana," she said softly.

But Hana didn't budge.

"Let's go," Uri urged again.

The major waved his pistol.

"Clear out of here," he barked. "Leave these people in peace."

Judith slowly turned around. She followed Uri to the jeep in silence.

April 28, 1948

The night passed quietly. Only occasional cracks of gunfire could be heard through the open window, from far away, in the direction of the New City. The sound of a heavy diesel engine slowly grew louder, then ebbed again, a British armored scout car patrolling Sheikh Jarrah.

Hana lay awake in bed. The pain from her healing stab wound was bearable, since Nurse Sarah had slipped her medicine to last a few days.

She had left the door open to her bedroom and was listening to her father breathing uneasily as he slept on the living room sofa. She heard him muttering names, as if in a fever, and occasionally his breathing seemed to stop. Then it returned, his throat rattling.

She had tried to get her apartment back in order after it was ransacked by Jewish intruders, but her father had stopped her. *It's pointless,* he kept saying, *pointless, pointless.*

She tried not to think about it, tried not to keep having the same thoughts. They would have to decide, soon. Her father pressured her about it every day. The more she considered it, the more she found that there wasn't much to deliberate, not with David dead. He had been her bridge to another world, to their world, the Jews' world. But this bridge had been burned just as he had been burned to death in that bus. What options did she have left? Live here, alone? Or with her father, who didn't even wish to live anymore?

Deir Yassin belonged to the Jews now. Her mother was dead as well, murdered. What had once been her home village was now inaccessible even though it only lay a few miles to the west. Her father was right. It was pointless.

Hana stood up and went into the kitchen. She pulled out the sharp carving knife and went back to her bed. Gently, as if probing, she ran the sharp blade across the veins of her left arm. Judith had attempted it, and she hadn't succeeded. But Hana was a nurse. She knew what she needed to do to truly make the cut deadly. She pressed the blade harder to her lower arm, making a small incision. Suddenly she stopped.

She thought she felt a slight movement in her abdomen. She caught her breath. Again she felt something moving. It had moved, her baby had moved.

She released slow breaths, cautiously, deeply breathing in and out as if wanting to make certain. Suddenly, it was important for her to know that everything in her body was working right.

Her child, his child, it was living inside her—and with it, a piece of him as well. Her sorrow combined with a previously unknown tenderness, all for that tiny being inside her belly.

I'll stay with you, she whispered. *I'll live for you, always.*

She lowered the knife.

Judith took a drag of her cigarette, the glowing embers illuminating her worried face. The New City was submerged in deep darkness. Power for street lighting had been switched off long ago. Uri was out on a patrol. They were trying to drive the Arabs out of Katamon, the urban area west of the New City where many middle-class Arab families lived.

Yes, she thought, *the Arabs did have to go.* They couldn't remain in Katamon. The Haganah's plans were clear. They'd been directed to create interconnecting Jewish areas in Jerusalem, and Arab Katamon would have been a foreign body inside the Jewish New City.

Judith released smoke from her lungs. There was no alternative, she thought once again. There was no place for the Arabs in this part of Jerusalem. It was simple reality. Simple, yet grave.

But once the British had gone, was there no place at all for Arabs in this new state? Here in Jerusalem, or anywhere?

She ran her fingers through her thick hair. This made her shirt sleeve slide up, and she noticed the spot where she could still make out the prick for her blood draw.

Hana was an Arab too. They were bound by their blood. Fate, or whatever one wanted to call it, had brought them together. If the British hadn't intervened in Sheikh Jarrah, Hana Khalidy would now be a refugee, somewhere, anywhere, like so many thousands of others.

But the British would be gone in a few days. The Haganah was firmly intent on taking back Sheikh Jarrah after they withdrew.

What would happen to Hana then?

April 30, 1948

Mohammed Khalidy looked at his watch and rose from his armchair. He pulled on the suit pants that hung loose from his once well-rounded belly, and carefully buttoned up his jacket.

"It's time," he said with determination in his weary eyes, the kind that would not tolerate any objections.

"We're going, today," he said. "I've arranged everything, transportation, money, our accommodations in Amman."

He'd done it all, Hana thought bitterly. Among all the victims, he counted as one of the few privileged ones. He had a bank account in Transjordan, and his sister must have helped out, since she'd been living in Amman for a long time. Her father had seen to everything. She was supposed to be grateful. But now, life as she'd known it would be gone forever. It wasn't his fault, of course. She had gotten involved in the Jews' world, given up everything for nursing and for the Jewish hospital's mission. She had loved one of them, and she was now going to have a half-Jewish child. And yet the rift had widened, a deep chasm that she was no longer able to surmount.

She heard honking from the street.

"That must be Ali," her father said.

A few minutes later came the knock on the door. Ali had only survived the massacre of Deir Yassin because he'd moved his family into the neighboring village a few months before. Now, he looked distraught.

He was unshaven, wearing an old suit and felt slippers. His eyes kept darting back and forth.

"The Haganah," he said finally. "They came this morning, at dawn. They gave us two hours before the village was to be cleared." He stared at the ground. "I brought them with me," he said. "My wife and both my children. They're sitting in the car."

Mohammed Khalidy went up to him and placed a hand on his arm. "Don't worry. We'll get by all right, together."

Ali raised his head. He looked close to tears. "On Radio Damascus they were saying we were supposed to go but could come back soon. We should leave our villages so that we don't get harmed when the Arab armies come and drive the Jews into the sea once the British pull out."

Hana looked to her father. He said nothing. A propaganda war had been raging on both sides for weeks. The whisper campaigns, radio proclamations, intimidations, and threats were distressing the population. That turned into hysteria, panic.

"We can't waste any more time," he said eventually.

East of Jerusalem, the road descended steeply into the Jordan Valley. In the distance, the smooth waters of the Dead Sea reflected the hot springtime sun. After the unusually heavy rainfall of the past few months, the normally barren hills of Judaea were covered with green that flocks of Bedouin sheep now pounced on.

The rear end of the overloaded Chrysler was sagging low. Ali's wife held their youngest child on her lap in the back seat, and her thirteen-year-old son sat between her and Hana. Mohammed Khalidy sat up in the passenger seat next to Ali.

Ali suddenly stepped hard on the brakes. A heavily loaded donkey was bucking on the roadway before them, a screaming fellah striking him with a stick. The animal wouldn't budge from its spot. Standing behind the donkey was a whole family, three women balancing sacks on their heads, one holding a small child. An old woman, clearly exhausted, lay in the blazing sun on the side of the road. Next to her was a baby wrapped up in a bundle of clothes. Ali tried steering the Chrysler around the refugees.

"Wait, stop," Hana said. She climbed out, holding a bottle of water, and leaned down to the old woman. Her face showed deep lines, the hair under her headscarf a pale gray. She drank greedily.

"Where are you trying to go?" asked Hana.

The old woman gave a helpless shrug. "Away," she whispered. "Only God knows."

The baby began screaming. The old woman held it feebly in her arms and tried to calm it. She reached for the water bottle and gave it to the baby.

"Don't you have any milk?" Hana asked.

The old woman waved away the notion. "Milk? Where from? They took everything from us, our goats, our cows."

The baby began screaming again. Hana took it from the old woman's arms and cradled it. A young woman took the sack off her head and stepped over to them.

"Her name is Sulima, she's eight weeks old," she said. "I'm her mother, that's her grandmother."

Hana unwrapped the cloth around the baby. It kept screaming.

"She's hungry. She really needs milk," Hana told the fellah woman. "I know, I'm a nurse."

"We've been on the road for five days," the woman said. "I . . . I have no more milk."

Hana stroked the baby's head. The donkey had calmed down, grazing on the side of the road. The man stood next to it, his face blank.

Hana took the baby over to the car and showed her father. "She'll die if we don't do something soon. We have to take her with us." She pointed at the old woman. "And the grandmother too."

The younger woman raised her hands and released a sharp cry.

Hana turned to her. "We don't want to take your baby from you. But we can't simply let her die."

The woman lowered her head in silence. Hana searched her bag for a pencil and wrote on a scrap of newspaper from the car. "This is our address in Amman. You can find them both there."

The woman took the page and looked at Hana with embarrassment. "I cannot read," she said. "No one in our family can."

Hana read the address to her several times, asking her to repeat it back. "And if you forget, you must find someone who can read it," Hana said. "You will have to."

She gestured to the old woman. "Come on, we'll move you together. Let us help."

The old woman tried to get up but slumped back down again. "I can't," she said, her voice breaking.

Ali climbed out of the car and pulled her up using both arms. She hobbled, supported by Ali, over to the Chrysler, and slid onto the rear seat without a word. After assuring the terrified mother once more, Hana, baby Sulima in her arms, got in next to the grandmother and pulled the car door shut with difficulty.

Hana cradled Sulima tight. She gently pressed the child to her belly and hoped that her own baby could feel it. It would be like this soon, when her own child was born, when she could cradle it in her arms. A wave of affection flooded her. Feeling such warmth, she fell asleep.

Ali suddenly slammed on the brakes. Hana woke with a start and looked out the window anxiously.

A seemingly endless migration of refugees was blocking the road. Streams of people pulled heavily loaded-down handcarts, donkeys, and horses.

"Up ahead is Allenby Bridge," Ali said. "And beyond that, Transjordan."

The Chrysler made only halting progress. They weaved their way through the lines of exhausted people. On the banks of the Jordan, a makeshift tent city had developed. *There must be thousands of refugees here,* Hana thought. *Sulima's family will be here as well.*

Their car finally reached the narrow bridge. Young soldiers wearing the uniform of the Arab Legion stood on the other side, observing the refugees who kept thronging across the bridge to Transjordan.

The old woman's head had slid down onto Hana's shoulder.

Acting on an uneasy feeling, Hana grabbed the old woman's hand and tried to feel for her pulse.

"Stop, Ali. Stop right now," she moaned.

Her father turned to her.

"She's dead," Hana said.

Hana couldn't stop trembling. Was this their future too? Only more death, more ruin? Maybe she should've taken that knife to her arm after all. She placed a hand on her belly while cradling Sulima in her other arm, the baby starting to cry. No, she wanted to live, she had to live, for this little life inside her, and perhaps for this one she held. No matter what the future might bring. "I will be there for you," she whispered. "For you, my little one. You can depend on me."

The Chrysler came to a stop in front of an armored Arab Legion scout car that was parked along the approach to the bridge. A lieutenant jumped down, a young Bedouin.

"We have a dead woman in our car!" Hana shouted out the window.

The lieutenant opened her door, let Hana out, and then gently pulled out the dead woman. He carried her into the shadows of the armored car and laid her on the ground. Then he came back over to them.

"We're going to show the Jews. You can depend on it," he said. "Our holy Jerusalem belongs to us."

May 12–13, 1948

Once they reached the door, Uri suddenly put his arms around Judith, lifted her up, and carried her over the threshold, covering her with gentle little kisses. He kept carrying her through the apartment, searching for the bed. He laid her down carefully there and began removing her clothes.

She felt like she was in some sappy American romance movie, yet she enjoyed it. For a moment, she was able to tune out everything that was happening and indulge in the fantasy of them as a carefree couple.

She savored his passionate caresses, these seeming even wilder, more impetuous to her than on their first night. She felt such desire—for him, for life. She had seen too much death. Now she wanted to leave her nightmares behind, using his body, using the force of his emotions, digging her fingers into him, becoming one, at least for now. She screamed when she came, and could not, would not calm down for a long while. The quivering inside her finally waned, and she laid her head on his chest. She felt as if she'd washed up on an island in the middle of a storm, one so small that the wind could still sweep her away whenever it wished.

Uri gave her a blissful smile and pulled her even closer with one arm. He used his free hand to search for cigarettes in his pants on the floor.

"My last one." He lit it and handed it to Judith.

Cigarettes were getting expensive. Earlier that year, the Haganah had insisted that the Jewish military governor allow cigarette shipments on the embattled delivery trucks, even when it meant less foodstuff getting into Jerusalem. But the city had been cut off again, for weeks now, and in the streets, people could be seen snatching cigarette butts off the ground.

Judith held the smoke in her lungs a long time. Then she gave the cigarette back to Uri.

The Haganah had assigned them an apartment that the family of an Arab bank employee had been living in until a week ago. He had fled with his wife and four children to Beirut after Jewish attackers set fire to the building next door.

Uri rose from the bed. She heard him in the kitchen. After a while, he came back with a cup he was careful not to spill.

"Breakfast for the lady," he said, grinning. "I found a few scoops of coffee in the back of the cabinet. There was even sugar."

He handed her the cup and then crawled back into bed with her. He kissed her, lightly, with no inhibitions. Judith took a sip and gave him the cup, and they drank the precious coffee together this way.

"You know what I'd really like to do?" Uri asked.

She stared at him.

"To shower. To simply stand under a shower. Doesn't matter if it's a trickle. Just to be able to wash up and not have to count every last drop."

Judith stroked his beard stubble.

He laughed. "You're right. Shaving would be another luxury."

The starry night was giving way to half-light, the sky fading from dull gray to an increasingly deep blue. Soon, the first orange-red streaks heralded the dawn of a cloudless May day.

"Of course, having our own country would be nice, too, without daily shoot-outs, without ration cards, with our own army and our own police, even our own criminals as far as I'm concerned. Just some kind of state to call our own, where no one's trying to kill us or tell us what to do—not the United Nations, not the Arabs, and certainly not the Brits."

He placed an arm around her, kissed her again. "And our own family."

Judith freed herself from his embrace and looked him in the eyes. "Our own family? What are you trying to say?"

"Well, just what I said," he replied, and gave her a nervous laugh.

"You mean, a family, you and me . . . ?"

"Yes, that's exactly what I mean." He kissed her. "I might not be the best at all that," he said. "And maybe it's not exactly the best time, but I think this is what they used to call a marriage proposal."

Judith felt herself getting choked up. She began to tremble uncontrollably. Her hands searched his upper body for something to hold on to but failed.

"What's the matter?" he asked, startled. "What's wrong with you, Judith?"

Images raced through her head, like in a movie, images of a family, smiling, carefree, in the sunshine, at a lake. Images from a world infinitely far away, apparently buried forever, and yet, suddenly so very near.

"Judith, for God's sake . . ." She now heard his voice. "Tell me. I'm sorry, did I say the wrong thing? Is it Yael? I miss her terribly, you have to understand that, but we found each other in spite of all that pain. She'd want us to be happy."

The movie came to an abrupt halt. Judith stopped trembling. A deep sigh forced its way out of her chest, and then came the tears. She sobbed, not holding back, her head pressed into the pillow.

Uri, helpless, caressed her. He pulled the covers over her quivering shoulders and reflexively searched for the pack of cigarettes before remembering in frustration that it was empty.

"Please, Judith," he tried again, "just tell me what's wrong."

She didn't respond. She was far away from him, in another world.

Sunlight had crept into the room. Uri's eyes fell on his watch on the nightstand. There was a meeting scheduled for six o'clock that morning, and they needed him there. He gently pushed back the covers, stood up, and slipped into his unwashed clothes. Then he sat on the edge of the bed and stroked her hair. She seemed to have calmed down somewhat.

"I have to go," he said softly.

Judith turned and stared at him, her eyes filled with tears. "I'm sorry," she whispered. She squeezed his arm. "Do you think we're actually going to get there?"

Uri wrinkled his brow. "Get there? What do you mean?"

"Our state, a country, the one you want, a place for us. A place where I don't always have to be afraid. Where no one can do the things to me they did before."

Uri hugged her. "Yes. We'll get there. I—" He searched for the words. "I'm going to protect you. I will always keep trying. Please, you have to trust me. You don't need to be afraid anymore. You have me, we have each other. You only—you only have to want it."

He sounded helpless, despite his words. "Please. I know it's not the right time, not the right time at all to be leaving. I should be staying here with you, I know, but I have to go. You know the Brits are pulling out tomorrow."

Judith kept squeezing his arm. "Just give me some time, Uri, all right?"

He hesitated, but then kissed her. And she finally let him go.

Jonathan Higgins tossed a file into the overfull wooden crate next to his desk.

"So, that's that," the sergeant said. "Thirty-one years and now it's closing time. Our good General Allenby surely couldn't have imagined this when he reported to Jerusalem back in 1917."

He slammed the crate shut. It was the last of so many he'd filled in the past few days. The British Mandate government had thoroughly prepared for withdrawal. Over two hundred thousand tons of material had been packed up and readied for delivery back home. The British were saying goodbye to yet another part of their shrinking empire.

"Hard to believe we're heading home, out of bloody Palestine, away from these nervy Arabs, these impertinent Jews, out of this place, back to good old Britain. Wonder if anyone will thank us? We brought civilization to this godforsaken desert, paved roads, real governance. And now? Now they're all happy we're finally clearing out. God save the King." He turned to Lieutenant Goldsmith, sitting in his chair behind the empty desk. "I've requested my discharge. It'll do for a little house in the country. Perhaps I'll even start playing a little golf." He cleared his throat. "What about you, sir, if you don't mind my asking? The big careers are now being made in Germany, what with the Commies causing loads of trouble in Berlin. The 'Cold War,' they're calling it."

Josef dodged the question. "Me? I plan to take a look around, see what the future holds."

Higgins sat atop the crate and sighed. "It's quite the miracle—been in this bloody country over two years now, and guess what? I'm still alive! The Jews tried to kill me all sorts of ways, even blew up this bloody hotel, at least part of it. And tomorrow morning at seven, it belongs to them—or the Arabs, depending on who marches in here first. A nice little race, no doubt. And you know something, sir? If I may: I don't care; couldn't give a shit."

A private came in and saluted.

"Here, help me with this," Higgins told the man. Together, they hauled the crate out of the office to a truck waiting outside.

Josef picked up the receiver of the phone on the empty desk, anxiously testing whether it still worked. The usual tone sounded in his ear. He quickly dialed a number.

"Tomorrow morning at seven," he said softly when a voice answered in Hebrew. "Be quick, but don't make trouble. The withdrawal itself must proceed without a hitch."

Josef rested his face in his hands. The time had come—he finally had to decide. He took a deep breath. He owed the British for taking him in as a child, and he had attempted to pay them back. He'd worn their uniform for years. He had risked his life for them in the war. The red beret of his airborne division lay on the desk in front of him. He'd always been proud of that beret.

But he felt something inside him, something stronger than that loyalty. And tomorrow he would have to show it. Josef knew there was no turning back.

May 14, 1948

Sergeant Higgins puffed out his chest and saluted. The Union Jack slid slowly down the flagpole. It was seven in the morning. A small group of international reporters had gathered before the King David Hotel to observe the historic moment. A soldier folded up the British flag. Higgins lowered his salute.

In front of the hotel stood a convoy of vehicles. It was to begin rolling any moment. Josef was watching everything from the lobby of this hotel that had served as British headquarters. He now saw Sergeant Higgins come over, giving him a puzzled look.

"What's wrong, sir? It's time, we're moving out."

Josef looked him squarely in the eyes. "I'm staying here, Higgins." He stretched out a hand to the sergeant. "Best of luck."

Higgins shook, reluctantly.

"I'm one of them, Higgins. This is where I belong now."

Higgins took a step back. He seemed to consider something a moment. Then he returned his hand to his cap and saluted. "I only learned one word of that bloody language. Apologies, sir," he said, his voice raw. *"Mazal tov."*

"Mazal tov, Higgins," Josef replied, and saluted as well.

They could hear engines starting up outside. Higgins rushed out to catch them.

Josef heard the solemn tones of bagpipes in the distance. Soldiers of the Highland Light Infantry, along with so many other British troops, were marching to the clang of bagpipers as they left their post in the Hospice of Notre Dame one last time, so close to the medieval walls of the Old City. The last units had now left their bases. The British were withdrawing from this city of three world religions in two large columns: one headed north, passing Ramallah and on to the port of Haifa, and the other to the south toward Egypt.

Josef felt his throat tighten as he watched the last of the trucks disappear down the road. The sound of rapid footsteps ripped him from his gloomy thoughts. A troop of young men with machine guns came running toward the King David Hotel. They were soldiers of the Haganah, storming the abandoned British positions just minutes before the Arabs could. The Haganah had been carefully preparing for the takeover. On this historic morning, this operation was decisive for bringing the heart of Jerusalem under Jewish control.

"We can't thank you enough, Josef. Without your information, we wouldn't have been able to pull this off."

Josef felt a hand on his shoulder.

"Welcome home," Uri said. He hugged Josef.

For a brief moment, they stood together without speaking.

Then Uri broke the silence. "You don't happen to have a cigarette, do you?"

Josef gave him a pack of Players.

Uri pulled one out and lit it, then handed back the pack. "Just imagine, half a can of kerosene for ten cigarettes at current rates. Keep a good eye on that little fortune of yours."

Uri squeezed Judith's hand under the table. A coy smile played on her lips, but her eyes were serious. He wondered if she'd ever be able to laugh without inhibition. He would, once all this was finally over, do everything he could to bring a smile to those eyes. On the other hand, he loved that earnestness of hers. *Say yes,* he thought—*please, Judith, say yes. You must, you simply must say yes.*

A tense silence filled the room. The Haganah commanders were hunched around a radio. The words came from a man just thirty miles away from Jerusalem, but the signal was weak. They strained to hear David Ben Gurion's faint voice through the static and crackles.

At four o'clock that afternoon in the Tel Aviv Museum on Rothschild Boulevard, Ben Gurion had unfolded a page of text that had been bitterly negotiated a few hours before. At issue was the "Rock of Israel," a phrase from Psalm 19:15 that was to appear in the Declaration of Independence. The religious communities wanted *Rock* to refer to God, but leftists insisted on a clear separation between religion and state, saying *Rock* should serve as a metaphor for Israel's strength. In the end, the Rock was named but not interpreted any further.

Yet no one was talking about that dispute anymore because, shortly before the beginning of Shabbat, the 650,000 Jews across Palestine huddled around radios to listen to David Ben Gurion.

Uri squeezed Judith's hand tighter as the historic announcement began.

"Like all other peoples," Ben Gurion said, "the Jewish people have the natural right to determine their own history, under their own sovereignty. Accordingly, we, the members of the People's Council, representatives of the Jewish community of Eretz Israel and of the Zionist movement, are here assembled on the day of the termination of the British Mandate over Eretz Israel and, by virtue of our natural and historic right and on the basis of the resolution of the United Nations General Assembly, hereby declare the establishment of a Jewish state in Eretz Israel, to be known as the State of Israel."

Then he named the date of the Jewish calendar: the fifth of Iyar, 5708.

Uri kept holding Judith's hand tight in his. He only let go when everyone rose and sang "Hatikvah," the national hymn of the newly founded state.

Someone turned off the radio. They could hear gunshots outside. Now that the British had withdrawn, battles were being fought all over Jerusalem.

"We have our own state, our very own state. Israel. Listen to how that sounds—no more Palestine," Uri told Judith in a low voice. "The homeland you always wished for."

They went out into the hallway. Uri took Judith in his arms. "Please, Judith, say yes. There's no better day than today."

She freed herself.

"Uri, please be patient with me. The most important thing is that you've kept yourself alive," she said. "You might not believe me right now, but I do love you."

May 21, 1948

Shrapnel whizzed over Judith's head, smashing into the wall of a building. She threw herself to the sidewalk. About five hundred shells daily were falling on the Jewish part of Jerusalem.

Judith heard a donkey's bloodcurdling scream. The animal had collapsed, hit by the ricocheting shrapnel. It had been pulling a cart with a water tank, since some of the water supply had to be carried by horse and donkey due to the fuel shortage. A gaunt old man stared helplessly at his bleeding animal. Judith ran to see if she could help. The old man knelt over the donkey and shook his head.

"Nothing to be done," he said. He caressed the donkey's bleeding neck. "My God, Yossele, what's next?" he wailed. "You go on ahead, I'll be there soon."

The donkey was bleeding heavily, but his legs kept kicking frantically as if trying to fight his own demise. Judith took out her pistol, carefully aimed, and shot the animal in the head.

She placed a hand on the old man's arm. "Make sure you get him to a butcher, quick."

The man winced but didn't respond.

Right at that moment, Judith noticed a thin trickle widening along the street. The Arab Legion gunners had hit their target: the water tank was breached.

She turned back to the sidewalk where she'd been lying, then rushed over and picked up the loaf of bread she'd dropped. She clamped it under one arm and ran down Ben Yehuda Street, keeping close to the walls just as everyone did in Jerusalem these days.

The bell at the front door wasn't working because there was no electricity, but the door was open. Judith ran up the stairs and knocked, out of breath. The door opened a crack. Shimon looked up at her, a mix of fear and curiosity in his eyes.

"Is your mother here?" she asked.

Shimon nodded and let her in. Tamar came down the hallway, wiping her hands on her apron.

"Quick, grab as many cans and pitchers and pails as you can find," Judith said. "There's a water tank leaking a few streets over, got hit by artillery."

She handed the bread to Shimon and fished around in her shoulder bag for a small bar of chocolate, melted a little from the daytime heat. She'd found it in the kitchen of her new apartment where the Arab family used to live.

"Here, this is for you and your sister."

Tamar rushed into the kitchen and came back with several bottles and a bucket. They ran down the stairs and out to the street. A small crowd had gathered around the tank and was collecting the precious water. The old man sat in silence next to his donkey, stroking its head.

"One and a half gallons," Tamar said. "That's the latest ration. One and a half gallons per day, for everything. And it's getting hotter every day."

Judith helped her carry the water bucket. A huge explosion shook the windows of the surrounding buildings—another shell. The two of them picked up their pace, careful not to spill the water. Judith heard a piercing howl above her, followed immediately by another explosion, this time farther off.

They finally made it back inside the apartment. Shimon had set the chocolate on the table next to the bread but hadn't touched it.

"Go ahead, eat it," Judith said, "before it completely melts. Just leave half for your sister."

Shimon took the bar and carefully unwrapped it. He bashfully broke off half and began eating his share.

"I still have some tea left," Tamar said, "and a little wood for the fire. I could make some for us now that we have water again."

Judith nodded in agreement. After a while, Tamar came back from the kitchen with the tea and poured it into two cups.

"No sugar, I'm afraid," she said.

They drank in silence. Through the open window, they could hear birds chirping. For one single moment, it seemed as if life were normal. Tea on a May day in Jerusalem.

After a while, Judith broke the silence. "Where's your husband?"

"On duty, south of town. I heard the Arabs are advancing on Bethlehem. They'll be here soon if our people aren't able to stop them."

"The Egyptians, the Iraqis, the Syrians, the Lebanese," said Judith. "They're advancing on us from everywhere. And the Arab Legion from Transjordan on top of that." She was amazed at how coolly she added up all the armies attacking the new Jewish state. "Now King Abdullah suddenly deems it the appropriate time to join in the fight. Oh, and a few Brits are sticking around too—commanding the Arab Legion. They're the ones aiming this artillery fire at us."

Tamar set down her cup. She had gone pale. "You sound well informed." She leaned in. "How bad is it, you think?"

Judith leaned back. She chose her words carefully. "Jerusalem is cut off, Tamar. You see it yourself: we're out of everything. But we can't give up. That's exactly what they all want. If Jerusalem falls, we'll never have a homeland. We need to hang on, somehow. We have to."

Judith marveled that she was now the one issuing rallying cries. She drank her tea and gently set the cup back on the table. She debated whether to mention the secret plan to change the encircled city's fate.

"We're trying to build a new road. Right through the mountains, past the barricades. Right now, it's just a dream, nothing more. But if we could pull it off—"

She gave Tamar a spontaneous hug. "I have to go. Keep the children safe. I'll come back as soon as I can."

"Thank you," Tamar said softly. "And thank you for the bread."

May 23, 1948

Uri prodded the boy in the ribs. Chaim opened his eyes slowly, squinting. He was small, practically a kid. Next to him on the cold ground lay two more boys, maybe sixteen years old. They belonged to Gadna, the Haganah youth organization.

"What's—what's wrong?" he stammered.

"All hell's broken loose," Uri said. "Get up, see for—"

The staccato of machine gun fire interrupted him.

Chaim grabbed his weapon. He fished around in his pocket and pulled out a few cartridges.

"Six," he said. "That's all I've got, six lousy bullets."

"And the others?" Uri said. "What about them?"

Chaim shrugged. "Same. No one's got more than a handful." He pressed a hand against the wall and tried to stand.

"What's wrong with you?" Uri asked.

"I haven't eaten for two days," Chaim said. "We don't have anything left." He slumped back down.

Uri stepped over and propped him up. The other two boys briefly raised their heads, then fell back asleep.

For days, a battle had been raging for the massive building that housed the Hospice of Notre Dame across from the Old City of Jerusalem. Operated by nuns, it was originally supposed to serve as lodging for French pilgrims. Yet its thick stone walls and over five hundred rooms proved more fortress than hospitable lodging, and its strategic location in the heart of Jerusalem meant both sides were desperate to take the structure. The Arab Legion kept firing artillery at it from the battlements of the Old City. They had penetrated the sprawling hospice many times already, and the Haganah had driven them out repeatedly, fighting from room to room.

A cry rang out from a lower floor: "They're back again!"

The machine gun staccato increased. Uri reached into the bag on his shoulder and pulled out several cartons of ammo.

"Here, this is everything I have left," he said, and thrust them into Chaim's hands.

Chaim took them with a mix of wonder and gratitude.

Uri checked his Sten machine gun. The magazine was half-full. He took one more look at Chaim and the other two boys, then ran out of the room.

At the bottom of the stairs, he spotted two men silhouetted against the sunlight streaming in. Uri thought he could see kaffiyehs on their heads. He fired a burst. The two Arab Legion soldiers fell to the floor.

He heard a shout in Hebrew from the other end of the long corridor. And from outside came the drone of a heavy diesel engine. Uri knew what it meant: the Arab Legion was sending in their tanks.

He bounded into a room that gave him a view of the street. On the wall, a cross hung next to a painting of the Virgin Mary, the narrow cot revealing that this had been a French nun's refuge until a few days ago. He spotted a khaki-colored Arab Legion tank out on the street, followed by regular infantry.

Uri emptied his magazine and hit one of the soldiers, but the rest of his shots just ricocheted off the tank's steel plating. He could only watch helplessly as the tank kept rolling toward the hospice.

He heard a sound behind him. He aimed his Sten at the door, but then lowered it once he remembered he had no ammo left. He reached for his knife. A figure in a khaki uniform stood in the doorway, a type of thin tube slung on her back by a leather strap.

"The Haganah sent reinforcements," said Judith. "I came with them. They told me I could find you here with the Gadna kids."

She handed him the tube. It was a British bazooka. Uri held it a moment, dumbfounded. A hail of bullets burst through the window, the ricochets bouncing around the narrow room in search of a target. Uri threw Judith down and himself over her.

The bazooka clattered to the floor.

Uri sat up and peered over the windowsill. The tank had almost reached the building. Uri picked up the bazooka and took careful aim. Then he held his breath, pulled the trigger. The projectile struck below the turret. Nothing seemed to happen for a moment, then the shell exploded inside the tank. Flames shot out in all directions.

Uri lowered his head below the sill and closed his eyes a moment. He felt a hand on his arm. He looked into Judith's face. Her eyes were earnest.

"I say yes, Uri," she whispered.

Uri needed a moment to grasp what she was telling him. "You're saying yes?" he said, to make sure.

Judith nodded.

He stretched out his arms to pull her close.

A massive explosion stopped him, followed by a blast wave. Part of the hospice facade collapsed and crashed into the street. Where a wall had been a few seconds before, there was now a huge gaping void.

Uri lay curled up on the floor. He wiped dust from his eyes and felt for Judith. She lay on her stomach and wasn't moving. Uri carefully turned her over. Gray-brown mortar covered her face, stone grit clung to her hair, dark blood trickled from her head.

"Judith," he whispered, "Judith, can you hear me? Please wake up." He caressed her, helpless. "Please, wake up," he repeated. "Wake up! You better wake up. It's me, Uri, you hear, please hear me."

She didn't move. A deep void opened up inside Uri. *All this for what?* he thought, *for what?* He heard rapid footsteps.

Chaim came in aiming his gun. "You need a medic?"

Uri shook his head, "Help me get her downstairs."

Chaim grabbed her legs, Uri held her upper body. Staggering from fatigue, they reached the ground floor.

May 28, 1948

Youssef rested one hand on the grip of his curved dagger. *Such laughable figures,* he thought with a mixture of contempt and admiration. Before him, down one of the narrow alleys, stood a small group of exhausted young Jews, most men but also some women. Youssef could now watch them in peace. Here they were, the so-called heroes of the Haganah, only a few dozen. Their faces gaunt, barely able to stand. These were the defenders of the Jewish Old City. Now, after ten weeks of fierce fighting, they had finally given up.

"Slaughter them, the pigs!" a teenage boy screamed at him.

"Let's hang them!" screamed another, picking up a rock and throwing it at the Jews.

Youssef felt his fingers trembling. *Go, take one for yourself, plunge your blade into their hearts.* He took a step forward. Shots rang out.

Two officers wearing the red-and-white checked kaffiyehs of the Arab Legion were aiming their machine guns, ready to shoot into the enraged crowd of Arabs about to pounce on the Jews.

Another Arab Legion officer, his kaffiyeh adorned with the crown insignia of his King Abdullah of Transjordan, pulled his revolver and pointed it at Youssef.

"You there, get lost," he said. "And the rest of you too. These Jews are prisoners of the Arab Legion now. No one touches them. They're under my protection. Do you understand?"

The crowd grumbled but obeyed the officer. He had, after all, achieved what the unorganized Arab fighters hadn't been able to: with his soldiers of the Arab Legion from Transjordan, he'd broken the Haganah's bitter resistance and taken the Jewish Quarter in the Old City of Jerusalem.

Abdullah el-Tell, son of a rich landowner family, was, at thirty-one, the youngest major in the Arab Legion, which took its orders from a British commander, General John Bagot Glubb. King Abdullah had personally ordered el-Tell to take Jerusalem. This was his moment of triumph. Fighting for such a reward brought the highest honor. Within the medieval walls of the Old City stood the shrines of the three world religions: the Christian Church of the Holy Sepulcher, the Muslim Dome of the Rock as well as the Al-Aqsa Mosque, and the Jewish Wailing Wall, on whose stones the great Jewish Temple had once stood.

The Jews had tried every means of getting reinforcements into the Jewish Quarter. And the Arabs had made every effort to prevent it. But only now, with the Haganah forced to surrender, it became clear just how few of them had been holding on for so long and with even fewer weapons.

Along with those disarmed Haganah fighters, now gathered the people whose fate had been sealed by the defeat. A couple thousand Orthodox Jews had long lived in the cramped houses of the Jewish Quarter. They had dedicated their lives to studying the Torah, and wanted nothing to do with politics or with the Zionists. They only wanted to serve their God and wait for the Messiah, who would one day make his entrance through the gates of Jerusalem.

Yet now, after two thousand years of waiting and praying, they were forced to leave. The Wailing Wall, once a short walk away, would now be out of their reach.

Youssef watched the columns of people begin their trek. The younger men had to go into captivity in Transjordan along with the Haganah fighters, while the older inhabitants of the Old City were to pass through the ancient stone gates for their march into the Jewish New City, where Jews would now be held by the soldiers of the Arab Legion.

Youssef couldn't hold back any longer. He ran into the nearest synagogue, held a match to one of the curtains, and watched the flames eat away at the cloth.

Many copied him. Youssef's eyes glistened. God the Almighty and Exalted had heard his believers. A massive black cloud of smoke was rising above the Jewish Quarter.

June 3, 1948

The heat of early summer filled the city. The smell of uncollected trash grew stronger. It made its way in through the wide-open windows.

Judith lay at the end of the corridor and watched two nurses run by, rolling a bed holding a bleeding, screaming child, yet another victim of the constant artillery barrages. Hadassah Hospital had evacuated its six hundred patients to the New City. But they didn't have enough rooms to house all the wounded, so temporary beds had been set up everywhere. Judith had a bandage around her head that hadn't been changed in some time. They were lacking bandages and medicine. She looked around in dismay, sad to see Hadassah so diminished. She wondered if it would ever again occupy its grand old building, ever again be a place where Jews and Arabs could make the kind of connection she and Hana had.

A familiar face appeared, leaning over her.

"How are you doing today?" Nurse Sarah asked.

"Better, much better," Judith replied. The ache in her head had lessened considerably.

"You got really lucky. A severe concussion but nothing broken, and that cut on your head's healing rather nicely."

Nurse Sarah turned to go, obviously in a hurry. Judith grabbed her hand.

"Have you heard anything from—her?" she asked in a low voice.

Nurse Sarah pulled her hand back. She stood there a moment, her head lowered. Judith thought she saw tears in her eyes.

"No, nothing. Only that she left, for Amman I think, to her relatives," she said finally. "I went to her apartment once, but it was empty." She swallowed hard. "Plundered."

"Isn't she supposed to be having her child soon?"

"Yes, in the next few weeks, I think."

Nurse Sarah pulled out a hankie and wiped at her eyes.

"Excuse me, I—I can't help it. It just hit me suddenly. She's—she was such a lovely person. I miss her a lot. Everything that's happened—I thought that here, at least—" She turned to leave. "Sorry, I have to go," she said, and again wiped at her eyes as she rushed off.

Judith looked out the open window at the empty street. After a while, an ambulance bearing the Magen David Adom emblem came speeding up. She'd barely noticed it. *Will it be a boy?* she wondered. She really hoped so, and hoped Hana would name him David, in spite of everything. She closed her eyes and fell into a half-sleep.

Something woke Judith. She glanced around and saw she'd been moved to a small room. Someone was touching her hand. Uri stood before her with a concerned look on his face. He leaned over and kissed her on the forehead, right below her bandage. She wrapped her arms around his neck and held him tight.

"Oh my God, Uri," she whispered. "How did you manage to get here?"

Uri looked away in embarrassment. "Well, um, they told me half an hour and then come right back. South of town we've finally driven back the Egyptians for real—Ramat Rachel is ours again." He sat on the edge of the bed and took both her hands. "We need a rabbi."

Judith sat up. "A rabbi?"

"Yes, a rabbi. Unless you know some way of having a Jewish wedding without one?"

She hesitated, then shook her head. "Are you telling me that, for us to get married, it needs to be a religious ceremony?" she said. "This is supposed to be a new and modern country we're fighting for, where you can choose to be religious or not. Where there's no one always telling you how to live, whether with God or without."

"You're right, of course, but this is a state for Jews of all different origins, so what binds us together is our historic religion. That's why we need a rabbi, and as soon as possible. Because I'd like to get married to you right now."

He took Judith in his arms and kissed her. But Judith wasn't satisfied.

"So, with this wedding, I'm supposed to put myself in the hands of God? We can't be man and wife without him being there?"

She wrapped her arms around her pulled-up legs and held them tight. "I wonder where God was when I was in Dachau. Our God, not to mention the Christian God the Nazis claimed to believe in. The God that allowed my mother to be gassed. Where was he?"

Silence reigned in the small room a long while. They then heard a shell land in the distance.

Uri sighed. "Looks like the Arabs are now looking after their God and ours and the Christians' as well. Over there"—he waved a hand toward the east—"just a mile from here, they're now in control of the Old City and all the important shrines along with it. Here in the New City? You could say we're godless."

Judith moved closer to him.

Uri placed an arm around her. He said, tentatively, "The part with the rings will have to wait, unfortunately." He squeezed her tight. "But there's no getting around that rabbi."

June 9, 1948

Judith looked at herself in the mirror. Nurse Sarah had managed to get her enough water to wash herself. Her dark hair was shining, the adhesive bandage that had replaced her wound dressing was small and mostly covered by her hair. Nurse Sarah had even seen to it that her khaki uniform was washed and ironed. Insignia of the newly founded Israeli army had been sewn on it a few days before. She'd been assigned the rank of sergeant.

But Judith frowned. Was this the way a bride was supposed to look? She crossed the apartment and opened the drawer to a dresser, which, apart from the bed, counted among their few furnishings. But it was empty except for a pair of underwear. She thought about the old dress she'd worn back on the ship. It was in Yardenim, inaccessible for the moment.

She gave up and buckled her belt, on which hung her British revolver. She locked the apartment door behind her and set off.

The June day was hot, the streets still devoid of people. She heard whistling above her and threw herself to the ground, crawling behind an overflowing trash can. The shell landed in the street about fifty yards away, where it did no damage beyond making a crater in the street. Everyone was staying inside whenever possible.

Judith waited one more moment just in case the Arabs fired again. Then she stood up and looked down. Her freshly washed uniform was now all dirty. She patted the dirt off and started on her way again.

When she reached Ben Yehuda Street, she knocked three times on the apartment door. Tamar opened up.

"Come in," she said with obvious delight. She got a glass of water and set it on the table for Judith. "Don't have any more tea left, unfortunately."

Judith drank in slow gulps. Then she set the glass down.

"I'm getting married," she said.

It took Tamar a second to process the news. "Married, now?" she asked in disbelief, but then quickly added, "That's so wonderful."

"You're right. It's not exactly the best time. But then we thought: What better time?"

Tamar was quick to reply: "Right, right, sure."

Judith took another sip of water. "It's just that, I—I mean, look at me. I'm supposed to get married wearing this cobbled-together uniform?"

Tamar gave Judith a once-over. Then she smiled. "Wait here, I'll be right back."

She disappeared into the bedroom and came back a short time later with a white dress over one arm. "Stand up a second."

Judith stood, bashful.

Tamar held the dress up to her. "My old wedding gown. Looks like it might fit. Maybe a little too wide, but that's what a sewing kit is for."

Judith took the dress and went out into the hall with it, standing before the mirror. She held it up and smiled at her reflection. Tamar stepped behind her.

"You'll be such a beautiful bride," she said. "So do you know where the big event is to take place?"

Judith hesitated. "At our place, over in Katamon. Though it's not exactly hospitable there yet."

Tamar touched her shoulder. "It would be an honor for me if you had it here. It doesn't exactly look like a palace at the moment here, either, but it'll do."

Judith threw her arms around Tamar. "That would be so lovely, but I really couldn't accept."

"Come on, of course you can! In fact, you have to. It's settled. Now, when is it supposed to be?"

"Day after tomorrow," Judith said, embarrassed.

They could hear the patter of quick footsteps outside the apartment. Shimon pushed open the door. He was out of breath, his face red.

"I saw trucks," he panted. "A long line of trucks, loaded down full. The grocer on the corner says they're bringing all kinds of food. They must have come on that new road."

He ran into the apartment, looking for his sister. "Just imagine," they heard him saying, "trucks all full of food."

Ayelith came into the living room with her doll. "Does she get some too?" she asked, stroking her dolly's hair.

Judith and Tamar looked at each other, eyes wide. Tamar went over to the radio. Yossi had found batteries at an abandoned British base, a precious commodity considering the power cuts. They turned on the receiver, which was tuned to Kol Hamagen, the Haganah radio station in Jerusalem. After a moment, the music was interrupted.

"There will be a cease-fire," said the voice on the radio. "It's to take effect the day after tomorrow."

June 11, 1948

Youssef had already performed his morning prayer. Now he watched the first rays of sunlight break on the golden cupola of the Dome of the Rock. The cupola seemed to glow brighter the higher the sun rose above the mountains of Judaea. Feeling a deep satisfaction, he observed the early morning spectacle with fascination. The third most important shrine in Islam had been secured.

He stood on the city wall south of the Jaffa Gate, with the Old City of Jerusalem below him to the east, the New City to the west. These massive walls had withstood all the Jews' attempts to retake the Old City. Youssef looked over the blackened ruins of the Jewish Quarter. God had imposed his just punishment—the Jews had been driven out. They could go build themselves a new Wailing Wall.

The previous night had been as noisy as ever. Artillery fire had increased again in the past few days—the closer they got to the cease-fire, the heavier the barrages. Arab commanders were secretly hoping to force the Jews into capitulating before the cease-fire could go into effect. Even in this exalted moment of daybreak, the sounds of battle permeated the Holy City.

Youssef turned and looked to the west. Only a half mile away, those first rays of light danced around the panorama of the New City, the King David Hotel directly before him, and beyond that, the prominent, looming tower of the YMCA. He squinted and thought he could make out the Jewish Agency building farther west.

He turned to the northeast. He cringed every time he saw Mount Scopus. That blasted hospital stole the woman that was rightfully his with its insidious promises of Jews and Arabs working together in harmony. *Zionist lies,* he thought. *This land is ours alone.* At least he'd salvaged some of his dignity, by cutting down the woman who'd betrayed him and leaving her to die alongside the convoy of Jewish doctors from her precious Hadassah.

The minute hand kept advancing on the watch he'd acquired from one of the Jewish apartments in the Old City. It said 5:45 a.m., still fifteen minutes until the cease-fire. Youssef bit at his lip, picturing the Jews sitting down there waiting for the Arabs to stop firing their guns. He felt a wild rage rise up inside him. *It was true,* he wanted to shout. They had saved Old Jerusalem from the Jews, a thousand times true, and he had done his part. They had shown the Arab world that it was possible.

Yet down in the New City, they lived on, those one hundred thousand Jews, despite the monthlong blockade, despite the attacks from all sides, despite the deployment of professional soldiers from the Arab Legion.

The soldiers were standing right next to him here on the battlements, those soldiers of King Abdullah from Transjordan, calm and composed, holding their rifles, smoking. The clever king had gotten what he wanted: those parts of Palestine that the United Nations had promised the Arabs were now under his control, and he could come to Jerusalem and pray in the Dome of the Rock whenever he wanted—a triumph, more than anything, over his many rivals in the Arab world.

Traitors, Youssef wanted to scream. *Your king is a goddamn traitor, along with all the other rulers and their lackeys inside their palaces in the Arab capitals.* How could they even consider a cease-fire? Hadn't they promised to drive the Jews into the sea? Hundreds of thousands of their compatriots, from Tiberias and Jaffa, from Haifa and Jerusalem, were now homeless, driven from Palestine. Whether in the souks of Damascus or the bazaars of Cairo, on the banks of the Tigris in Baghdad or the streets of Amman, millions of Arabs would never understand it, Youssef was certain of that. *They don't care about us at all,* he thought. *They just want Jerusalem.*

The impending cease-fire was supposed to last a month. *Four weeks,* Youssef thought. *More time for the Jews to supply the starving city with all that they needed, with food, water, and of course, with soldiers and weapons.*

He watched his minute hand land on six o'clock. He was holding a machine gun, one he'd wrenched from the hands of a dead Haganah man when they'd attacked the Hadassah convoy.

He took a deep breath, then positioned his gun firmly on the wall and emptied his whole magazine toward the west, at the Jews' city.

Tamar Schiff squinted at Judith. She removed one pin after the other from her mouth and stuck them into the baggy sides of the white dress.

"Don't worry, we'll get this right," she said. "Now take it off, I've still got an hour."

Judith did as Tamar said, slipping out of the dress and pulling her old khaki shirt back over her shoulders. Ayelith had been eagerly watching the fitting, and she held her doll up to Tamar.

"She should get married too. Can you make her a pretty dress?" she asked.

Tamar put a hand on Ayelith's head. "You have someone in mind she should marry?"

While Ayelith screwed up her face in thought, her mother focused on the dress. Her deft hands swiftly sewed the excess fabric together.

"Okay, done. Put it on," she said, and handed Judith her wedding dress.

Judith pulled it on and turned in a circle.

Ayelith's eyes sparkled. "Look, so beautiful," she said to her doll. "Such a beautiful bride."

Tamar smiled. "You're right, Ayelith, absolutely right. And now for the veil." She draped the white veil over the bride, covering her hair and face. "It's perfect, Judith. Now your groom can come."

"I don't know how to thank you. Please, call me by my Hebrew name now: Yuhudit."

The rabbi was in his midsixties. He had spent his whole life in the synagogues of Jerusalem. His fair skin was wan and wrinkled, his side-locks light gray like his beard, interspersed with pale yellow. He kept looking nervously at the clock ticking loudly on the wall, its pendulum swinging back and forth. He didn't come to this part of the city often, didn't interact with people who only went to synagogue on Yom Kippur. Shimon stood between his parents, next to Ayelith, looking as impatient as the rabbi.

Uri, still in uniform, had only bounded up the stairs a few minutes before the wedding, a borrowed black suit under one arm. While quickly changing in the bathroom, he realized that the sleeves were far too short. It was the first time he'd ever worn a suit. He had to ask Yossi to knot the tie for him. Then Uri looked at himself in the mirror and grinned. This morning was already bringing events he never could've imagined a few hours before. Within sight of the Old City, he had seen soldiers of the Arab Legion making friendly conversation with soldiers of the new Israeli army. There had been occasional gunfire shortly after the cease-fire, but the longer the morning went on, the clearer it became that all weapons truly were at rest. Merchants were opening their shops and putting out the newly acquired goods, cafés were setting up tables and chairs despite having little to offer, and people were strolling the streets still littered with busted brickwork, shattered roof tiles, shrapnel.

Now Uri stood, a kippah atop his head, beneath the chuppah, one man holding each of its four poles. Again the rabbi looked at the clock. When the big hand finally landed on the twelve, the clock began to chime. All eyes turned to the bedroom door. It slowly opened. Josef Goldsmith led in his sister wearing her bridal gown.

Uri stared. He thought he knew her, but the woman he now saw? He felt his palms suddenly get damp.

Judith stood next to him under the chuppah. Uri wanted to lean over and kiss her, but the rabbi's strict and almost angry look stopped him.

The rabbi uttered some brief religious formalities, although, clearly having been warned by Uri the day before, refrained from any additional speeches. As Jewish tradition prescribed, Uri stomped on a glass, that symbol of mourning for the destruction of the Temple.

Finally, something like a smile crossed the rabbi's face, and he nodded to Uri. Uri pulled Judith to him, to lift the veil and to kiss her.

But right at that moment, the apartment door flew open and Shimon's friend Menachem burst in. He stood still a moment, confused by the presence of so many formally dressed people. But he didn't let himself be deterred.

"Come on!" he shouted at Shimon. "Come on, hurry! There's a soccer game on, a real soccer game, and you're playing goal!"

Shimon glanced up at his father but didn't wait for his consenting nod. He ran out with Menachem instead, their happy footsteps clattering down the stairs.

AUTHOR'S NOTE

To whom does Jerusalem belong? And who is right when it comes to a just resolution to the Middle East conflict?

Such questions began the very day the State of Israel was founded, and they haven't changed even seventy years later. This land is still being fought over, the conflict still escalating into violence. While the Jewish state has firmly been established, a solution for the Palestinians, who also dream of their own state, is moving ever further from reality. Jerusalem remains at the heart of it all. In recent times especially, the city's status has once again become a bone of contention in world politics.

The city is the symbol for a history full of drama, going back three thousand years now, to when King David first conquered the city for the Jews. Since then, control over Jerusalem has changed hands again and again.

The first time I was in Israel, I noticed something immediately: on the edge of the narrow road to Jerusalem there still stood, so many years later, the wrecks of armored trucks. They remain there today, silent witnesses to how desperate the struggle for the Holy City of three religions was in 1948, how narrowly the Jews had escaped losing their capital. Those wrecks got me curious. I wanted to know their story.

I returned again and again, including in October 1973, when the armies of Egypt and Syria invaded the country during the Yom Kippur

War. I experienced firsthand how close the Jewish state was to military defeat, especially in the north, and yet was still able to emerge victorious.

It's this pattern that shapes the history of Israel: repeatedly being attacked, repeatedly reacting to the threat of being driven into the sea by the Arabs, and repeatedly triumphing.

Even the founding of Israel itself began with a war. This was the direct consequence of the 1947 United Nations decision that divided the British Mandate between Jews and Arabs.

The Jews insisted on finally getting their own homeland—on claiming, once and for all, the biblical land of their forefathers. Encouraged by the (later broken) promises of the British Mandate authority and morally strengthened in their claim by the Holocaust before a world audience, they set out early on to acquire land in Palestine. This was soon reflected in the number of inhabitants: in the early 1920s, Palestine had been home to around six hundred thousand Arabs and eighty thousand Jews. By the 1940s, the number of Arab inhabitants had doubled, and the Jews did everything in their power to increase their population through new waves of immigration, both legal and illegal. After the founding of the State of Israel, some 750,000 Arabs left the conquered area and the number of Jews reached 650,000—in other words, a massive population shift had taken place. No wonder the Israelis called the struggle for control in what was then Palestine a "war of independence," while the Arabs called it the Nakba, the "catastrophe"—one that continues for Palestinians to this day.

Nothing remains more controversial, however, than the question of who is at fault. For a long time, it was part of the myth surrounding the founding of the state that the vast majority of Arabs left the ancestral land voluntarily during the war—driven by the promises by Arab leaders that they could return to their homes after a few weeks once the Jews were beaten back.

No Palestinian ever voluntarily handed their home to the Israelis, of course. But it took more than forty years for Israeli and Palestinian historians, some working together, to begin painting a more realistic picture. They came to the conclusion that a mixture of fear, propaganda about atrocities, false promises, and forceful expulsions triggered the exodus that's still at the core of the unresolved Palestinian question in the Middle East today.

Both sides used all means possible to achieve their goals: the Zionists, under the determined leadership of David Ben Gurion, consciously entered into military conflict in order to see the UN decision realized, and with it their dream of their own state; while the divided Arab leaders wagered that their far-greater numbers would prevent this.

Jerusalem was at the heart of the conflict. Israel without Jerusalem—unthinkable. The third holiest site in Islam in the hands of the Jews—never! And so, the fight for the city turned fiercer and increasingly desperate. Neighbors and friends became adversaries overnight.

This conflict has been documented in comprehensive detail ever since. The archives are largely open, leading to a wealth of new assessments of the facts believed to have been known. And the dispute about whose interpretation of these facts should prevail continues unabated.

This book is a novel. It doesn't attempt to take sides, but rather portrays the human face of this historic drama—in all its many facets. The main characters in this novel are fictional. Kibbutz Yardenim and the Arab village of Deir El Nar aren't found on any map. And yet the story occurs within a concrete historical framework: it leads up to the two major massacres in the battle for Jerusalem—the attack on the Arab village of Deir Yassin outside the city gates and the attack on the doctors and nurses of Hadassah Hospital. These were the two most shocking massacres the world saw in this bloody struggle; they were certainly not the only ones. Brutal murders, rapes, looting, terrorist attacks on innocent people—they too were part of this war.

The peace activist Uri Avnery experienced that period as an Israeli soldier and impressively describes his experiences in his extremely readable book *1948: A Soldier's Tale; The Bloody Road to Jerusalem*.

Dov Yosef, the military governor of Jerusalem appointed by Ben Gurion, gives the most comprehensive insight into the tense situation of a city cut off from all supplies in his account, *The Faithful City: The Siege of Jerusalem, 1948*, doing so with facts and figures and in the sober manner of his actual profession, as a lawyer.

The War for Palestine: Rewriting the History of 1948, is a joint work by British, Israeli, and Palestinian historians published by Cambridge University Press that I found as helpful for understanding the conflict as I did Tom Segev's *One Palestine, Complete*.

The memoirs of Golda Meir, *My Life*, and Abba Eban, *My Country*, describe the critical years of 1947–48 from the perspective of those directly involved in shaping them.

On the journalistic side, *O Jerusalem!*, by Larry Collins and Dominique Lapierre, counts as a classic among the numerous other works about the struggle for the Holy City—they complement the other well-known sources with their own gripping and comprehensive research.

The internet has become an indispensable source as well these days. More and more Palestinians are speaking out there, telling their stories, as are British soldiers, with their accounts of active duty in Palestine. *The British Record on Partition*, published by The Nation Associates in 1948 and now accessible online, is highly informative, for example, as are the numerous records from British military and police files.

The activities of German Wehrmacht and SS members, either involved in fighting or serving as instructors on the Arab side, are documented by a number of sources and show that, after the Holocaust, these people had no qualms about continuing to participate in the extermination of the Jews.

The series Dachauer Hefte provides important insights into events surrounding the liberation of Dachau concentration camp and is partially available in English, titled *Dachau and the Nazi Terror: 1933–1945; Testimonies and Memories*.

My numerous trips to the region, to Israel, to the Palestinian territories, and to surrounding states, have helped me to better get to know the people on the ground and to understand the roots of the ongoing conflict—even when it's sometimes hard to understand why two peoples simply cannot find common cause. This, despite solutions that finally seemed within reach, at least in the 1990s, when statesmen on both sides were even awarded the Nobel Peace Prize, only to fall back into the old hostile patterns of behavior.

In all the bitter disputes in the seventy years since the founding of the State of Israel, one institution has shown that it may be possible for those involved to view people as humans first and foremost, and to make the issues of nationality, religion, and ethnicity secondary. The Hadassah Hospital in Jerusalem, founded by and largely maintained by Jews from the United States, was then and remains now an island of humanity amid a sea of mistrust and hostility. I thank Ron Krummer for showing it to me.

Peaceful coexistence is achievable. The Arab and Jewish doctors, nurses, and staff of Hadassah Hospital demonstrate this day after day, courageously and unswervingly. In recalling this shining example, in showing that hope is possible even in the Middle East, this book hopes to make a contribution as well.

Werner Sonne
Spring 2018

ACKNOWLEDGMENTS

I'd like to thank Andrea Weilguni and Liza Darnton from Amazon Publishing for making this book travel around the world and in the United States, where the dedicated women of the Hadassah Women's Zionist Organization of America have founded and are still supporting the Hadassah Hospital in Jerusalem as a symbol of hope and reconciliation. My thanks also go to Steve Anderson for doing a great job translating the German version into English, and to Anna Rosenwong for her sensitive help in easing the book into English.

ABOUT THE AUTHOR

Photo © 2017 Niklas Sonne

Werner Sonne worked for German broadcaster ARD for more than forty years as a radio and TV correspondent, during which time he covered the German government while living in Bonn and Berlin. He was also based in Washington, DC, and the former Eastern Bloc in Poland, and he had assignments in Moscow. He started to travel the Middle East extensively in 1973 when he reported on the Yom Kippur War in Israel and kept returning to the troubled region's front lines—including during the Afghanistan conflict. From 2004 to 2012, he hosted ARD's Berlin-based *Morgenmagazin* show. Since then, he has written about foreign and security policy for daily newspapers and magazines and has penned nonfiction books on similar topics. He is also the author of several political thrillers and historical novels.

ABOUT THE TRANSLATOR

Photo © René Chambers

Steve Anderson is a translator, an editor, and a novelist. His latest novel is *Lost Kin* (2016). Anderson was a Fulbright Fellow in Munich, Germany. He translated *Where the Desert Meets the Sea* while on a residency at the Europäisches Übersetzer-Kollegium (European Translator College) in Straelen, Germany, with support from the Kunststiftung NRW (Arts Foundation of North Rhine-Westphalia). He expresses his heartfelt thanks to both organizations for their tireless efforts toward advancing the craft of literary translation. He lives in Portland, Oregon. Learn more about him at www.stephenfanderson.com.